Moranthus is an elf who has lost everything. With his lover dead and his career stagnating, he jumps at a chance to redeem himself by rescuing a human prince from the goblins hunting him—even if failure means death or eternal exile from his homeland.

Gerrick, a human soldier who bears an uncanny resemblance to his prince, has always chosen duty over desire. As the sole parent of his young daughter, he needs the extra coin that working as the prince's body double provides—even if it may one day cost him his life.

When a case of mistaken identity puts the prince in the hands of a goblin raiding party, Moranthus's and Gerrick's paths collide. With winter closing in and miles of hostile goblin lands ahead, they must set aside their differences and work together to bring the prince home safely.

Their deepening connection comes with a growing certainty that rescuing the prince may be fatal. Moranthus and Gerrick must each find a way to reconcile his heart's desires with his homeland's needs—or die trying.

Dawn's Light

Duskblade, Book One

Shannon Blair

A NineStar Press Publication
www.ninestarpress.com

Dawn's Light

ISBN: 978-1-64890-211-6
© 2021 Shannon Blair
Cover Art © 2021 Natasha Snow
Published in February, 2021 by NineStar Press, New Mexico, USA.

Also available in Print, ISBN: 978-1-64890-212-3

WARNING:
This book contains sexually explicit content, which may only be suitable for mature readers. Depictions of graphic violence, self-inflicted wound/suicide, and suicidal ideation

*For anyone who has ever been in the closet. You are beautiful,
and you deserve to be loved for all that you are.*

One

Moranthus had spent the better part of a fortnight chasing his quarry along the Dawn's Gate edge of the Ghostwood. His meager diet of chalky waybread and over-salted jerky did little more than take the edge off his hunger, and spending weeks on horseback had left him beyond saddle sore. His days blurred together like the colors of the glowstone he kept cradled in the center of his palm. Though it was his only reliable guide at the questionably mapped edges of this unfamiliar country, the strain of determining where each of its shades faded into the next, counting off one less mile between him and his ever-moving destination, left him with a near-constant headache.

The wide, hilly landscape around him certainly didn't offer much else to guide him on the rare occasions he glanced at it to ensure he hadn't strayed too far from the Ghostwood's edge in his search. Dawn's Gate's northern plains didn't look so different from the southern steppes of Moonridge, his homeland, but in the absence of the bone-chilling winds that screamed across Moonridge's southern steppes, the still air around him felt foul and stagnant, as though a dozen people had breathed it before him and sucked all the life from it.

But Moranthus wouldn't have traded any of it for the world. This was the first real hunt he'd seen in over a decade, after he'd made a pariah of himself by getting caught on the losing side of the coup that had killed his Patriarch and set his Patriarch's illegitimate daughter on Moonridge's throne. A few minor discomforts were nothing to complain about.

Even the solitude came as a welcome change after finding himself at the center of attention in every human village he passed through. The adults gave him veiled stares and treated him with just enough politeness to make him feel unwelcome. Their children's endless questions over what had made his ears so long and pointy and whether he'd gotten his purple skin from frostbite, of all things, made him feel like one of the framed butterflies his Patriarch had kept in his study. Moranthus wondered if they treated all elves that way. Or if they knew the shaved sides of his head marked his probationary status in Moonridge and didn't want him trying to find a place for himself in their community. Not that anyone in Moonridge had treated him much better lately.

Just over two months earlier, he'd lounged on the narrow, rickety bed pressed against the left wall of his rented room, happy to be home after the latest in a series of jobs only marginally more interesting than watching snow melt. Beside him, his amethyst cameo of his former Patriarch sat in its usual place near his pillow. Moranthus absently rubbed the carved likeness of his Patriarch with his thumb, missing the days when his work left him feeling fulfilled instead of frustrated. In his service, Moranthus had spent his days tracking down fugitives, missing persons, and lost or stolen valuable objects.

His Matriarch's latest orders had gotten his hopes up by sending him in search of a messenger who had vanished en route to his destination while carrying sensitive correspondence. But when Moranthus found the messenger's belongings and gnawed bones strewn about an abandoned wolf den, the "sensitive correspondence" in question turned out to be nothing more than a dinner invitation to the head of a minor noble household. Moranthus had been reduced to a glorified follow-up letter.

The room's low ceiling and windowless walls made him wonder if it had been part of an attic before its conversion into a living space. The cramped space around him—occupied by a table and single chair pressed against its right wall in addition to the bed and chest of drawers that lined its left—felt comfortable enough compared to the inns he stayed in on the road. After ten years, he hardly noticed the draft his poorly sealed walls let in. The fire he kept blazing in the small fireplace against his back wall kept the worst of the cold out anyway.

The smell of blood from the butcher's shop beneath him wafted through the gaps between his thin floorboards, mingling in a not entirely unpleasant manner with the crisp, sweet taste of the bowlful of plums he'd made into his evening meal. As he finished each plum, he tossed its pit across the room, where it bounced off his doorknob with a sharp *ping* before clattering along his floor. It made a completely unreasonable amount of noise, really. But that was the point.

He'd done it as his latest mild act of revenge against the butcher downstairs, who had woken well before dawn that morning for what seemed to be the sole purpose of loudly and thoroughly fucking his wife. For the past several years, the butcher had made a point of waking Moranthus that way every morning after Moranthus returned from a mission and wanted nothing more than a good, long sleep.

Moranthus still hadn't decided whether the butcher did it as a backhanded reminder that Moranthus wasn't getting any, or as a bizarre way of marking his territory. More than once, he'd considered pulling the butcher aside and explaining that, if he had any intention of running off with a member of the butcher's household—which he did not—he would've been far more interested in the charming young fellow the butcher had recently brought in as an apprentice. If the charming apprentice in question hadn't already taken up with the butcher's wife, anyway. But pointing out that the butcher had an attractive apprentice and an unfaithful wife would probably get him banned from the butcher's shop, and he didn't want to go to the trouble of finding another reputable place to buy meat in the lower district of Aurora, Moonridge's capital. Or a new landlord, for that matter.

The first knock at his door caught Moranthus off guard. He couldn't remember the last time he'd had a visitor. He'd halfway decided to dismiss it as a trick of the wind, or a child throwing rocks as an ill-advised form of amusement, when a second knock echoed through his room, followed by several more in rapid succession.

Moranthus slid off his bed and retrieved the dagger he kept beneath his pillow before padding, barefoot, across the floorboards between him and the door, careful to avoid the ones that creaked. No one who'd come to his door unannounced was likely to have anything pleasant in store for him. Not anymore.

He opened his door to find one of his Matriarch's messengers standing outside, an official-looking satchel in his arms. In that moment, Moranthus wanted nothing more than to tell the bastard that his next set of orders could wait until he asked for them and slam his door shut again.

Instead, he sighed and asked, "What do you want?"

"I am looking for Moranthus. I've come to the wrong place, I take it?" The messenger frowned as he cast a disdainful glance over Moranthus. His eyes lingered on the shaved sides of Moranthus's head and the thick stripe of red hair—the only thing separating him from a clean-shaven full exile—that ran down its center, woven into a disheveled, three-strand commoner's braid. Outside of Aurora's upper district, Moranthus rarely bothered with the elaborate, seven-strand affair that marked him as a veteran duskblade. In Lower Aurora, it only served as a marker of how far he'd fallen.

"Not at all. You've already found him, in fact." Moranthus flipped his dagger so its blade rested in his palm and presented its pommel—engraved with a stylized snowhawk, the duskblade insignia—to the messenger for inspection.

The messenger's face snapped into a toothy smile, oozing false cheer as he presented the satchel to Moranthus. "Excellent. I come bearing orders from our most esteemed Matriarch," he said, each syllable accompanied by a tap of his well-fitted, overembroidered right boot. The steep, narrow streets that wound their way through Lower Aurora—slick with mud and whatever other refuse trickled down from the upper city—had left it and its twin covered in a layer of filth that would never quite wash off. It served him right for wearing that sort of footwear on the job.

He was a mousy little thing, with pale, watery eyes set in a bland, but well-proportioned face, his ears perfectly pointed and skin a flawless shade of dusky lilac. Probably hadn't set foot outside Upper Aurora before their Matriarch had sent him on this delivery, no doubt as a punishment of some sort. Moranthus would've much preferred the sight of the butcher, his face flushed ruddy-violet from exertion and his blood-stained apron draped over his ever-growing paunch. At least he'd earned his place in the world.

"So I noticed." Moranthus made no move to accept the satchel.

The messenger blinked at him, brow furrowed in an almost comical display of confusion. "Would you like to invite me in then? I'd prefer to conclude my business here as soon as possible."

"Not particularly, but I take it I don't have much choice in the matter."

"You don't. There are certain…details our Matriarch insisted I explain to you in person. To prevent any misunderstandings."

Moranthus opened his door wide and gestured for the messenger to step through. "Let's get this over with." Before he lost his temper at being forced to offer hospitality to a highborn busybody, who'd no doubt leave grimy footprints all over his floor.

The messenger made himself comfortable in Moranthus's chair, his hands folded over the satchel on his lap. Well aware the messenger expected him to remain standing as a way of acknowledging that the messenger acted as an extension of their Matriarch's will, Moranthus seated himself on his bed and leaned back against the wall behind him. The frustrated glare it earned him made him confident he'd chosen the right course of action.

"So, what's this all about?" Moranthus gave the messenger the most ingenuous smile he could manage. Best not to press his luck too far.

The messenger took a deep breath, pinching the bridge of his nose as though he meant to fend off a headache. "Our Matriarch has, for reasons far beyond the comprehension of one such as myself, chosen to entrust you with a highly sensitive mission of the utmost urgency. I would advise against treating it with the same flippancy you have shown me thus far."

Moranthus sat up straight, eyeing the satchel with a sense of curiosity he hadn't felt in years. "Is that why she was so adamant about you explaining my orders to me?" When they'd last spoken, their Matriarch had told him in no uncertain terms that he should consider himself lucky she'd spared even his life after he'd chosen his master so poorly. She'd then evicted him from his hard-won room in Aurora's palace and made a point of restricting him to assignments well below his rank, most of which took him as far away from Aurora as possible. Putting this sort of trust in him wasn't like her. "Because that won't be necessary. I'm sure our Matriarch has told you all sorts of wild stories about me—most of which, in her defense, are probably true—but I assure you, I am perfectly capable of reading and understanding whatever's in that satchel of yours."

"The orders themselves aren't what she asked me to explain," the messenger replied. "In fact, I couldn't explain them if I wanted to. Our Matriarch felt that sharing the exact nature of your orders with me would compromise their security. They should be self-explanatory once you've taken the time to read over them."

"So, if I can't ask you anything about my orders, what *did* our Matriarch want you to explain to me?"

"That a great deal depends upon your success in this matter, and that you may find yourself in a more…favorable position upon your return so long as you do not disappoint her. She also instructed me to give you this, to be used in the unfortunate event of your failure." The messenger retrieved a razor from a pouch on his belt and tossed it onto the bed beside Moranthus. Even tucked inside its wooden handle, its steel blade had a cold, sobering shine. "Does it clarify the gravity of the task that lies before you?"

Using only his fingertips, Moranthus picked up the razor, casting a wary eye over the ceremonial carvings that adorned its handle. So, *that* was his Matriarch's game. Either he returned home with news of his success, or he faced the grim choice he'd so narrowly avoided ten years ago: death or exile. Whichever he chose, the razor's edge would suit his needs. "That it does. I suppose I'd best get to work," he said. His voice sounded hollow, like a distant echo carried on the wind.

"Indeed, you should. Sooner, rather than later, if you've any sense left in that space between your ears." The messenger got to his feet and placed the satchel on Moranthus's table. "This contains your orders, as well as everything you'll require to carry them out. I wish you the best of luck. You're going to need it." With that, the messenger let himself out of Moranthus's room, leaving the door open behind him.

The autumn air it let in felt warm compared to the ice in Moranthus's veins.

His Matriarch's orders were maddeningly sparse. Apparently, Dawn's Gate's settlements closest to the Ghostwood, which acted as the goblin territories' eastern border, had gotten ransacked more than usual by goblin raiding parties that year. Orthenn, the third son of the King of Dawn's Gate—and hardly more than a child at his twenty-seven years of age—had taken it upon himself to lead a scouting mission through the Ghostwood to discover which warlord those raiding parties belonged to.

Moranthus's Matriarch had it on good authority that a goblin warlord had somehow caught wind of Orthenn's planned route and intended to send out a raiding party to kidnap Orthenn. And so, for what was no doubt a very good reason—that his Matriarch had neglected to share with him— instead of sharing that information with Dawn's Gate's king and letting him sort the matter out for himself, she'd decided to task Moranthus with intercepting Orthenn before a goblin raiding party absconded with him. Once that was taken care of, Moranthus needed to bring Orthenn north to the border Dawn's Gate shared with Moonridge, where they'd rendez-vous with a detachment of Moonridge frostguards who'd take Orthenn back to his father as a gesture of goodwill.

Even after having pondered it for weeks of solitary travel, Moranthus couldn't wrap his head around why his Matriarch had gone to such trouble on behalf of the King of Dawn's Gate. She'd justified staging a coup against her father by claiming he'd weakened Moonridge by relying on diplomatic negotiations instead of trusting in the legendary prowess of Moonridge's soldiers to ease any tensions between Moonridge and Dawn's Gate or the goblin territories along Moonridge's western border. Strengthening diplomatic ties between Moonridge and Dawn's Gate by ingratiating herself to Dawn's Gate's king went against everything she believed in.

And if Moranthus's mission failed, she risked destroying the peace her father had spent the centuries of his reign working so hard to forge with Dawn's Gate. Dawn's Gate's king didn't know a goblin warlord was scheming to kidnap Orthenn, after all. Ordering Moranthus to stage a counterkidnapping—because, with all the formalities and sugarcoating washed off, that was what Moranthus was about to do—without consulting Orthenn's father put Moranthus in an awkward position. He doubted Orthenn and the soldiers under his command would take kindly to a strange elf dragging Orthenn up to Moonridge without so much as a by-your-leave. If any of them managed to get word of that back to their king before the frostguards returned Orthenn to his father, relations between Dawn's Gate and Moonridge had the potential to turn very violent, very quickly.

Really, his Matriarch would've done better to arrange for Orthenn's entire company to be rescued along with him, or quietly disposed of, to prevent them from making any misguided attempts at rescuing their prince. Fewer loose ends to deal with that way. Moranthus might have even said as much if people who questioned his Matriarch didn't have a nasty habit of ending up dead.

But then he would've been saddled with at least four or five heavy, tramping frostguards at his back, slowing his pace to an agonizing crawl. Duskblades operated best in solitude, without the distraction of other fighters encroaching on their space and the shouted orders of commanding officers who held no real authority over them. He would've gotten along with a group of frostguards like a snowhawk got along with a pack of wolves.

With a bright flash of light, Moranthus's glowstone shifted into the pale, blue-green hue that indicated he was within a mile of Orthenn's location. It didn't matter why his Matriarch wanted Orthenn rescued or why she'd gone about rescuing him this way. She'd sent Moranthus on a mission, and too much depended on his success for him to be distracted with matters that for the time being were above him.

As the glowstone's light faded to its usual dull glow, Moranthus's horse, Storm, stopped to snatch up a mouthful of the wispy grass that softened the noise of her hooves. With a flicker of a smile and a pat on her neck, he slid off her back instead of urging her onward. She'd carried him as far as she could, and he welcomed the chance to stand on his own two feet again. Even if he'd had a longer distance left to travel that day, he wouldn't have begrudged her a rest. Tall and stocky, with a thick, mottled-gray coat, she'd been bred to jog at a steady pace through snow and over rocks, not for sprinting across open fields. She'd been a gift from his Patriarch just before the coup, and he'd never forgive himself if he lost her to overexertion.

To his left, Dawn's Gate's western plains extended in an endless sea of yellow-brown. In summer, they supposedly glowed with vibrant, green life, with grasses that reached as high as a man's waist, but on the verge of winter, they were as barren as the frosted fields of his homeland. Late autumn in Dawn's Gate could've passed for summer in northern Moonridge, but in his sturdy leathers and hooded, fur-lined cloak, Moranthus found the warm weather more stifling than comforting.

On his right, the gnarled, twisted oaks and drooping willows of the Ghostwood sprawled across the land as far as he could see. The sun's slow descent below the horizon cast dark, eerie shadows between their branches, plunging the Ghostwood into a deeper darkness than its midday twilight.

Even in Aurora, as far to the north as even elves dared to settle, tales of foolhardy travelers venturing into its depths, never to return, were sung by third-rate bards to eager children who were delighted and terrified, in equal measure, by their descriptions of starving, man-sized wolves and vengeful spirits.

Or at least, those were the kinds of songs Moranthus's father had always favored. In adulthood, Moranthus had come to fear the real threats he faced while traversing Moonridge's northern pine forests more than fictions dreamed up by a man who'd died without ever setting foot in the wilds. But he still felt a shiver of unease run down his spine at the thought of passing through a place that had spawned so many of his childhood nightmares.

Still, unless he wanted to shave the rest of his head and make a new home for himself in Dawn's Gate or the goblin territories, his only path forward lay within the Ghostwood. His Matriarch's orders had been clear as a spring-fed stream on that matter. With a chance at regaining some semblance of his old life on the line, he couldn't afford to let a few ghost stories stand in his way.

Moranthus patted Storm's flank as he removed two days' portion of waybread from her saddlebags. He doubted it would take him long to reach Orthenn's encampment, but he didn't want to risk going hungry if traversing the Ghostwood took longer than expected. "This is where we part ways, my friend. Try not to get yourself into too much trouble while I'm gone."

Storm flicked her tail in acknowledgment and gave him a brief, curious glance as he walked toward the Ghostwood without her. Tethering her wasn't necessary. Moonridge horses were trained to never stray far from where their masters left them before they were saddle broken and were smart enough to know that straying off on their own in such a cold, unforgiving land would lower their chances of survival. She'd stay where he'd left her, or at least not wander too far for him to call her back with a whistle. Tethering her would only make her an easy target for any hungry creature or unaffiliated goblin that roamed the Ghostwood's edge.

When he reached the tree line, Moranthus stopped, gazed into the darkness before him, and almost went back to grab Storm's reins and lead her into the forest with him so he'd have some comfort when its trees closed in around him. But finding a path through the undergrowth large enough for her to pass would only slow him down, and she'd make too much noise for him to reach Orthenn's camp unnoticed. With one last check to ensure that his bow, sword, and dagger were all in their proper places and securely fastened to his leathers, he took a step forward and passed into the Ghostwood.

Two

Nights on the road were hard on Gerrick. Having a six-year-old daughter back home made them harder. He didn't understand why his brothers-in-arms expected him to forget his home life while he was on duty. For the five years he'd spent under Orthenn's command, he'd never taken much interest in campfire talk. They shouldn't have thought tonight would be any different. But they'd still started poking fun at him when he kept silent as their conversation shifted from the bear they'd killed that afternoon to the girls a few of them had left back home and the brothel most of the others had visited in the last town they'd passed through.

The bear, Gerrick had taken an interest in. They were eating it for dinner that night, and he'd landed the killing blow on it. It would've been unmanly of him not to do a bit of bragging about that. He couldn't pretend he didn't like the sound of them calling him "bear blood," either, even though he knew they wouldn't keep at it long enough for the name to stick. The bragging must've gotten their hopes up though. Then he'd disappointed them by going back to his old, quiet self when their talk turned to women.

It wasn't that Gerrick wasn't interested in women. He just didn't have any women in his life to talk about. Gerrick had broken things off with his daughter's mother months before his daughter was born. His daughter's mother had died and left their daughter in Gerrick's care less than a year later. Gerrick hadn't found another girl before then, and he hadn't had the time to find one since; raising his daughter on his own kept him too busy for that.

He didn't see the appeal of brothels, either. Not when he still felt too guilty about fathering one child out of wedlock to risk it happening again with another girl. His brothers-in-arms never tired of teasing him about that. Tonight was no exception. And worse than usual.

Before their teasing turned to accusing him of wanting a man in his bed in place of a woman, like it always did, Gerrick left his seat by Orthenn's campfire and walked into the dense forest surrounding the camp. He explained himself by telling the others he wanted to scout the perimeter of their camp as he lit himself a torch. They didn't believe a word of it. He didn't have the energy or patience to care. A man could only sit through so much mockery before it broke him. Gerrick couldn't let himself break where anyone could see him. Leaving the camp was his only choice, whether his brothers-in-arms liked his excuse for it or not.

A hand grabbed his shoulder after the trees closed in around him. He put his free hand on the hilt of his sword as he shrugged the hand off and turned around, but he didn't expect he'd need it. If it was a goblin, he would've already killed Gerrick.

He let go of his sword when he recognized Aldous, the closest thing he had to a real friend in Orthenn's company. Even in his torch's dim light, he couldn't miss the bushy, graying mustache that covered most of Aldous's face.

"You need to stop taking this so hard, lad," Aldous said, lifting the corners of his mustache with a sympathetic smile. No one else could've called Gerrick "lad" and walked away from it without a bloody nose or blackened eye. But Aldous had ten years on him and let Gerrick's daughter stay with his wife and five children when their duty to Orthenn took them away from home. Aldous had earned that right. "It's just a bit of fun. You know that."

Gerrick scowled. "It's gone on too long. Find some new fun."

"Maybe it has gone on a bit long. But it's also been a bit long since you've had a woman, and it's taking a toll on you."

"I'm fine."

Aldous snorted. "And I'm the Matriarch of Moonridge. I swear, lad, you're wound so tight that if someone shoved a lump of coal up your backside, it'd come out a diamond. Buying yourself a woman for a night or two might do you some good."

"It wouldn't. I'm not spending good coin to pretend I don't know some poor girl is only pretending to like me. I have a daughter to provide for."

"I have five sons, and I'm getting by on the same pay as you. You could afford to spend a little on yourself if you wanted to."

"I *don't* want to." Gerrick turned on his heel and started walking again. "If you like brothels so much, why don't you visit them?"

"Because my wife's been trying to get a daughter out of me since I married her, and if I go and father one on some other girl, she'll never forgive me." Aldous laughed as he followed after Gerrick. "You're sure you won't let us keep yours? I promise we'll take good care of her."

"I'm sure." Gerrick shook his head, but couldn't keep from smiling. The offer was a joke between them now, but Gerrick had almost taken Aldous up on it when he'd first joined Orthenn's company. It was hard work, raising a child on his own. But after five years of watching his daughter grow, knowing he'd made her into everything she was, he wouldn't give her up for anything in the world.

Aldous shrugged. "Can't blame a man for trying. You're going to want to find a mother for that girl eventually, though, aren't you? That's not going to happen if you never go out looking for a woman who likes you enough to put up with that stony face of yours without you paying her for it."

"You think I haven't already tried that?"

"If you have, you haven't tried very hard, lad. You wouldn't look half bad if you cleaned yourself up right, and there's plenty of women out there who wouldn't mind getting a daughter along with a husband." Aldous thumped Gerrick on the back. "Take my wife's sister, for instance. Still never been married, and she's wonderful with the children. You should meet her sometime."

Gerrick covered his face with his free hand and let out a frustrated groan. He should've known Aldous would bring that up again. It happened with everyone who'd known him long enough to get past poking fun at him for taking on a woman's job by raising his daughter on his own. They always had a sister, or a cousin, or a maiden aunt who could give his daughter the motherly affection she needed. As though Gerrick didn't love her enough for two parents. As though him being a man meant that a woman could take one look at his daughter and understand her better than he did after knowing her all her life. And as though Gerrick should be grateful for a woman to marry him as a last resort and barely tolerate him for the rest of both their lives.

If that was the best he could hope for in a wife, Gerrick was better off alone. His daughter had gotten to six years old just fine without a mother; if it came to that, she could get by without one for the rest of her life too.

"How many times do I need to tell you no, Aldous?" Gerrick asked.

"I'm not saying you need to marry her straight off." Aldous held his hands up in a defensive gesture. "It'd just be nice if you'd let me introduce the two of you before you decide you're not interested. I wouldn't ask if I didn't think the two of you would get along."

"I'm still not interested. Stop bringing it up."

"I'll stop if you'll give her a chance. Is that so much to ask, after I've helped you with your daughter all these years?" Aldous had Gerrick there. They both knew it. Aldous bringing the favor into things was a low thing to do though.

"I'll think about it," Gerrick replied. "After this scouting mission's over. Bring it up again before then, though, and it's not happening."

Aldous clapped him on the shoulder. "Thank you, lad. This'll be a good thing for you; just you wait and see. Now let's get back to camp while there's still some dinner left."

As Gerrick grunted his agreement, a strange shadow in a nearby tree caught his attention. He took a step toward the tree, bringing it within the hazy, yellow circle of light his torch gave off. A freshly killed rabbit was draped over a fork in one of its branches. Something, or *someone*, had gone hunting near Orthenn's camp.

"What do you make of this?" Gerrick asked.

Aldous squinted at the rabbit for a moment, then shrugged. "An owl could've dropped it, or a lynx might've stashed it there." He cast an uneasy glance at the forest around them and lowered his voice as he added, "Or we've just missed crossing paths with a goblin."

"Do you think he's still nearby?"

"I couldn't say. But if he is, that's all the more reason to get back to camp. Orthenn needs to know about this; he'll decide what needs to be done about it." Aldous started walking in the direction of Orthenn's camp.

Gerrick took one long, last look into the shadows between the trees, then followed after him.

Three

Inside the Ghostwood, Moranthus found some comfort in the knowledge that it wasn't so different from the dense Moonridge pine forests he'd tracked more than his share of fugitives through. It was darker, of course, and the leaf litter beneath his feet absorbed the sound of his footsteps more than it should have. But that wasn't necessarily a bad thing. He'd have an easy enough time keeping hidden if he ran into any trouble, at least. Then again, he supposed it would also make it easier for any trouble in his path to stay hidden from him. Anything could be hiding in the shadows around him, and he'd never see it coming until it was already within striking distance of him.

The air grew stiller and more stagnant as his glowstone led him deeper into the Ghostwood until he reached a place it seemed the wind had never touched. A deafening silence, broken only by the sound of his breathing and muffled footfalls, filled his ears. At some point, he'd started clutching his dagger to his chest in a white-knuckled grip. He couldn't remember removing it from its sheath.

He shouldn't have given a second thought to carving notches into tree trunks to mark the path he'd taken through the Ghostwood. But as the stifling darkness closed in around him, the notches began to feel less like trail markers and more like desecrations that, in one of his father's songs, would've gotten him cursed or killed by an ancient forest guardian. The glowing fungus that grew among the tree roots deep within the forest gave off an eerie light that sharpened the shadows between the trees and gave them a hostile life as they shrank from the brighter light of Moranthus's glowstone.

After hours of what felt like aimless wandering, Moranthus's glowstone finally gave off the warm, yellow light that meant he was within a hundred paces of his quarry. At first, he thought it must be mistaken. He didn't feel any closer to another living creature, human or animal, than he had since he'd lost sight of Storm. Still, he pressed onward until he could just make out the glow of a campfire in the gloom ahead of him and the sound of rough, male voices that didn't travel half as far as they should have.

He eased his grip on his dagger and let his sword arm drop to his side to keep from looking like a threat if, by a stroke of ill luck, Orthenn or one of his men caught sight of him as he scouted the perimeter of their camp. He slunk through the trees until he stood as close to their fire's ring of light as he dared, closing his left hand around his glowstone to keep its light from revealing his position.

Orthenn's company had found a clearing of sorts and—judging by the rumpled state of their bedrolls and the myriad of crude carvings in the bark of the trees nearest their fire—had been using it as a base of operations for a not-insignificant amount of time. A large pot dangled over their fire, giving off a rich, pleasant aroma that made his mouth water.

Moranthus counted eleven of them, all wearing a green tabard edged with the deep orange of Orthenn's family line over at least a hauberk of the sturdy chain mail Dawn's Gate's blacksmiths had perfected. A pair of them kept a half-hearted watch on the forest around them in between swapping jokes and stories with their comrades. Most sported a scruffy coating of hair along their cheeks and jawline in a range of near-identical browns and blonds.

Picking Orthenn out from his companions would pose a greater challenge than he'd anticipated. Moranthus's Matriarch had included a drawn likeness of Orthenn in his orders, but that likeness had shown Orthenn clean-shaven and dressed in princely finery. That didn't give Moranthus much to go on now, when Orthenn would be sporting a full beard and wearing the same uniform as his men. All he could be certain of was that he was looking for a pale-complexioned man with blue eyes and fair hair. That could've described almost half the men in Orthenn's camp.

Moranthus risked a glance at his glowstone, then shoved it into a pocket in his leathers. Its glow had reached the faint, white color that meant he was within twenty paces of Orthenn. It had gotten Moranthus as close to Orthenn's location as it could; Moranthus had to find his own way forward now.

He crept around the outskirts of the camp with footfalls that were swallowed by the lively noise of its inhabitants, keeping to the shadows until he stumbled onto a sight that froze the blood in his veins. Crouched in a clump of bushes, too fixated on the camp to notice his approach, was a goblin scout. His gray-green face was streaked with dirt, and his eyes were crossed over his long, hooked nose as he scribbled something onto a crumpled sheet of parchment with a stick of charcoal.

Moranthus bit back a frustrated sigh. He couldn't risk making his move until he'd dealt with the goblin. If the goblin saw Moranthus near Orthenn's camp, Moranthus's mission would be doomed before it fully began. At best, the goblin would bring news of Moranthus's rescue attempt back to his comrades, and Moranthus would have a full raiding party on his heels after he got Orthenn out of the Ghostwood. At worst, the goblin might make use of the bow and quiver of arrows—no doubt coated in some form of poison—strapped to his back and bring Moranthus's hunt to an abrupt, fatal end before he'd even gotten Orthenn out of his camp.

Taking painstaking care to avoid any sudden movements until the last possible moment, Moranthus sheathed his dagger, took hold of his own bow, and nocked an arrow onto its string. He held his breath as he took aim at the goblin's heart, then let the arrow fly. It sank into the goblin's chest with a solid *thud* and sent him toppling to the ground with an ear-splitting scream.

As one, every man in the camp went silent and turned to stare in the goblin's direction. Moranthus cursed himself for not aiming well enough for an instant kill as he stepped backward, hoping to disappear into the shadows between the trees before any of Orthenn's men started wondering where the arrow that felled the goblin had come from. In retrospect, a few frostguards might've been a welcome asset to his mission.

A twig broke under his heel with a sickening *snap*. Moranthus winced and stifled a frustrated growl at his own carelessness as the entire camp's attention shifted to him.

A soldier with a bristling, sandy beard called out, "You, there. Step into the light."

Moranthus kept still and silent, just in case the order had been directed at the still-twitching goblin scout.

The soldier placed a hand on the hilt of his sword. "I won't ask you again. Step into the light. Now."

Moranthus did as he was told, a litany of potential lies and excuses flowing through his mind. He held his hands in the air, still clutching his bow, in a gesture of surrender as he walked toward the campfire. "I assure you I mean you no harm."

"We'll be the judge of that, elf. What brings you so far from home into such a dangerous place?" The soldier—no, Moranthus would call him Bristles—kept his hand on his sword. As he spoke, his companions huddled together, a blond bear of a man at their center. It was hard to tell at this distance, but he looked like a good match for Moranthus's likeness of Orthenn. They'd given their prince's identity away. Moranthus just needed to find a way to get to him.

"Does it matter?" Moranthus squared his shoulders and raised an eyebrow in a show of mock offense. "I killed a goblin scout for you. You're free to thank me whenever you'd like."

"That was some damn convenient timing on your part. How do we know you're not working with them and using this as a trick to get in close before stabbing us in the back?"

"Because there would be easier ways to do that than wasting a perfectly good scout on a bit of playacting?"

"And how do we know that your scout's really dead?"

"Send someone to check on him if you don't believe me. If he's not dead yet, he'll be getting there in a moment or two."

Bristles gestured to a short, stocky brunet at the cluster's edge. "Go and test his claim."

The brunet nodded, trotted over to the goblin, and gave him a harsh kick in the side. The goblin didn't stir. "Looks dead to me." He shrugged and walked back to his place in the cluster around Orthenn.

Bristles nodded, running a hand over his beard. "So, you haven't gone goblin, or at least not enough to have any qualms about killing them. That still doesn't explain why you *are* wandering the Ghostwood. Alone. After dark." He set his mouth into a grim, hard line.

Moranthus responded with a small frown of his own. Talking his way into the good graces of Orthenn and his men hadn't factored into his plans. But if he'd learned one thing in his century and a half as a duskblade, it was that sometimes, in an act of deception, the truth—or a slanted interpretation of it—was the most convincing falsehood available to him. "I have a message for Prince Orthenn. Will you allow me to speak with him?"

Bristles laughed in his face. "And who might this message of yours be from?"

"His father."

Bristles went silent, locking his blue eyes onto Moranthus's yellow in an obvious attempt at intimidating him into backing down from his claim. Moranthus held his gaze, setting his face into a stony mask of neutrality. One crack, and he'd lose everything.

Several agonizing heartbeats later, the man Moranthus assumed to be Orthenn pushed his way past the men clustered around him and stepped forward to stand at Bristles's side. "Let's hear it then."

Moranthus's lips curled into a smile as Bristles shook his head and took a step back. His troublesome guard notwithstanding, Orthenn seemed like a trusting sort. He shared Bristles's coloring and hawkish features, but his expression looked stern instead of sour, and he had a shorter beard. Moranthus could've easily mistaken them for brothers.

Moranthus took Orthenn's approach as an invitation to lower his hands into a more natural position and gave Orthenn his full attention. "Wonderful," he said. "I'm glad at least you've decided to be reasonable about this."

"Don't get ahead of yourself. I didn't say I believe you. Just that I'm willing to hear you out," Orthenn replied.

"Of course. I understand your skepticism, given the circumstances." Moranthus gave a short, breathy laugh in acknowledgment of the awkward position he'd put himself in. "This certainly isn't how I'd have chosen to introduce myself."

Orthenn sighed. "Just give me the message." His eyes had a tired look to them.

In that state, he'd respond best to a short and to-the-point approach. All the better. Moranthus wouldn't have to bog himself down with unnecessary details, which would make it easier to keep his story from changing if he had to tell it a second time.

"Perhaps we could discuss this somewhere more private?" Moranthus asked, casting a wary glance at their uncomfortably large audience. He tried to anticipate whether they'd try to sway their leader's judgment. Bristles, at the very least, seemed to have enough influence over Orthenn to make a problem of himself. And Moranthus doubted any of them would like the thought of Orthenn abandoning them at the behest of a stranger from a foreign land.

Bristles scoffed, as though he'd read Moranthus's mind and wanted to confirm his misgivings. "Why, so you can slit his throat in peace?"

"I thought we'd already established that I have no intention of harming any of you," Moranthus said through gritted teeth. "If I wanted to, I could easily have turned my bow against one of you instead of that goblin. But I didn't, did I?"

"Settle down, both of you." Orthenn held up a hand in a similar gesture to the one Moranthus's Patriarch had always used to signal that he'd run his mouth too much. "Elf, whatever you have to say to me, you can say in front of my men. I'd trust each and every one of them with my life; you don't need to fear any betrayal from them."

Moranthus bit back the urge to address him as "human" and see how he liked it. He'd been trained better than that and endured worse insults with a smile on his face. It would take more than a simple "elf" to break him. "Very well. We are in your camp, after all. I came here, on behalf of your father, to ensure your safety as you return home."

"You'll be waiting on me awhile, then. We won't be finished here for at least another week."

"Perhaps I didn't make myself clear. Your father wants you to return home now, and it's my job to make sure you get there."

Orthenn blinked at him in confusion. "Why? Our mission here isn't finished yet."

Moranthus sighed. He would've preferred to avoid discussing the goblin lord until he'd gotten Orthenn out of earshot of his men, but he didn't see what other choice was left. "There are…rumors that a goblin lord has put a price on your head and sent a raiding party out to claim it. Your father would prefer not to put you at risk if there's any truth to them."

"What about my men? Aren't they also at risk?"

"Of course, they are. But presumably less so if you aren't with them."

"If you really think a band of goblins is going to stop and ask if we still have our prince before they attack us, you're a damn fool," Bristles said, aiming a sharp glare at Moranthus.

Moranthus didn't meet his gaze. "I was under the impression that I was having a conversation with your prince, not one of his pawns."

"He makes a fair point," Orthenn said. "A raiding party would have no way of knowing I'm no longer among them. Even if they did, it wouldn't stop them from attacking. I can't leave my company to face something like that while I run back to safety."

Bristles nodded, a satisfied smile on his face.

"If you run afoul of a raiding party, do you really think you'll make enough difference to justify defying your father?" Moranthus asked. "He made quite a point of insisting that I return with you."

"One man can make all the difference in the world," Bristles replied in Orthenn's place. "You dishonor him by belittling his skill."

Orthenn nodded. "He speaks the truth." He didn't seem to have any objection to allowing others to speak for him. That was unusual for a prince, but maybe human nobles didn't think as highly of themselves as elven ones did. Even before the coup, Moranthus's Matriarch would have had a severe punishment in store for any soldier who dared to undermine her authority. Harsh as her methods were, in that moment, Moranthus preferred them to the alternative.

"What do you suggest I tell your father?"

"Tell him I appreciate his concern, but I am committed to our soldiers and the task that lies before us. He's a fair man. He won't hold you responsible for my actions." Orthenn gave him a strained half smile. "You're free to stay here for the night if you'd like. I won't send you away without rest after you've come so far on my behalf."

"You're too kind, my prince." Moranthus found himself mirroring Orthenn's expression. If he couldn't talk Orthenn into leaving with him, Moranthus would need to resort to more drastic measures to get him out of his camp. He had a long night ahead of him. And it had the potential to be a bloody one.

Four

Gerrick kept a watchful eye on the elf as he stalked across the camp and seated himself on a clump of tree roots near its western edge. Now that Orthenn had dismissed the elf, most of Gerrick's brothers-in-arms had already gone back to their talk. Gerrick didn't understand how they could feel so at ease with a man with such questionable loyalties in their midst. The elf wasn't making a problem of himself now, but Gerrick didn't trust him to stay that way. They shouldn't, either. Then again, they didn't have the same responsibility for Orthenn as he did.

He was too restless to return to his seat by the campfire. After walking once around the camp's perimeter, squinting into the darkness in search of any more unwelcome surprises, he sat beside Orthenn on a fallen log at the camp's northern edge.

Orthenn grunted in acknowledgment of him, then went back to running a whetstone along his sword's edge, his mouth set in a grim line. He seemed to share Gerrick's concerns. That set Gerrick on edge more than the elf's lingering presence in Orthenn's camp.

"What are we going to do about him?" Gerrick asked, nodding toward the elf.

Orthenn didn't look up from his sword as he replied, "Hopefully nothing. If he knows what's good for him, he'll keep his word and leave us in the morning."

"And if he doesn't?"

Orthenn set aside his sword and turned to face Gerrick. "That's what I have you for, isn't it?" His voice had the same resentful edge it did every time he acknowledged the role Gerrick played in his company.

Orthenn had voiced his opposition to Gerrick joining his company when his father had first offered Gerrick a post there as an additional layer of security for him. Gerrick had seen the relief in Orthenn's eyes when he turned the offer down. He'd also seen the disappointment on Orthenn's face when he reversed his decision after his daughter's mother died and he found he had a child to provide for. Orthenn had warmed to him, little by little, in the years since then, but Gerrick doubted they'd ever be as close as Orthenn was to the other soldiers under his command. The ones who weren't a constant reminder that his status as a prince kept him from fully living the soldier's life he wanted.

"It is." Gerrick ran a hand over his beard, surprised at how bristly it had grown. He'd need to shave before going home if he didn't want to frighten his daughter when he picked her up from Aldous's house. "Do you think he's really working for your father?" It was a stupid question, but it was the best way to change the subject he could think of.

Orthenn scoffed. "Of course not. My father would never put that kind of trust in an elf."

Gerrick believed that. There'd been bad blood between Dawn's Gate and Moonridge for the five centuries that had passed since the grandfather of Moonridge's current Matriarch had annexed all of Dawn's Gate's lands north of the Wintersbreath River. He'd struck an agreement with one of Orthenn's ancestors to help protect those lands from goblin raids in exchange for his people being allowed to work any unused farmland in the area. The arrangement lasted until Dawn's Gate's next king refused to honor his father's agreement and ordered the eviction of the elven farmers and soldiers that had settled on his land. When they refused his orders, he sent his army in to force them out. Moonridge's Patriarch retaliated by sending his own army in to protect his interests there, leading to the most crushing defeat in Dawn's Gate's history. The Wintersbreath River had acted as Dawn's Gate's northern border ever since.

"Who do you think he is working for, then?" Gerrick asked.

"Hard to say. Probably not a goblin lord after the way he killed that scout, but it's still possible. I've never heard of a goblin warlord who wasn't willing to sacrifice a man or two to get a job done. If he isn't working with a raiding party, then his Matriarch's put him up to something. Your guess is as good as mine as to what. Let's hope we don't find out."

"Sounds like we're taking a bit of a risk, letting him stay here overnight."

"We are. But I'd rather keep him where I can see him than have him skulking about in the darkness." Orthenn went back to sharpening his sword. "Was that all you came here for, or is there something else?"

Gerrick thought back to the rabbit he and Aldous had found. "There might be something to his story about a goblin raiding party hunting you."

"What makes you say that?"

"When Aldous and I went out on patrol—"

"When you went off to sulk over a bit of friendly teasing, you mean."

Gerrick wanted to protest. He nodded instead. Orthenn didn't have any more interest in women than he did, but his status kept the rest of their brothers-in-arms from making the same fuss over it as they did with Gerrick. He didn't know what it was like to sit through the same "friendly teasing" for years on end. But it wasn't Gerrick's place to argue with him. "We found a rabbit someone stashed in a tree. There's a chance a goblin left it there."

Orthenn shrugged. "Or our pointy-eared friend there did some hunting earlier. That doesn't prove anything."

"What about the scout he killed?"

"That just proves there are goblins in the Ghostwood. We already knew that. There's no guarantee he was looking for us in particular."

"It's hard to believe it's just a coincidence though."

"What would you have me do?" Orthenn gave him a hard look. "I'm not running back to my father with my tail between my legs because of a few goblins. If a raiding party wants me, they're welcome to try to take me. We're some of the finest soldiers Dawn's Gate has to offer. They won't stand a chance against us."

"Not in a fair fight. But goblins fight dirty. If they attack us in the night…"

"We'll have someone on watch who'll notice and wake the whole camp. Tonight, that's me. You don't think I'm sharp enough to notice an entire raiding party coming toward us?"

Gerrick winced. He'd pushed Orthenn too far; there'd be no swaying him now. "Of course, you'd notice, my prince. I didn't mean any offense."

"Good. Since this has you so worried, you'll be joining me. Will that be enough to put your mind at ease?" There was no mistaking the warning in Orthenn's voice or the icy look in his eyes.

"It will. Thank you." Gerrick wouldn't have gotten much sleep that night anyway. The extra watch would at least give him something useful to do while he was awake.

"Then you're dismissed." Orthenn's expression softened. "Try to lighten that mood of yours. We'll be fine. The elf doesn't know what he's talking about; don't let him get to you."

Gerrick hoped Orthenn was right.

Five

Orthenn and his men gave Moranthus, and the clump of tree roots at the edge of their camp that he'd seated himself on, a wide berth for the rest of the night. They probably assumed he didn't pose a threat to them when they outnumbered him by such a wide margin. And now that Orthenn had dismissed him, Moranthus didn't seem to be of any further interest.

It reminded him of the way Moonridge's people—even the ones so close to the southern border that they might as well have lived in Dawn's Gate—had treated him after the coup. They were approachable enough when they thought he was just another elf going about his daily life, but they always went cold toward him as soon as they got a good look at his hair. If Moranthus had business with them, they'd still talk to him—albeit, as begrudgingly as possible—but he'd counted himself lucky if anyone else would even look him in the eye. His status as a veteran duskblade didn't mean anything anymore; even beggars were treated with more respect than half-exiles like him.

Moranthus ground a twig into the dirt with the tip of his right boot. At least that kind of treatment didn't sting as much, coming from Orthenn's men. Humans weren't overly fond of his people at the best of times; Moranthus wouldn't have gotten any warmer a reception from them if he still had a full head of hair. And their avoidance of him left him with more than enough peace and quiet to think things over.

Unless Orthenn's refusal to return home had just been a show of bravado to save face in front of his soldiers, Moranthus had lost his chance at extracting him without a fuss. He didn't like his chances of extracting Orthenn *with* a fuss either. Not when Orthenn had ten loyal soldiers under his command, and they all had enough muscle on them to overpower Moranthus in a scuffle. Even after taking the extra bulk of their armor into account, Moranthus looked like a spindly youth who hadn't filled out to match his height compared to them.

The skill and speed he could usually rely on to win his fights for him wouldn't mean anything against so many opponents at once. As soon as he went after one of them, another could just grab him, wrestle him to the ground, and sit on him until he surrendered or died of shame. If they didn't kill him first.

He'd need a subtler approach to have any hope of salvaging the situation. Some way of catching Orthenn alone and off his guard, where he'd be easier to reason with or, failing that, sub-due. He wished he'd had more time to survey Orthenn's camp before blundering his way into it. It might've given him some insight into what routine, if any, Orthenn and his soldiers followed and any ways such a routine might be exploited. As things stood, he'd need to base any plans he made on guess-work and rely on luck to see them through. And all before his time in Orthenn's camp ran out the next morning, unless he wanted his job to get a lot more difficult.

The sound of slow, heavy footfalls beside him snapped him out of his thoughts. He looked up from the deep impression he'd made in the soft dirt at his feet to find a stocky, brown-haired soldier—the same one Bristles had put on goblin-kicking duty earlier—standing over him, a bowl of stew in his hands. His eyes held a soft, apologetic look that did nothing to lift Moranthus's spirits. Being pitied was worse than being ignored.

"Have I taken your seat?" Moranthus asked. His voice had a sharp, tired edge to it that he hadn't intended.

"Um…no. I just…thought you might be hungry." The soldier averted his eyes from Moranthus's. "We had some stew left over, so you can have it. If you want. It's really not half bad." He held the bowl out toward Moranthus in a stiff, overly careful manner.

"That's not the most convincing recommendation I've heard, but all right." Moranthus took the bowl and held it close to his chest, his stomach growling as he felt its warmth on his hands and caught the meaty scent of the stew it contained. As an afterthought, he added a hasty "Thank you."

The soldier's face brightened; the corners of his mouth upturned in a boyish grin that made Moranthus wonder if he'd even aged past his teens yet. Someone so young had no business scouting a goblin-infested forest. Orthenn was a fool to have brought him there. "It wasn't any trouble. Wouldn't have made much sense to take a second helping for myself before you'd even had a first."

"I suppose it wouldn't have." Moranthus took a larger-than-necessary bite of stew in an effort to stave off any further attempts at conversation. Getting acquainted with a man he'd be leaving at the mercy of a goblin raiding party would just make things stickier than they already were.

"See? I told you it wasn't half bad." The boy sat down on the dirt next to him. "My name's Liam, by the way."

Moranthus spent as much time chewing his bite of stew as he could get away with. Which wasn't difficult, given the tough, stringy lumps of meat it contained. Probably bear, by the taste of it. At least he knew what sort of animals lived in the Ghostwood now.

When it became clear the boy had no intention of leaving, Moranthus swallowed, then sighed. "Moranthus," he said, hoping that a name was all Liam wanted from him.

A young human offering a bowl of stew shouldn't be so disconcerting; spending the last decade of his life in solitude had taken more of a toll than he'd realized. If he'd been alive to see it, Moranthus's Patriarch would've gotten a good laugh out of how badly his favorite duskblade's usual charm and quick wit had failed him. Then, before Moranthus had a chance to get upset, he would've gathered Moranthus into his arms and planted a kiss on Moranthus's forehead to apologize for making fun of him. Moranthus's heart hurt as he realized how much he still missed those days. Everything had seemed so simple back then.

"Is that a common name up in Moonridge?" Liam's voice put an end to that disastrous flow of thought before Moranthus got swept away by it. Moranthus almost felt grateful for that.

"Not particularly." Moranthus's parents had gotten his name from a lesser-known medicinal berry. Or a botched pronunciation of some obscure folk hero, depending on which one he asked.

"Oh."

A long silence passed between them. Liam at least had the decency to look awkward, as though he knew he had no one but himself to blame for the uncomfortable position he'd put them in. Moranthus tried not to make eye contact, instead focusing on the rapidly cooling bowl of stew in his hands. Questionable flavor aside, it was the first hot meal he'd had in weeks, and it might be longer still before he got another.

When Moranthus had finished most of the stew, Liam took a deep breath, opened his mouth to speak, then closed it again. He bit his lower lip, eyebrows furrowed in an almost comical display of concentration as he stared into the canopy of leaves above them.

Moranthus had seen the same expression more than once on his old apprentice, when she'd wanted to ask a favor of him but hadn't quite found the courage to follow through on it. It had taken him years to train her out of that. He'd never quite figured out whether she'd started doing it in the first place because he'd inadvertently done something to put her off or because there was just something intimidating about the way he carried himself. She'd stopped speaking to him altogether after the coup, but that didn't stop him from occasionally wondering where the last ten years had taken her. Under less tense circumstances, he might've found Liam's similarity to her endearing.

"Out with it," Moranthus said, more from a desire to end Liam's misery than to hear whatever it was that had frozen his tongue.

"Pardon?"

"If you've got something to say, then say it. I don't bite, unless you give me a good reason to."

"It's—" Liam cast a glance around the camp, lingering on Bristles for a moment. "It's nothing, really."

Moranthus raised an eyebrow at him. "Really?"

"No. It's just… I think you had the right of things earlier," Liam said, his voice barely a whisper.

"What do you mean?"

"That you were right about Orthenn going home." Liam winced at the sound of his own voice and cast another furtive glance around the camp. "I mean, if his da wants him back bad enough to send you all the way out here, it must be important, right?"

"Most likely."

"Then he should go, shouldn't he? We could manage without him if we had to. And if there really is a goblin lord after him..."

"Yes?" Moranthus didn't know what to make of Liam. If Moranthus could get any useful information out of him, he was a potential chink in Orthenn's armor. But if he'd just come to Moranthus in search of someone safe to voice his concerns to, he'd go running back to Orthenn the moment Moranthus attempted to make use of him. Better not to take any risks until he'd gotten a better grasp of the situation. Moranthus allowed himself to lean slightly forward to show his interest without making himself look too eager.

"Well, then he's better off where he's safe. We all are. What good's our king to us if he spends all his time tearing his hair out on account of worrying over his kidnapped son?"

"I'm sure he'd manage somehow." Agreeing too fervently with Liam would just scare him off.

"I dunno. Maybe." Liam let out a short, bitter laugh. "I know *my* da wouldn't kick up much of a fuss if I went missing in a goblin raid. He hasn't even spoken to me for the past year now."

Moranthus blinked at him, his expression lapsing into a blank stare before he could catch it and twist it into something more pleasant. He hadn't expected Liam to offer him *that* bit of information. It went quite a long way toward explaining why he'd come to Moranthus, of all people, to share his misgivings about Orthenn's decision though. Confessions like that always worked best on strangers when the man giving them wanted sympathy more than a reasonable explanation.

"I've said too much, haven't I?"

"You haven't." Moranthus gave him a small, unintentionally genuine smile. He'd been the one who'd pressed Liam into saying it, after all; he'd brought it on himself.

In another life, he could've left it at that. Offered Liam a sympathetic ear for his family troubles and then gone on his way, either to write his mission off as a failure or find a way to slip through Orthenn's defenses on his own. His conscience could've stayed as clear as a field of virgin snow. But he didn't. With a sick, twisty knot in his gut that had nothing to do with the stew, he asked, "Orthenn staying here really does worry you, doesn't it?"

He'd never used to feel like this, doing his job. Under his Patriarch's rule, he'd lived for the thrill of a new set of orders and done worse things to better people without hesitation. But then, the missions his Patriarch had given him had always made sense. Moranthus had trusted that any unsavory actions against individual people that those missions entailed would benefit Moonridge as a whole.

Moranthus had assumed he'd feel the same way about carrying out his new Matriarch's orders when she finally gave him a chance to, but the thought of tricking Liam into betraying Orthenn weighed more heavily on Moranthus's conscience than it should have. Had things really changed so much under his Matriarch's rule? Or had the isolation he'd faced under her rule just changed him?

He gave his thigh a discreet pinch to put an end to that line of thought. He had work to do. He could have a discussion with himself about ethics after he'd gotten himself back to Aurora. Otherwise, he'd spent the last ten years slogging through a sea of petty make-work for nothing.

"I guess it does. More than I thought it would anyway." Liam winced. "Don't tell anyone I said that."

"I wouldn't dream of it."

"You know, you're really not half bad for an elf. Not as uppity as everyone's always saying your people are."

"I suppose I'll have to take that as a compliment." The knot in Moranthus's gut twisted itself even tighter. "You wouldn't happen to know of any way I might change Orthenn's mind, would you?"

Liam was quiet for a moment, the corners of his mouth downturned in a thoughtful frown. "Can't say I do. I wouldn't worry about it too much though. This isn't the first time he's turned one of his da's messengers away. No one's likely to hold it against you if you come back without him."

"I'm sure you're right. I'd just hate to feel like I gave up without trying everything I could first. After coming all this way, it's a shame to be leaving empty-handed."

"If it's really that important to you, you could try talking to him again, maybe. He'll probably be in a better mood once he's had time to calm down from the fright you gave us, showing up the way you did."

"I can't imagine he'd want to look indecisive, changing his mind in front of everyone so soon after he's made a decision."

"You could try him later, once everyone else has turned in for the night then. He's got the first watch tonight, so you wouldn't be waiting too long."

Moranthus made a small grunt of approval in the back of his throat. That could work. That would work nicely. "Maybe I will. Thank you."

"It was no trouble." Liam paused, a guilty look in his eyes, before continuing, "There's something else you should know. I'm not supposed to tell anyone this, but Orthenn isn't—"

"Liam!" Bristles's voice pierced the hum of idle chatter hanging over the clearing like a well-aimed arrow. "That's enough talk. If you've got time to waste mooning over our guest there, you've got time to fetch us some more firewood. Get to it!"

Liam leapt to his feet, his face flushing a deep red. Whatever he'd been trying to say before Bristles interrupted him, Moranthus would never hear the rest of it now. He hoped it wasn't anything important. "I-I will, sir! And I wasn't—"

"*Now*, Liam. No excuses and no dawdling, unless you want your watch doubled tomorrow."

"Right, sir! I'm sorry, sir!" Liam dusted himself off and turned to leave.

Before he fully realized what he was doing, Moranthus reached out and caught Liam by the wrist. "Listen, if you do encounter a full raiding party and it doesn't work out in your favor…just do what they tell you. I don't know what you've been told about them, but goblins don't kill their captives if they can avoid it. You'll be worth more to them alive. Try to keep that in mind." He kept his voice low, but insistent, his eyes locked on the shaggy, badly cut hair that covered the back of Liam's head. A boy Liam's age really didn't have any business patrolling the Ghostwood or facing even an inexperienced goblin warrior, let alone a full raiding party.

Liam wrenched his arm free, as though Moranthus's touch had burned him. "You should be telling the goblins to do as we say after they've lost, not the other way around. If it comes to a fight, we'll be winning it, plain and simple." With that, he stalked across the camp and into the forest surrounding it without so much as a backward glance.

"Of course. My mistake," Moranthus murmured. He wasn't sure whether he meant it for Liam or himself.

Six

Moranthus finished his stew, then put his hood up and lay back against the tree's trunk. If Orthenn and his men thought he'd dozed off, all the better. He didn't need any further distractions or disappointments to keep him from the task at hand.

Liam had given him as clear a shot at Orthenn as he was likely to get; that was all that mattered. All he could let matter if he wanted a future for himself. Moranthus's Patriarch was gone, and nothing he could do would bring him back. He'd clung to the past long enough. It was time for him to find a way to live with the present and all the imperfection and uncertainty that went along with it.

He pretended to sleep as the sounds of the camp dimmed around him. Letting on that he was sitting awake, waiting for a chance to catch Orthenn alone, would've made him look suspicious and gotten Liam into more trouble than he was likely to face already. Little by little, the lively conversations, and the tramping footsteps that often punctuated them, faded to murmurs interrupted by an occasional snore.

Only the fire stayed consistent, crackling brightly as it gnawed through the firewood Liam had gone to fetch. Its sound carried Moranthus back to the rough-hewn stone hearth that had warmed his childhood home. He relaxed his posture as he recalled the nights he'd sat beside it on his mother's lap, lulled to sleep by the feel of her rough, washer-woman's fingers combing through his hair. His childhood home was long gone, and his mother was ash in one of the communal burning pits dug outside Aurora to dispose of the countless victims of the plague that had swept across Moonridge during Moranthus's adolescence. But it was a good memory all the same.

When the snores grew more frequent and the last hushed murmurs subsided, Moranthus cast a lazy glance around the camp. He counted nine occupied bedrolls scattered around the clearing. At the clearing's northern edge, on a fallen log covered in a thick coating of moss, sat Orthenn, staring into the inky darkness that loomed just outside the camp with an intensity that made his soldiers' earlier, half-hearted attempts at guard duty look laughable in comparison. Bristles had also remained awake, stalking along the camp's southern edge like a captive bear testing the limits of its cage.

He watched several repetitions of Bristles's patrol route, hoping he'd eventually stop and either give himself a rest or go to sleep like everyone else. When Bristles showed no sign of slowing down, let alone stopping, Moranthus accepted that he'd need to find a way to work around him. He might've admired the man's commitment to his work if it weren't so wretchedly inconvenient. It would certainly complicate matters if Bristles took exception to Moranthus having as private a conversation with Orthenn as the camp would allow. But he didn't see what other choice he had, and he'd wasted too much time already by waiting on Bristles.

With an exaggerated yawn, Moranthus got to his feet. He took his time straightening himself out, making a show of stretching and brushing a few bits of dirt off his cloak before walking across the camp toward Orthenn. Bristles gave him a scowl from the opposite end of the camp but was too far away to voice any complaints without causing a fuss that would wake the rest of the camp and earn him the ire of his sleeping companions. Moranthus had Orthenn all to himself, unless Bristles decided Moranthus was enough of a threat to Orthenn's safety to justify abandoning his post.

With a hard, sharp tug, as though he were removing a bandage that had stuck to a wound, Moranthus pulled his hood back. Even if Orthenn knew what the shaved sides of Moranthus's head meant, he'd respond better to a worried face than an expression rendered unreadable by the shadows of Moranthus's hood.

Orthenn cast a brief, tired glance at Moranthus as he sat beside him, then shifted his gaze back to the forest without a word.

Moranthus took a brief, half-interested glance of his own at the darkness between the trees, but couldn't make out anything worth his attention. Orthenn was deliberately ignoring him. He'd have to get things moving himself. "Do you have a moment?" he asked, keeping a note of uncertainty in his voice in an effort to win himself a bit of sympathy.

Orthenn sighed. "If I have to." He kept his eyes fixed firmly off Moranthus. So much for making things easier by taking his hood off.

"I won't trouble you for long; all I ask is that you hear me out."

"If you're going to try to convince me to leave again, you can save your breath. It's not happening."

"Is there really no way I can change your mind?" Moranthus would've hung upside down from a tree and juggled if he thought it would get Orthenn's attention. Trying to reason with Orthenn without being able to see his face well enough to read his expression felt like arguing with a stone wall. And he suspected that Orthenn knew that, maddening creature that he was.

"There isn't. But if it makes you feel better, you're welcome to try."

"There's no need to mock me, is there? You'd act the same in my position." Moranthus didn't see much point in hiding his frustration. Orthenn could think he'd won if he wanted to. Maybe he'd get smug and let his guard down a little.

"Calm down, would you? I've seen mother hens less fussy than you are."

"I'd feel much calmer if I didn't have to explain to your father why I've returned to him without his son."

Orthenn turned to face him, his expression caught somewhere between sympathy and irritation. "How long are you going to keep this up? I've given you my answer, and it hasn't changed. I can't rightly ask my men to finish out their task here if I'm not willing to see it through along with them. That's all there is to it."

"Be that as it may, I really don't think you've considered the consequences of—"

"He *said* he's done with you. I suggest you listen to him." Bristles placed a hand on the back of Moranthus's neck and gave it a light, but firm squeeze.

Moranthus winced at the feeling of Bristles's rough, sword-callused fingers digging into his skin, cursing himself for not paying closer attention to Bristles. He knew better than to let himself get snuck up on, and he had no excuse for losing track of an armored human. Even as an apprentice, he'd never have gotten away with such sloppy work. Fighting the urge to tear himself away from Bristles and tell him exactly where he could shove his shoddy excuse for a threat, he choked out a strained "Understood."

"Good." Bristles relaxed his grip. "Now, I'm going to let go of you, and you're going to leave Orthenn in peace. We've all heard more than enough from you. Give it a rest."

Moranthus cast a hopeful glance at Orthenn but got only stony silence in return. "All right," he said. "No more trying to talk him out of this." Bristles was right. The time for words had passed. He'd need to take a more hands-on approach to make Orthenn see things his way.

"There's a good elf." Bristles let go of his neck and took a step backward.

Moranthus sat still for a moment, taking deep, steadying breaths to keep his head clear. The beginnings of an idea stirred in his mind, and as long as he could move quickly enough and think up the rest of the plan as he went along, it had a half-decent chance of working. If he slipped up, things would likely end in a run-in with the business end of Bristles's sword, but with the way things had gone between them so far, there was a strong possibility of that happening anyway.

Moranthus cast an imploring glance upward to the watchful moon hidden somewhere above the trees, then rose to his feet. He took a single step forward, keeping Orthenn in his peripheral vision as he moved. Bristles's lingering presence behind him put him ill at ease, but that couldn't be helped. His heartbeat quickened as he moved his right hand to the hilt of his dagger, slow and smooth to keep Orthenn and Bristles from catching on to him. Straining his ears to pick up on any sign of them moving behind him, he tightened his grip on the dagger until his knuckles went pale.

Then, in a single, fluid motion, he turned on his heel, drew his dagger, and held the flat of its blade just under Orthenn's chin. Hard enough to put pressure on his skin, but not hard enough to cut him. No need to spill any blood if he could avoid it.

"On your feet, princeling. We have places to be," he said, his voice low and rough. He pressed his dagger just a hair harder into Orthenn's chin to break through the shock and get him moving.

Orthenn did as he was told, his eyes shining with betrayal as he stood. Moranthus didn't make the mistake of meeting them. It was easy enough to avoid when he stood about half a head taller than Orthenn. Orthenn's skin had paled to an ashy color that almost glowed in the firelight, and Moranthus could hear Orthenn's heart pounding in his chest. Orthenn was afraid of him to an almost troubling degree.

A metallic, scraping noise sounded just ahead of him. Bristles, no doubt, trying to make a hero of himself.

Without taking his eyes off Orthenn, Moranthus said, "I wouldn't do that if I were you. One more move, and your prince will be watering these trees with his blood."

Bristles scoffed. "Like you'd really do it. Kill him, and there's nothing left to protect you." Still, the scraping noise stopped.

Moranthus put a hand on Orthenn's shoulder and turned him until Moranthus stood at his back, grateful for the fallen log between them and Bristles. He shifted his dagger so its blade rested against Orthenn's throat and then gave Bristles his full attention. "Wouldn't I? I've already come this far."

"Why are you doing this?" Bristles kept his voice level and let go of his sword.

When he'd first entered their camp, Bristles and Orthenn had been eager enough to believe Moranthus had defected to the goblin territories. They wouldn't need any convincing to believe it again now that Moranthus was holding a knife to Orthenn's throat. As long as he kept Bristles alive while he dragged Orthenn out of the camp, he could count on Bristles to lead the rest of Orthenn's men on a rescue mission in the wrong direction and buy Moranthus the time he needed to get Orthenn across Moonridge's southern border.

"It's like I said," Moranthus replied. "A goblin lord's put a price on his head. I intend to collect it. He's worth more alive, of course, but I still stand to make a sizeable profit off his corpse, if it comes to that. The real question here is whether you're willing to cooperate with me."

Orthenn gave an almost imperceptible shake of his head. Moranthus wasn't surprised; anything else would've made him look like a coward. He trusted Bristles to look at his situation with more reasonable eyes. Bristles's job was to protect his prince's life, not his honor. As long as Moranthus had Orthenn under his control, Bristles would do anything Moranthus told him.

Bristles kept his eyes locked on Orthenn for a long moment; then he sighed and slumped his shoulders in defeat. "Just tell me what you want."

"There's a good human." Moranthus let his lips curl into a satisfied smirk. Maybe it was petty and more than a little foolish, taunting a man he'd backed into a corner, but it felt good. "First, I'll be needing your sword belt. You'll get it back once we're done here. You have my word."

Bristles ground his teeth as he unfastened the buckle holding his sword belt in place. He caught his sword by its sheath before it could slide off his hip, then tossed it to the ground beside Moranthus's feet. It landed with a soft, reassuring *thud*.

"Close enough." Moranthus squeezed Orthenn's shoulder. "I'm going to need yours, as well. You won't be needing it where we're going."

Orthenn spent a good, long while fumbling with his belt buckle, shaking hard enough that Moranthus could feel it through his armor. Moranthus wished he hadn't needed to frighten the man to such an extent to get him under his control. Once they got out of earshot of the camp, Moranthus would need to find a way to reassure Orthenn that he didn't mean him any harm, or they'd both have a long, uncomfortable walk to the border ahead of them.

When Orthenn finally got the damn thing off, Moranthus let go of his shoulder and snatched his sword belt out of his hand before he could drop it. Common as his sword looked, it was probably twice the quality—and cost—of whatever hand-me-down blade Bristles had found for himself. Best not to risk getting them mixed up in the dark. Orthenn would have more than enough to complain about without a lost weapon added to the list.

"Now then," Moranthus said, "I don't suppose you have any rope I could borrow?" He had a fair-sized length of cord tucked away in one of his pockets, but even if he cut it in half, he'd never get two sets of bindings out of it. Unless he wanted to risk leaving Orthenn's hands free, he'd need to find some way to supplement his supplies.

Bristles scoffed. "Next you'll be asking me to bind my own hands for you. You're an incompetent fool if you set out to kidnap a prince without bringing your own rope with you. Or are you just that lazy?"

Moranthus shrugged. "I doubt an incompetent fool would have made it this far. Now, will you be fetching that length of rope for me, or do I need to get it myself? Do keep in mind that if I have to drag your prince along with me while I sort through your things, I can't promise there won't be any…accidents along the way." He tapped the flat of his blade against Orthenn's throat. "I'd rather put his safety first if it's all the same to you. But if you insist…"

"Fine. You've made your point. I'll get you your damn rope." Bristles stalked past Moranthus and Orthenn, muttering a string of insults under his breath.

Moranthus turned Orthenn around again to better keep an eye on Bristles as he rummaged through a discarded pack by an empty bedroll. Bristles's entire demeanor made Moranthus uneasy. "I don't know what you were thinking, choosing him as your bodyguard," Moranthus murmured into Orthenn's ear. "If he doesn't know better than to antagonize a man who's holding a knife to his prince's throat, he shouldn't be allowed anywhere near you. You're sure I'm not doing you a favor by getting you away from him?"

Orthenn shuddered but kept silent. He hung his head when Bristles produced a sizeable coil of rope from the pack and trudged back across the camp with it slung over his shoulder.

"Careful now," Moranthus hissed, scrambling to adjust the position of his dagger so it didn't cut into Orthenn's neck.

Orthenn kept his head down as Bristles came to a stop in front of them, hunching his shoulders like a dog that expected a harsh kick from its master. Moranthus didn't need to see his eyes to know he'd screwed them shut.

"If this is the end, don't blame yourself for it. This isn't your fault," Orthenn said, his voice nothing more than a strained whisper.

"I have no one else to blame." Bristles's eyes took on a cold, steely glint that set Moranthus's teeth on edge. "Whatever comes of this…he'll get what's coming to him. I swear it."

Moranthus sighed. "This is all very touching, but I'm afraid our time here is running short. I assume you're all familiar with bindings, in some form, or can at least tie a secure knot?"

"So you really do expect me to bind my hands for you?" Bristles asked. "Why not just have me deliver Orthenn to your goblin friends while I'm at it?"

"Don't be ridiculous," Moranthus replied. "Of course, I don't expect you to bind anyone. That'll be your prince's job."

"Why me?" Orthenn asked. "You've got to be better at this sort of thing than I am."

"Because I'm not stupid enough to leave you unattended while I see to the matter. Don't worry. I'll be looking over your work once you're finished. I can make any adjustments I need to then."

"You ask too much of me. I can't—"

"Just get it over with." Bristles shoved the coil of rope into Orthenn's hands. "I don't want him touching me."

"You're sure?" Orthenn's voice took on a soft, pleading tone.

"I am." Bristles turned his back to them and extended his arms behind him, palms together. "Whenever you're ready, my prince."

"Smart man." Moranthus relaxed his grip on his dagger. "You'd do well to listen to him." Moranthus gave Orthenn one last pat on the shoulder, then eased his dagger off Orthenn's throat. "So long as you do as you're told, you'll have nothing to fear from me."

Orthenn gave Moranthus a harsh shove that sent him stumbling backward, but offered no further resistance as he bound Bristles's hands. From there, Moranthus talked him through tying Bristles to a tree at the camp's edge and working what was left of the rope into a makeshift gag to keep Bristles from waking the rest of the camp after Moranthus and Orthenn had gone. As a reminder, Moranthus kept his dagger on the back of Orthenn's neck throughout the process, only removing it to sever another length of rope from the coil and test the security of Bristles's bindings between each step.

With Bristles secured and silenced, Moranthus felt more confident in his control over Orthenn, who seemed almost disoriented without Bristles's constant commentary. Spending time apart from his bodyguard would probably do him some good. In the meantime, his face seemed frozen into an expression of vague worry, and his movements were abrupt and awkward. He filled his pack with as much of the camp's food supply—the same waybread Moranthus had been living off, for the most part—as it could hold before allowing Moranthus to bind his hands with the last of the rope.

Orthenn maintained an almost eerie silence as Moranthus led him out of the camp and into the dense forest surrounding it. Instead of craning his neck to peer into the darkness, and any threats it might have concealed, he kept his eyes fixed on the ground beneath his feet.

Moranthus expected Orthenn's heavy footfalls to overpower the Ghostwood's ominous silence. But the moment they left Orthenn's camp, their footsteps went as quiet as if they were walking barefoot across a rug. Moranthus hadn't been imagining things when he'd first entered the Ghostwood; sound really did travel differently there. That knowledge unnerved him more than the unmuffled sound of Orthenn's footsteps would have.

"I'm not really planning to sell you to a goblin lord, you know," Moranthus said as soon as they'd passed out of earshot of Orthenn's camp. "You can stop dragging your feet like a man walking to his execution any moment now."

"I don't believe you," Orthenn replied. He returned to his sullen silence as he continued trudging forward.

"All right. Pout all you want if it makes you feel better. We'll see how long you keep it up once you're safe at home tucked away in your own bed with your father's guards watching over you."

Orthenn offered no response, leaving Moranthus alone with his thoughts. Silent as it was, his company made Moranthus feel more at ease as they followed the trail of trees he'd marked out of the Ghostwood. Their journey out of it didn't seem to take half as long as his journey in.

They encountered no signs of life in the dense forest around them until they passed by the decayed remains of a large owl. Moranthus had no recollection of seeing the owl on his way to Orthenn's camp. It struck him as odd that it could have lain on the ground for so long without some other creature making a meal of it. Almost as though he'd been meant to find it as a warning. Or a glimpse into his own future if he cared to interpret it. The sight of the dead owl set Moranthus on edge more than he cared to admit, even after he and Orthenn had passed through the last of the Ghostwood's trees and stepped into the welcoming moonlight beyond their reach.

With a short, exasperated laugh, Moranthus shook his head at his own foolishness. All the dead owl really meant was that he'd let himself get too jittery in the years since his last real mission. Anyone would've been nervous, facing death or exile as a consequence for any mistakes in his work. But that was behind him. With Orthenn securely in hand, all that stood between Moranthus and a bright future in Moonridge were the miles between them and Moonridge's southern border.

"So, do you still think we're bound for the goblin territories?" Moranthus asked. "Unless your father has completely lost control of his borders, we're on the Dawn's Gate side of the Ghostwood. Welcome home."

Orthenn shrugged. "That doesn't prove anything. Maybe you just want to meet up with the rest of your raiding party first and help them burn down a village or two on your way home."

"That sort of attitude must do wonders for your soldiers' morale." Moranthus rolled his eyes before whistling for Storm. The sooner they put some distance between themselves and the Ghostwood, the better.

Orthenn tensed at the sound of approaching hoofbeats, but relaxed when Storm appeared, riderless, over the crest of a nearby hill. She let out a triumphant whinny and trotted toward them, pressing her face against Moranthus when she reached his side. Her breath washed over him in short, warm puffs as he ran his hands over her nose and forehead.

Moranthus gave Storm's flank an apologetic pat before attaching Orthenn's pack and sword belt to her saddle. Without a second horse, they'd have to walk to the border, and they could walk faster if Storm carried their belongings for them. As an afterthought, Moranthus removed his cloak, grateful to be free of its unnecessary warmth, and added it to the bundle of Orthenn's things on Storm's saddle. After double-checking that Orthenn's bindings and Storm's cargo were secure, Moranthus put a hand on Orthenn's back and led him away from the Ghostwood at a brisk walk.

For the next two days, Orthenn turned his back to Moranthus and slept, or pretended to, every time they stopped to rest and ignored any attempt Moranthus made at conversation while they walked. So far, he hadn't stopped eating, at least, but that gave Moranthus precious little comfort. He didn't trust the thoughtful, determined look Orthenn had set his face into during all those hours of quiet. It made him feel like he'd missed something.

On the morning of their third day outside the Ghostwood, Moranthus, weary from a sleepless night, set about checking Orthenn's bindings. Orthenn kept silent, as usual, as Moranthus ran his fingers over each of the knots he'd tied, testing their strength, and tugged at the rope around Orthenn's wrists to ensure that it hadn't loosened enough for Orthenn to slip out of it or tightened enough to keep Orthenn's blood from circulating into his hands.

Moranthus was almost disappointed when he found his rope work as secure as it was the night before. He checked every last wrinkle of Orthenn's clothing for a concealed weapon, or even a sharp stick or rock Orthenn could use to cut himself free. But his search didn't yield anything more interesting than a few prickly grass seeds that had gotten stuck to Orthenn's tabard while he slept. If Orthenn had concealed a means of freeing himself, either he'd hidden it somewhere Moranthus couldn't find it, or it wasn't something Moranthus knew to look for.

Moranthus allowed himself a frustrated growl as he hauled Orthenn to his feet. "I suppose it's safe to assume you still aren't speaking to me?" he asked.

Orthenn stretched as well as he could with his hands bound. "Unless you tell me who you're working for, I don't have anything to say to you."

"I've already told you that I'm working for your father." Indirectly, and most likely without Orthenn's father's knowledge or approval, but that was beside the point. "I'm not sure what else you want from me."

"You're lying. Stop making a fool of yourself by pretending I don't know that." Orthenn gave him a hard look. "Let me go now, and no one has to know you did this. You seem like a decent enough sort. Whoever you're working for…whatever they're threatening you with if you don't do this, you can get away from that. I'll help if I can. But you need to be honest with me."

Orthenn was in no position to be making those threats and offers, so Moranthus didn't dignify them with a response. "And what makes you so certain I'm not being honest when I say I'm working for your father?"

"If you were, you wouldn't have kidnapped me."

"I wouldn't have needed to kidnap you if you hadn't refused to follow your father's orders. If I could trust you to cooperate with me, I'd happily take those bindings off you."

Orthenn shook his head. "That's not what I meant. If you were really working for my king, you wouldn't have kidnapped *me*."

Moranthus's brow furrowed. "What do you mean?"

"The real Orthenn's still in the Ghostwood. I'm just his body double."

"No. That's not possible." Moranthus's orders hadn't mentioned anything about a body double. His Matriarch might be inexperienced, but she knew enough to not overlook such a significant detail when she'd formulated whatever scheme Moranthus was participating in. Unless she hadn't overlooked it and had meant for Moranthus to fail…but that would be stupid. If she really wanted him dead or exiled, she'd have just given the order. Not sent him on a fool's errand as a cruel joke.

"It's the truth. All the king's messengers know about me. You didn't, which means you aren't one of them." Orthenn shrugged. "You can still bring me to whoever you're working for if you don't believe me. They aren't going to be happy when they find out I'm just a nobody with a prince's face though."

Moranthus struggled to keep his breathing even as he rummaged through his pockets in search of his glowstone. Orthenn was lying—he had to be. Showing Orthenn that the glowstone was enchanted to track him, and only him, would be more than enough proof to shut him up. And soothe the frayed edges of Moranthus's mind.

But when Moranthus finally curled his fingers around the glowstone's smooth, round edges and held it out in front of him, instead of the bright, white glow he'd been expecting, it gave off a dull, violet light. A dull, violet light that meant Orthenn was still in his camp, if he wasn't already in the hands of a goblin raiding party. And Moranthus was two days' travel away from him, stuck with a worthless body double who'd outwitted him without uttering a single word.

Moranthus's chest tightened. His tongue felt as though it had frozen solid as he choked out an anguished "What have you done?"

His hand fell to his side, shaking. He couldn't bring himself to catch the glowstone—the glowstone he should have
checked before he left the Ghostwood—as it slipped through
his fingers.

60

Seven

From the moment he'd stepped into Orthenn's camp, the elf reminded Gerrick of a fox. It was those keen, yellow eyes, paired with his long nose and that smug look he never quite managed to wipe off his face. Until now.

Even without the smugness, the resemblance held. But now, instead of a fox that had just made off with a farmer's fattest chicken, the elf looked more like a fox caught in a trap, ready to gnaw his own leg off to escape. Gerrick had the sinking feeling that he was that leg.

The elf's hand settled on the hilt of his sword. He eased it halfway out of its scabbard.

"Are you all right?" Gerrick asked. He wished he'd overheard Liam's conversation with the elf back at Orthenn's camp. He might've at least gotten the elf's name out of it. That would've given him a good way to start talking the elf down.

The elf responded with a short, harsh bark of laughter, a feverish gleam in his eyes. "As all right as I can be, considering that you've just killed me."

"Don't exaggerate." Gerrick fought the urge to take a step backward. He didn't want the elf thinking he meant to run off. "I haven't killed you, and I don't want to. I don't know who you're working for, but—"

"Oh, but I'm afraid you do know. And I'm willing to bet he won't be too pleased with your little performance once he's caught wind of this."

"Don't try to tell me you're a royal messenger again." Gerrick gave the elf a hard look. He'd never put much stock in the tales of elven arrogance that were passed like bits of candy around Orthenn's campfire, but he couldn't think of a better reason the elf would expect him to swallow the same lie twice. "I'm human, not stupid."

The elf sighed and crossed his arms over his chest. "I'm not a messenger, and I assure you, I am quite finished with pretending to be one. If I intended to lie to you, I'd have chosen a far more convincing story than that."

"Then what are you? Let's have the truth and be done with it."

"Moonridge duskblade. Sent, at my Matriarch's request, to bring Orthenn home before he falls victim to a goblin raiding party. As a favor to your king. Which, with the exception of my Matriarch's involvement, I have already explained to you if I'm not mistaken."

Gerrick couldn't see any lie in his eyes. But he hadn't seen any lie in the elf's eyes when he'd first stepped into Orthenn's camp either. If he worked for Moonridge's Matriarch, it was possible that he really was trying to protect Orthenn. But if that was true, he should've known Orthenn had a body double. "Prove it."

"Are you really in a position to be asking me to prove myself?" The elf raised an eyebrow at him. "Last I checked, you were my hostage. And not a particularly valuable one now that you've decided to stop being Orthenn."

Gerrick winced. "What are you going to do with me, then?" There was no use putting it off any longer. If the elf meant to kill him, better to get it over with than give the elf the satisfaction of drawing it out.

"That depends entirely on how much you're willing to trust me."

Not much farther than Gerrick could throw him. "What do you mean?"

"I mean that you were right earlier. I'm not dead. But if I can't find a way to salvage this, I may as well be. *We* may as well be."

"And?"

"*And* I am going to have significantly less trouble salvaging this mess if I can rely on your cooperation."

"My cooperation with what?" Gerrick gave the elf an incredulous look. "I'm not going to help you kidnap Orthenn, if that's what you're asking."

"Not kidnap. Rescue." The elf spoke in the slow, overly cheerful voice of a father whose small child had just asked him an embarrassing question in a public place. The same voice Gerrick had fallen into when his daughter asked in the middle of a crowded market if she would ever get a new mother. "If I'm not mistaken"—the elf picked up his tracking stone and turned it over in his hand—"your prince should still be where we left him. Which means we haven't lost him yet. So long as we're quick about it, we have a chance of reaching him and setting things right before the goblins take matters out of our hands."

"Orthenn won't just let you back into his camp after what you've done. This is out of your hands already."

"That's where you come in. If he sees me alone, he'll assume that I killed you and attack me on sight. If I bring you back to him as my hostage, I'll never convince him that he can trust me. But if I have you at my side of your own free will, and you're willing to vouch for my intentions…I might still have a chance at reasoning with him."

Gerrick couldn't betray Orthenn like that. He'd failed in his duty as Orthenn's body double already by telling the elf who he was. But he hadn't been able to stop himself. The elf had gone out of his way to get Gerrick out of Orthenn's camp without bloodshed, and he hadn't treated Gerrick badly after taking him hostage. He probably wasn't a bad man at heart. Just a man working for a bad cause. And he looked like he was young enough that he could still turn his life around if he had someone to set him straight. The way someone should've set that cutpurse straight before he attacked a city guard trying to arrest him and robbed Gerrick's daughter of her mother. Gerrick had wanted to set the elf straight. That had been a mistake; he knew that now. But maybe it wasn't too late to put things right.

"Why would I vouch for a man who kidnapped me?" Gerrick asked.

"Because it'll get those bindings off your wrists."

Gerrick's wrists started to itch, as though they'd heard the elf's words and wanted Gerrick to know their thoughts on the matter. He didn't trust the elf, but the elf seemed to trust him well enough. He didn't see much harm in letting the elf keep trusting him if that trust helped him get back to Orthenn's camp.

Gerrick couldn't talk the elf out of going after Orthenn again, and that tracking stone of his would lead him back to Orthenn's camp with or without Gerrick's help. But if Gerrick went with him, he could keep the elf from getting within striking distance of Orthenn a second time. The elf would let his guard down eventually. When he did, Gerrick would be ready to turn on him, the same way the elf had turned on Orthenn.

"You're not afraid I'll run off?" Gerrick didn't want to agree to the elf's plan too easily.

The elf shrugged, a cold smile on his lips. "You're welcome to try. I can't imagine you'd get far on foot. Unarmed. Without supplies. Assuming I don't just chase you down and take my chances using you as a hostage, of course. You'd never outrun me."

"Fair enough."

"Do we have an agreement, then?"

Gerrick forced a tense half smile onto his face. "You're taking me with you whether I agree to this or not. I might as well have my hands free. But I can't promise Orthenn will listen to me. He's…steadfast. Hard to sway once he's made up his mind."

The elf tried and failed to stifle a laugh. "You can just call him stubborn if that's what you mean. I promise I won't tell anyone."

"I said what I meant."

"Of course, you did. But, steadfast or stubborn, you have my word I won't hold you responsible for Orthenn's actions. Just tell him he can trust me, and I'll see to the rest." The elf was direct by elven standards. Didn't waste time getting to his point.

"All right. We have an agreement." Until the elf gave him an opportunity to break free of it.

"Good. I'm glad you're willing to be reasonable about this." The elf unsheathed his dagger and crossed the short expanse of grass between them in several quick, confident strides. "And I'm glad we were able to resolve this little misunderstanding before things got messy."

"So am I." Gerrick kept his gaze fixed on the red braid draped over the elf's shoulder as the elf sawed through his bindings. He didn't trust himself to keep his lie hidden if he met the elf's eyes.

As the last of Gerrick's bindings fell from his wrists, the elf took a step back and returned his dagger to its sheath. "So, does Orthenn's body double have a name?"

Gerrick rubbed at the abrasions his bindings had left on his wrists. "Gerrick." His name sounded strange to his ears after spending the last two days going by Orthenn's. It was good to have it back.

"Moranthus." The elf extended a hand toward him. "Ready to save your prince from himself?"

Gerrick clasped Moranthus's arm and gave it a single, firm shake. "I am."

Gerrick spent the rest of the day struggling to keep pace with Moranthus as he led them back toward the Ghostwood. The slow, meandering course Moranthus had set for them over the past two days quickened into a hard march along a straight path that, as far as Gerrick could tell, didn't exist outside Moranthus's head. Instead of skirting around the steepest hills, Moranthus climbed over them, eyes fixed on that damned tracking stone of his like he couldn't feel the slope of the ground beneath him.

Gerrick pushed himself into maintaining a pace just shy of a run so he could keep himself at Moranthus's side and keep an eye on the tracking stone. He hoped that by watching its colors change, he could make sense of how it worked. He got nothing out of the ordeal but a splitting headache and a stitch in his side that only worsened as the day wore on.

The tracking stone's colors didn't shift in any pattern Gerrick could make sense of. Half of them blurred together to the point that Gerrick wasn't sure they'd changed at all. The damn rock was a waste of time. He trusted his eyes and ears to get him to the Ghostwood, and Orthenn's camp, more than some fiddly magic trinket.

But, distracted as Moranthus was by his tracking stone, Gerrick wasn't fool enough to think Moranthus wouldn't notice if he tried to sneak off and grab his sword and pack from Moranthus's horse. The horse had taken one look at the latest hill her master had decided to lead them over before making a show of trotting around it and waiting for them on the other side. Gerrick wished he could have done the same.

They didn't stop to make camp until nightfall. They might not have stopped at all if Moranthus had had his way. Gerrick kept pace with him for as long as he could, but as the sun sank below the horizon, he fell farther and farther behind.

Eventually, Moranthus took pity on him. When he looked over his shoulder and saw Gerrick trudging along a good fifty paces behind him, he stopped. With a frustrated sigh, he whistled for his horse and set about unsaddling her for the night.

Gerrick cast a longing glance at his sword and pack as Moranthus let them fall to the ground. He didn't have the energy to do anything with his sword if he got it back, but he missed its comforting weight against his hip.

Spending a full day on his feet made the biscuit of waybread and small strips of jerky that made up his dinner taste better than they had any right to. Gerrick had almost finished his portion by the time Moranthus sat beside him, holding an untouched biscuit of waybread in one hand and a razor in the other.

Moranthus flipped the razor open, holding it away from himself like he thought it might bite him. Its blade shone like fresh-spilled blood in the reddish light of his tracking stone. His face settled into a small, worried frown as he flipped the razor shut again and ran a thumb over its handle.

"Something wrong?" Gerrick wasn't interested in hearing what was troubling Moranthus, but the sight of Moranthus silently staring at a blade was unnerving. Elves couldn't grow beards; Moranthus had no business carrying a razor. The sides of his head didn't keep themselves shaved, Gerrick supposed, but he still shouldn't have brought something so flashy into the wilds. The whole thing felt wrong to Gerrick.

Moranthus shoved the razor into some hidden pocket in his leathers. "You mean, aside from the obvious?" He turned to face Gerrick, a tired look in his eyes. "Nothing at all. I've never felt better, knowing there'll be two rulers wanting me dead, or worse, if I don't get back to your prince in time. But please, don't let that get in the way of your rest and relaxation. I'd hate to spoil such a lovely night for you."

"We'll get there soon enough. What good's all this hurry if you're half dead from exhaustion by then?"

"Better half dead than all dead." Moranthus gave him a wry smile. "Which of your soldier friends *was* Orthenn anyway?"

"The one you left bound, gagged, and tied to a tree." Gerrick didn't see any point in trying to hide something that obvious. If he hadn't said it, Moranthus would've worked it out easily enough on his own. Orthenn was the only man in his company for whom Gerrick could pass as a double.

"Shit." Moranthus covered his face with his free hand, muffling his voice. "It *would* be him, wouldn't it? Skies above, I've carved myself a thin sheet of ice to stand on."

"It's not all that bad." Moranthus didn't deserve any sympathy from Gerrick. But Gerrick wouldn't get Moranthus to let his guard down if he didn't try to get on Moranthus's good side. "You talked your way into his camp once, didn't you?"

"And just look how well that ended for me." Moranthus grimaced as he took a bite of his waybread. "This is horrible."

"It is. But you get used to it after a while."

"Is there any game in these parts?"

"There are rabbits. Maybe a pheasant if you're lucky. Why?"

"I'm going hunting. Give me a shout if you need me or the glowstone changes color." In a single, deliberate motion, he picked up his tracking stone and placed it on the ground between them. He tapped a finger against his tracking stone, his eyes narrowed in a way that made Gerrick feel like a fresh-faced recruit caught sneaking out of the barracks after curfew. "I assume this goes without saying, but I'd advise against making me regret this."

Gerrick tried not to look surprised. He hadn't expected Moranthus to give him a chance to escape so soon. "I said I'd help you, didn't I? I won't go back on my word."

"Good." Moranthus gestured toward Gerrick with his waybread. "Do you want this?"

"If you don't."

Without further warning, Moranthus tossed the waybread at him. Gerrick caught it just in time to keep it from hitting his face.

Moranthus got to his feet, a surprised look on his face. "Good catch."

Gerrick watched with disappointment as Moranthus slung Gerrick's sword belt over his shoulder before striding out of their camp. It was a fine blade, and he hated to lose it. But if he wanted to get away from Moranthus tonight, he didn't have a choice. Orthenn would issue him another when they returned to Dawn's Gate.

He didn't need a sword for what he was planning to do anyway. He was running away from Moranthus, not fighting him. But he wouldn't gain anything by doing it on foot. Moranthus had a horse with him. He'd have no trouble catching up to Gerrick when he returned to their camp and found him gone.

Gerrick's only hope for staying out of Moranthus's reach was stealing the horse. Moranthus hadn't done anything to secure her tack, arranged in a neat pile on the far side of his bedroll, and Gerrick knew he could keep her under control once he'd gotten a bridle on her. Compared to the hulking, ill-tempered courser—bred to be an exact match for Orthenn's monster of a horse—Gerrick left stabled in the last town Orthenn's company passed through on their way to the Ghostwood, she was slow and docile. Better suited for pulling a farmer's plow than carrying an elven brigand along the edge of the Ghostwood. A horse like that wouldn't have much fight in her.

Gerrick waited until Moranthus vanished over the crest of a nearby hill before making his move. The horse stood in a nearby clump of grass, eyeing Gerrick as though she didn't trust him any more than her master did. She kept her eyes on him as he got to his feet, shouldered his pack, and pocketed Moranthus's tracking stone. Gerrick didn't have any use for the tracking stone, but if he left it behind, it would lead Moranthus right back to Orthenn. He couldn't let that happen.

The horse's ears pricked forward in interest when Gerrick reached her tack, but she kept herself mercifully quiet and still. Gerrick picked up the horse's saddle along with her bridle so he wouldn't have to waste time by coming back for it later.

The horse took a step backward as Gerrick approached her, her saddle draped over his arms and bridle slung over his shoulder. Reluctantly, Gerrick set the saddle on the ground. He extended his right hand and tried again, careful to keep from making any sudden movements that might spook her. The horse held her ground, but flattened her ears back against her head, nostrils flaring at his scent.

"Steady now," Gerrick murmured as he came within an arm's length of the horse. "You're all right." He reached up to put a hand between her ears so she would lower her head and make it easier for him to get her bridle on.

Instead, the horse reared up, sending Gerrick staggering backward, and squealed as she struck out at him with her hooves.

Eight

Moranthus started at the sound of Storm's high-pitched squeal, missing a clear shot at a plump rabbit. It didn't matter; whatever had spooked his horse was infinitely more worthy of his attention than a wasted arrow and a lost meal. He drew another arrow from his quiver as he raced back to the camp. He was too far from the Ghostwood to worry about goblins, but that didn't rule out human bandits or hostile wildlife. And if he'd let himself get caught up in hunting rabbits to the point that he failed to notice some sign of danger nearby, and Storm paid the price for it, he'd never forgive himself.

When he reached the camp and found Gerrick shouting a stream of nonsense syllables as he tried to stay clear of Storm's flailing hooves, Moranthus wasn't sure whether he wanted to laugh at him or run him through with his own sword. But, whatever else Moranthus decided to do, he needed to calm Storm down before she strained herself. And stop her from trampling Gerrick, even though a good trampling was exactly what Gerrick, as a horse thief, deserved.

With a sharp whistle, Moranthus ran toward Storm. In his haste, he didn't notice her saddle in his path until his foot caught on its seat and almost sent him sprawling on the ground. As he struggled to regain his footing, Storm showed no signs of relenting in her pursuit of Gerrick. If anything, Moranthus's presence encouraged her. With another squeal, she charged at Gerrick, who barely managed to scramble out of her path. Moranthus threw himself between them, keeping Gerrick at his back. He hoped, for Gerrick's sake, that Gerrick wasn't stupid enough to attack him while he was distracted.

As Storm wheeled around to charge again, Moranthus waved his arms over his head. "That's enough! You're safe now; he won't bother you again."

Storm snorted and pawed at the ground, her body held as stiff as a tree trunk.

Moranthus lowered his voice into a warning tone. "Storm. *Enough.*"

With another snort, Storm relaxed her posture. Moranthus stepped to the side, allowing her a clear view of Gerrick. Storm cast a wary glance in Gerrick's direction but showed no outward signs of further aggression toward him.

"There's my sweet girl." Moranthus let himself smile, confident that Gerrick couldn't see his face, and walked to Storm's side to give her a nice, long scratch behind the ears. She'd done the right thing by defending herself. He didn't want her to feel like he'd scolded her for it. "You didn't let him get you. You're safe now, I promise."

Without looking at Gerrick, he asked, "So, would you like to explain why you tried to steal my horse?"

"What makes you think I tried to steal her?"

"Oh, I don't know." Moranthus gave Storm a pat on the neck, then turned around. "Maybe it's got something to do with you holding her bridle and me almost tripping over her saddle on my way here?"

Gerrick dropped Storm's bridle. "I hoped to escape while you hunted."

"And you needed my horse for that?" Moranthus fixed his eyes on Gerrick in the harshest glare he could manage. He couldn't afford to lose Gerrick's cooperation, but he couldn't afford to let Gerrick think he'd allow any more escape attempts either.

"I couldn't risk you taking me hostage again and using me to get to Orthenn."

"You still think I'm trying to kill him, don't you?"

"Maybe you're not, but I don't trust what your Matriarch has planned for him."

Moranthus shrugged. He couldn't argue with that when he didn't fully trust his Matriarch himself. "You're probably right not to trust her. But, whatever she hopes to gain from this, I can assure you that, for the time being, the only plan she has for your prince is for me to return him to his father."

Gerrick sighed. "I wish I could believe that."

"Do you think I dragged you out of the Ghostwood and two days down the road toward your capital for the fun of it, then?"

"Maybe you just wanted me to let my guard down. Or you were trying to meet up with someone who'd finish your job for you."

"You're just determined to assume the worst of me, aren't you?"

"I'm not. But you're asking me to take a lot on faith."

Moranthus paused and took a deep breath to compose himself before replying, "Short of dragging you up to Aurora and having my Matriarch explain to you that she ordered me to return your prince to his father, and nothing more, I'm not sure what proof of my intentions I have to offer that would satisfy you."

"You could at least give me *something* more to go on than your word alone."

"All right." Moranthus reached into the front inner pocket of his leather jerkin and took out the crumpled envelope that contained his orders. With a flick of his wrist, he tossed it to the ground at Gerrick's feet. He probably shouldn't let anyone else see them, but then, he probably shouldn't have made off with Orthenn's body double instead of the real Orthenn either. He'd passed far beyond the point of "shouldn't haves," and he expected he'd pass farther, still, before he could set things right. *If* he could set things right. "I don't expect this to mean anything to you, but those are my orders. The same ones my Matriarch sent me, and the same ones I've been following since I left Aurora. Marked with her official seal, which you probably won't recognize."

Gerrick cast a wary glance at Moranthus as he bent down to pick up the envelope. His eyes lingered on its seal for a moment, brow furrowed, before he flipped it open and slid out the folded sheet of parchment it contained. He brought the parchment close to his face, then shook his head. "It's too dark for me to read this."

"Try using the glowstone for light, then. You've stolen that, too, after all. You might as well get some use out of it."

"Fine." Gerrick walked back to their camp and resettled himself on his bedroll. With a frustrated huff of breath, he fished the glowstone out of his pocket.

Moranthus tried to keep his breathing even as he watched Gerrick read, and then reread, his orders. The man took his job as Orthenn's body double seriously; Moranthus couldn't deny him that. Moranthus might've respected him for it if his devotion hadn't all but destroyed Moranthus's chances of going home at the end of his mission.

When Gerrick held the parchment up to the glowstone's light a third time, Moranthus made his own way back to their camp, stopping to pick up Storm's bridle and saddle as he passed by them.

"Is that convincing enough for you?" Moranthus asked, setting Storm's tack on the ground next to his bedroll for the second time that night.

He could almost feel the edge of a razor against his skin as Gerrick put his orders back in their envelope. Gerrick ran his thumb over the ridges of the envelope's wax seal. "These do look real," he replied. "Real enough to warrant Orthenn having a look at them, at any rate. I can't speak for Orthenn, but for what it's worth... I believe you."

"Do you mean that this time, or are you just going to turn on me again the next time I let my guard down?"

After a long pause, Gerrick replied, "I mean it."

Moranthus sat on his bedroll. "I suppose that'll have to do." He knew better than to trust a man who'd tried to steal his horse, and he knew better still than to travel with a man he couldn't trust. But he needed Gerrick, whether he trusted him or not.

Gerrick responded with a noncommittal grunt and held the envelope out toward Moranthus.

"Thank you." Moranthus snatched his orders out of Gerrick's hand and tucked them back into the inside pocket of his jerkin.

Heart still racing from his abrupt return to the camp, he turned his face to the stars above him in an effort to calm himself. Before the plague, his father, on the rare nights he was at home, would lift Moranthus up onto the roof of their dingy little house and point out all the constellations they could see, telling Moranthus a story about each of them. Those nights had, more often than not, ended with Moranthus falling asleep in his father's arms, the half-spun tale of some sparkling, long-dead hero weaving through his dreams.

Over a century later, he'd forgotten half the stories, and more of the constellations, but the stars themselves were etched deeper into his memory than even his parents' faces. The sight of them, in all their unchanging glory, never failed to bring him a sense of comfort. Even if they didn't shine quite as bright so far from home.

The moon's pale face, however, cast as much light as ever as it looked down on him, taunting him with the prospect of several more empty, sleepless hours between him and the first light of day. Those hours would bring Orthenn's goblin pursuers closer to Orthenn, if they hadn't reached him already.

Moranthus shook his head. He should never have needed to return to Orthenn's camp in the first place. His Matriarch had no excuse for overlooking a potential complication as serious as a body double in Moranthus's orders. Under his former Patriarch, such a significant oversight, intentional or otherwise, would've been unthinkable. But then, his former Patriarch would never have doubted Moranthus's loyalty enough to even consider exiling him either.

And his Matriarch *must* have devised his mission as a fool's errand that, when Moranthus inevitably failed to accomplish it, would justify her decision to exile him. He knew her well enough to know she was far too cunning—far too *careful*—to put one of her plans into action without first accounting for even the most insignificant obstacles in its path. She'd never have succeeded in overthrowing her father otherwise. Which meant she would have *also* accounted for the possibility of him succeeding where she'd intended him to fail. Whatever her game was, she stood to gain something no matter how his mission ended.

If Moranthus was lucky, his Matriarch hadn't lied when she'd hinted at restoring him to his former status after Orthenn made it back to his father. If he wasn't, and he found another razor waiting for him when he delivered Orthenn to the frost-guards responsible for escorting him home, then so be it. At least she'd need to exile him in person, that way. And explain to the rest of his order why she'd exiled a duskblade for successfully completing a mission she'd personally sent him on. That alone would be worth chasing Orthenn down a second time, goblins be damned. He'd take on the entire raiding party by himself if he had to.

"So, goblins?" Gerrick asked, as though he'd overheard Moranthus's thoughts.

"Yes, goblins. Did you have trouble reading my orders, or has it just taken this long for that part of them to sink in?"

Gerrick gave him a tired look. "How many of them?"

"Assuming it's a typical raiding party, there'll be fifteen to thirty of them, depending on how well-off their warlord is. Minus the scout I took care of for you, of course." Moranthus shrugged. "Those orders are all I have to go on. You know as much about this as I do now."

"You're sure the scout belonged to the same raiding party that's after Orthenn?"

"Well, I certainly hope he did. Your prince's chances of evading one raiding party are slim enough. If he's managed to run afoul of two at once, we'll never reach him in time."

"Then they're too close to him already. I was wrong to press you into stopping for the night." Gerrick tossed the glowstone onto the ground between them and got to his feet. "We should get moving."

"No. You were right earlier, even if that wasn't your intention." Moranthus motioned for him to sit back down. "If there's a chance we'll find a goblin raiding party waiting for us in Orthenn's camp, there's no use in exhausting ourselves before we get there. Get some sleep if you need it. I know I won't be getting any after what you just tried."

"How am I supposed to sleep knowing there's a goblin raiding party hunting Orthenn?"

"I'm sure you'll manage somehow. You can barely keep up with me when you're well rested; if you don't sleep tonight, it'll only slow us down tomorrow."

For a moment, Gerrick remained standing, his fists clenched at his sides. Something in Moranthus's words had struck a nerve. Moranthus braced himself for an argument.

Then, with a frustrated sigh, Gerrick muttered "Fine" and dropped to his bedroll. Without another word, he lay down and rolled onto his side so that his back was toward Moranthus. The pattern of his breathing made it clear he was nowhere near sleep, but he'd at least get some proper rest, whether he wanted it or not. And he'd give Moranthus some much-needed time to himself to gather his scattered thoughts into something that could at least feign a sense of coherence.

Moranthus picked up the glowstone and let it rest in the center of his palm. He traced its familiar sanded-smooth edges with his fingertips, hoping he hadn't made a mistake in assuring Gerrick that their pursuit of Orthenn could afford an entire night's delay. The cool, red light that radiated, unchanging, from its center supported his decision for the time being, but he knew from experience how easily, and quickly, that could change.

For what wasn't the first time in his career, he wondered why the enchanters in charge of making the damned things hadn't worked out a way of showing their targets' physical and mental conditions instead of just their locations. It already took upward of a decade to train an apprentice duskblade to read a glowstone with an acceptable level of accuracy. Adding a bit more complexity couldn't slow the process by more than a year or two.

Keeping his eyes locked on the glowstone in a silent plea for it to hold its color, Moranthus settled on his bedroll for what he hoped would be a long, dull night's watch.

In spite of his best efforts, Moranthus must have fallen asleep at some point. After closing his eyes on darkness in what he thought was only a blink, he opened them to the pale light of dawn crawling over the horizon. The glowstone shone up at him. Its red color had darkened over the hours he'd left it unattended. Orthenn was on the move.

Moranthus picked up the glowstone and gave Gerrick's shoulder a good shake with his free hand. "Wake up."

Gerrick woke with a start, a befuddled look on his face as he pushed himself into a sitting position. "What…" his voice trailed off into a yawn.

"The glowstone's changing. Orthenn isn't where we left him. We need to get moving." Moranthus got to his feet and set about packing up their camp.

Gerrick nodded. With another yawn, he pushed himself off his bedroll. He stood still and stretched for a moment, joints audibly popping, then started to help. He broke camp like the soldier he was—methodical, in spite of his haste, his every movement measured and deliberate. Moranthus admired his efficiency. With his help, they were ready to travel before Moranthus had fully shaken the sleep from his limbs.

"Orthenn might just be out on patrol," Gerrick said as Moranthus loaded the last of their gear onto Storm. His voice held a hopeful note that did nothing to soothe Moranthus's frayed nerves.

With Orthenn miles beyond his reach and still moving, according to his glowstone, hope was the last thing Moranthus needed. He'd set out on his mission with enough hope to fill every crevasse in the impassable glaciers north of Aurora, and it had led him in the wrong direction time and time again. Hope was the entire reason he'd stranded himself at the edge of a foreign land with a stubborn prince's horse-thieving body double for company. Hope could go and fuck itself. Until he'd seen with his own eyes that Orthenn hadn't been carried off by a goblin raiding party in the night, Moranthus decided to assume the worst. That way, at least he wouldn't be caught off guard when things went wrong.

"If the rest of your soldier friends are letting him go on patrol so soon after I kidnapped his body double, it's a miracle somebody else didn't snatch him before I caught up with you," Moranthus said without so much as looking at Gerrick.

"He wouldn't have given them much say in the matter." Gerrick sighed. "I'm surprised they kept him in our camp as long as they did."

"Do you expect me to find that reassuring?" Even if Orthenn was just out on patrol, it meant he was making himself an easier target for a raiding party. The man was a greater risk to his own safety than the goblins hunting him were.

"I don't expect anything of you. I'm just saying that this might not be as bad as you think it is. We might as well keep calm until we know for certain what's happened."

Moranthus took a deep breath and counted to ten before replying, "And what if Orthenn isn't just 'out on patrol'? Will finding what's left of his goblin-ransacked camp feel better because you kept yourself calm until we got there?"

"You say that like you don't think Orthenn's a match for whatever scoundrel's leading the raiding party on his tail."

"Yes. Because unless that raiding party belongs to a spectacularly inept goblin lord, he isn't. The 'scoundrel' leading them has probably spent more time in the Ghostwood than Orthenn's spent outside his father's castle."

"Are you saying we should just give up hope?"

"Of course not." Moranthus tangled his fingers in Storm's mane to ground himself. "Just… We need to accept that we probably have a longer road ahead of us than we anticipated." A road that ended in facing a goblin raiding party instead of fleeing from one.

"Or a shorter one if you're wrong. I won't accept that Orthenn let a few goblins get the better of him until I've seen it for myself."

"When did you become such an optimist?"

"I didn't." Gerrick's stony face cracked into a fleeting, rueful smile. "But until now, you've been wrong about almost everything. I'm hoping that pattern holds."

For a moment, Moranthus just stared at Gerrick. A part of him wanted nothing more than to smile along with Gerrick and believe that showing Gerrick his orders had been enough to cleanse the bad blood between them. But another part of him—the sensible part, if he could still claim to have one—knew better than to think things could ever be that simple. Gerrick had tried to steal Moranthus's horse the last time he let his guard down around him. He kept his expression neutral as he said, "You know, I think I liked you better when you were afraid of me."

Gerrick shrugged. "If you didn't kill me for trying to steal your horse, you're not going to. Other than that, there's nothing you could do to me that I'm afraid of."

"Are you certain of that?" Moranthus raised an eyebrow at him.

"Certain enough."

"Then I hope you don't give me reason to prove you wrong."

Nine

Late that afternoon, they reached the Ghostwood's edge. The cold, dark shadows between its trees looked almost welcoming in the bright sunlight. Gerrick knew better than to trust them. And from the look of things, so did Moranthus's horse.

Storm had stopped cold in a tall clump of grass around a hundred paces away from the tree line. She kept her eyes locked on the Ghostwood, and her ears pricked forward, even as she lowered her head to graze. Like most animals, she wanted nothing to do with the eternal darkness and unearthly silence of that place; even the fiercest warhorse balked at the prospect of entering the Ghostwood. That was why Orthenn and the rest of his company had traveled the last stretch of their journey there on foot.

"What are we going to do with the horse?" Gerrick asked.

"We take her with us, of course." Moranthus kept walking toward the Ghostwood as though nothing was amiss.

Gerrick grabbed Moranthus by the shoulder and jerked his thumb backward. "You sure about that?"

With a sigh, Moranthus half turned. He looked surprised when he saw how far away Storm was. "That's unusual. She never stops following me without me telling her to."

"I don't think she likes the look of this place. Can't say I blame her."

"She probably just thinks I'm going in without her again." Moranthus whistled for Storm.

Storm looked up from her grazing, but stayed where she was.

"Come on, girl. You're coming with me this time. There'll be plenty of grass for you in the forest." Moranthus whistled again, a worried look in his eyes.

Storm went back to her grazing, still keeping a wary eye on the Ghostwood.

"You're wasting your breath," Gerrick said. "She's afraid of the Ghostwood. All horses are. Why not just leave her here?"

Moranthus glared at him. "If a raiding party has your prince, there's no telling how long we'll spend in pursuit of them. Leaving her alone out here is no better than leaving her to die. She *is* coming with us."

Gerrick shrugged. "If you say so." He hoped Moranthus was wrong about needing to chase down a goblin raiding party. But he didn't trust that hope enough to argue with Moranthus over it.

He impatiently shifted his weight from foot to foot as he watched Moranthus approach Storm. Every moment he stood idle was a moment spent away from Orthenn's side and his duty as Orthenn's body double. Letting Moranthus kidnap him in Orthenn's place had seemed like the right choice at the time. And he hadn't had any real choice in the matter to begin with; Orthenn had all but ordered Gerrick to let himself get kidnapped.

Gerrick doubted that his king would care much for Gerrick's excuses if he lost his son to goblins as a result of Gerrick's absence though. Whatever his reasons were, a failure was a failure. If Gerrick couldn't return home at Orthenn's side, it was better he didn't return at all. Letting his king think he'd died in service to Orthenn would at least spare Gerrick's daughter from suffering the consequences of her father's shortcomings.

Storm let out a whinny when Moranthus reached her, and she relaxed her posture as he ran a hand over the white blaze on her forehead. But when Moranthus took hold of her reins and tried to lead her toward the Ghostwood, she pulled herself in the opposite direction in a show of defiance. Moranthus dug his heels in and kept his grip on her reins. He wouldn't have the strength to hold her there for long. Gerrick hoped he at least had the sense to get their things off her saddle before she bolted.

Then, Storm let out a long, shuddering breath and took a step forward. Her reins went slack in Moranthus's hand and stayed that way as he led her to the Ghostwood's edge. Gerrick tried not to look impressed.

Moranthus flashed a grin at him. "What'd I tell you?"

Gerrick responded with a noncommittal grunt and reached for his sword. He'd need easy access to his weapon if they ran into trouble in the Ghostwood, and he didn't trust Storm not to run off if she got spooked again. Storm sidestepped, flicking her tail in annoyance. Moranthus barely got his feet out of her way in time to keep from getting stepped on.

"What are you doing?" Moranthus snapped.

"If we're going in there, I need my sword. You're going to need my help if there's any fighting, aren't you?"

"You don't need your sword, and I don't need your help. I'm more than a match for anything we're likely to encounter. Just stay out of my way, and you'll be fine."

"You can't be serious." It was dangerous for a full company of soldiers to enter the Ghostwood. If Moranthus planned to go in there with only an unarmed man and a horse at his side, he was a madman.

"Oh, but I am. If you think I'm giving you a weapon after you tried to steal my horse last night, you're a bigger fool than I've been giving you credit for."

"You don't know what's in there."

Moranthus ran a hand over his hair and let out a frustrated sigh. "Gerrick. It is a forest. I have been tracking men through forests since before your grandparents were born. How different can this one be?"

Gerrick shook his head. "As different as night and day. I'm not going in there unarmed. You wouldn't, either, if you were in my place."

"This wasn't a problem for you when I led you out of the Ghostwood. Why is it a problem now?"

"You were holding a knife to my throat last time. I didn't have a choice."

Moranthus gave him a hard look. "What makes you think I'm giving you a choice this time? If you want to save your prince, you're going in there. Sword or no sword. Unless you'd rather I went on without you?"

"I would if you won't give my sword back." Moranthus couldn't get back into Orthenn's camp without Gerrick's help; he'd said it himself. He wasn't going to go on without Gerrick. They both knew that.

Moranthus shrugged. "I suppose I'm leaving you behind, then. If you change your mind, you know where to find me."

With that, he stepped into the Ghostwood, Storm trailing behind him.

Gerrick watched as they vanished into the shadows between the trees, an uneasy feeling in his gut. Moranthus was bluffing. He had to be. But if he wasn't…

Gerrick ran after Moranthus before he had a chance to think better of it. He tried to ignore the way the hair on the back of his neck stood on end when the Ghostwood's dark silence closed in around him. If traveling through the Ghostwood unarmed was what it cost to protect Orthenn, then he'd endure it without complaint. Moranthus's stubbornness was probably going to get them both killed, but at least Gerrick would die loyal to his prince and country.

He caught up with Moranthus a moment later. "Wait for me," he called out, not trusting the muffled sound of his footfalls to get Moranthus's attention.

Moranthus stopped and turned to face him. His posture had stiffened since entering the Ghostwood, and his eyes had a haunted look in spite of the smirk on his face. "So, you'll be coming along, after all?" The thick, heavy air made his voice sound faint and distant.

"Yes." Gerrick paused for a moment to catch his breath before continuing, "You'd better know what you're doing."

"Of course, I know what I'm doing. It's like I said: I've been tracking men through forests for most of my life. We'll be fine." Moranthus sounded confident. But the nervous glances he kept casting into the shadows around them made it seem like even he wasn't convinced that was true.

Ten

Moranthus didn't bother marking any tree trunks as they followed the red light of his glowstone deeper into the Ghostwood. It would only have wasted time, when the glowstone alone could keep them moving in the right direction until they reached Orthenn. And if Orthenn proved to be unreachable, Moranthus had lost any place he might have had in the world beyond the Ghostwood's edge anyway. There'd be nothing for him to find his way back to.

The still, heavy air around them swallowed what little noise Moranthus's footfalls made. It quieted even the sound of Storm's hooves to the point that he would have sworn she'd wandered away from him if he hadn't held her reins in his hand and felt her warm breath on his arm. Sound didn't just travel differently in the Ghostwood; it traveled *wrong*. A silence that deep should amplify noises, not muffle them. It made him wonder if there was some truth to the legends surrounding the Ghostwood's origin. All three of them.

Moonridge, Dawn's Gate, and the goblin territories all agreed that the Ghostwood grew on the site of a massive ancient battle between the armies of Dawn's Gate and several goblin clans. The battle had raged for days, claiming countless lives on both sides, until only a handful of soldiers were left. The survivors called a reluctant truce, and as they withdrew, a vast forest rose out of the earth between them, forming a natural wall between human and goblin lands. It was said that each of the Ghostwood's trees marked the final resting place of a human or goblin soldier. Its constant, foreboding presence served as a grim reminder of the bitter cost of war and the long history of bad blood between Dawn's Gate and the goblin territories.

If you asked a human, they'd say the Ghostwood was the earth's attempt to stop goblin clans from raiding human settlements. If you asked a goblin, they'd say the Ghostwood was meant to keep humans from spreading their greedy, wasteful ways to lands that couldn't support them. And if you asked an elf, they'd say the Ghostwood was the earth's way of giving itself a moment's peace from the humans' and goblins' constant squabbling.

But whatever the reason for its existence, the Ghostwood hadn't fulfilled its purpose. To this day, Dawn's Gate and the goblin territories existed in a near-constant state of conflict that seemed destined to continue for as long as the sun and the moon and the stars shone in the sky.

A dry, crackling *snap* beneath his feet ripped Moranthus out of his thoughts. After spending at least an hour engulfed in the unearthly silence around him, it felt like someone had snuck up behind him and blown a war horn directly into his ear. With a sharp intake of breath, he started and took a step backward. He clenched his hand in a vise-grip on Storm's reins to hold her steady as she snorted and tossed her head in alarm.

Moranthus allowed himself a quick glance over his shoulder—where Gerrick stood glaring daggers at him, one hand hovering in the empty space where his sword belt would normally hang, but otherwise unharmed—before casting his gaze downward in search of the source of the first real noise he'd heard since entering the Ghostwood. Whatever it was, the Ghostwood hadn't muffled it. That was worth looking into.

On the leaf-strewn ground in front of him lay the half-eaten remains of an owl. The same one he'd passed by on his way out of the Ghostwood three days earlier, if he wasn't mistaken. Its remaining feathers had the same mottled gray pattern, and its remains had a similar level of decay to them. It had to be the same bird. Which meant that they couldn't be far off the path Moranthus had followed through the Ghostwood on his way to Orthenn's camp.

Moranthus crouched down and took a closer look at the ground around the owl.

"What are you doing?" Gerrick's voice had a harsh, irritated edge to it.

"Trying to figure out where this came from." In anticipation of the inevitable "Why?" that would be the next thing out of Gerrick's mouth, he added, "If we can find the place it died, we might be able to retrace our steps back to Orthenn's camp from there."

"How's a half-eaten owl going to do that?"

"Simple. It's probably the same half-eaten owl we passed by on our way out of here. Of course, it wasn't half-eaten then, but that's not the point. Didn't you notice it?" Moranthus cast an incredulous glance over his shoulder at Gerrick. A dead bird of that size was a hard thing to miss, even for a human.

"I had other things to worry about." Gerrick frowned, meaningfully rubbing a hand over the chafe marks Moranthus's rope work had left on his wrist.

"Fair enough." Moranthus turned his attention back to the owl. If he looked at it from the right angle and held his glowstone close to the ground, he could just make out what looked like a trail of disturbed leaves leading off to its right.

He stood back up, pocketing his glowstone for the time being. The midday sunlight penetrated the dense canopy of leaves above him well enough for him to find his way through the trees without its light.

"Orthenn's camp, or whatever's left of it, should be this way." Moranthus set off in the direction he hoped the owl's corpse had come from.

"So, we're following your best guess."

Moranthus didn't bother with a response. He knew that Gerrick would follow him, whether he was sure of himself or not. Gerrick didn't have any choice in the matter at this point. He'd never find his way through the Ghostwood—let alone back to Orthenn—without Moranthus's help.

In the Ghostwood's perpetual twilight, every tree they passed looked almost identical to the others. As their search went on, Moranthus wondered if they hadn't just been circling the same patch of forest the entire time. More than once, what Moranthus hoped was a notch made by his dagger turned out to be nothing more than a light-colored patch of bark or the work of an animal sharpening its claws. And once they'd lost sight of the owl, the ground had ceased to be of any use to him. Moranthus had all but decided to give up the search as a lost cause when he heard the regular, heavy rhythm of Gerrick's footsteps slow, then come to a stop.

Moranthus sighed. "I know. We aren't going to find Orthenn's camp at this rate, and all I've accomplished with this is wasting both our time."

"This *is* a waste of time," Gerrick replied. "But I think I've found one of your markers."

"Let's see it, then." Moranthus fought to keep himself patient as he turned Storm around and led her to the tree where

Gerrick had stopped. Getting frustrated over how difficult it was to turn her among the Ghostwood's close-packed trees would just put her more on edge than she already was.

Gerrick stepped away from the tree and gestured to a notch in its bark. "I don't know what else that would be."

Moranthus only needed a glance at the notch to recognize the mark of his dagger. "Neither do I. Now let's see if we can find another."

They had little difficulty locating the next marker, or the ones after it. Before long, they reached the edge of Orthenn's camp.

From the look of things, Orthenn and his soldiers hadn't left willingly. A handful of embers still glowed among the ashes of their camp's central fire, and the cooking pot that had once hung over it lay upside-down and abandoned in the dirt. Their empty bedrolls still surrounded the fire's remains, each with the contents of a turned-out pack—minus any food it might once have contained—strewn over it. Arrows protruded from many of the trees on the clearing's outskirts, and the ground the bedrolls didn't cover bore the unmistakable signs of a scuffle. Fallen leaves had been torn up and flung into unnatural piles in several places, and the patches of dirt beneath them bore deep gouge marks.

One patch of ground was dark with what could only be blood, and at the camp's northern edge were a pair of makeshift graves. Or what would have been a pair of graves, if something hadn't dug up and partially eaten the corpses that had been buried in them. From this distance, it was hard to be certain, but they looked goblin. What was left of their skin had a greenish shade to it, and the sword stuck into the ground beside one of the graves was of goblin make. Orthenn hadn't let himself be taken without a fight.

"He's really gone." Gerrick's voice wavered. "They all are."

"It looks like they were at least taken alive," Moranthus replied. He hoped that would comfort Gerrick enough to keep him focused on the task at hand instead of everything that might have gone wrong with his fellow soldiers. The last thing he needed was for Gerrick to go all weepy on him. They didn't have time for that. *Orthenn* didn't have time for that.

"For now." Gerrick's voice had stopped wavering, but it still sounded quieter than usual.

"If the goblins didn't kill them when all this"—Moranthus gestured to the ransacked camp—"happened, then they aren't going to. If they can help it. Just hope your prince doesn't talk them into trying anything stupid before we find him."

"Can we get on with finding him, then? You've seen his camp; we can move on now."

"Not just yet. I want to take a closer look at this."

Moranthus hesitated for a moment, then tied Storm's reins to a sturdy-looking branch. After the way she'd resisted going into the Ghostwood, he didn't want to take any chances.

Once she was secured, he made his way to the far side of Orthenn's camp, where the two goblin corpses had been unearthed. He doubted the bodies would have anything useful left on them after being buried, dug up, and partially eaten, but they were still worth checking. If he found anything that linked them to a particular warlord or hinted at what they wanted with Orthenn, it would give him an edge over the surviving members of their raiding party.

But when he reached the far side of the camp, he found himself far more interested in an arrow protruding from a tree near their graves. An arrow fletched with the distinctive white feathers of a Moonridge snowhawk.

Moranthus wanted to believe it was just a coincidence. And for all he knew, it really was. Northern goblin clans often ventured into Moonridge for the purpose of buying, trading for, or—depending on the clan and the warlord at its head—stealing elven goods. It only made sense that an elven arrow or two would end up in goblin hands at some point.

But a northern goblin clan shouldn't have any interest in kidnapping a human prince. Transporting such a valuable hostage over such a large distance was risky work, and their warlord would need an extraordinary amount of luck for Orthenn's ransom to reach him without being stolen by one of his southern neighbors en route to its destination. A northern clan wouldn't have any direct contact with Dawn's Gate, either, which ruled out the possibility of one kidnapping Orthenn as a result of bad blood between its warlord and Orthenn's father.

But unless a southern warlord had gone far out of his way to obtain elven weapons for his soldiers, the arrow meant that a northern clan had kidnapped Orthenn. In spite of having no logical reason for doing so. And if a northern clan really was behind this, there was a chance their warlord had ties to Moonridge and had bought the service of an elven soldier or two along with their arrows.

Moranthus frowned. He didn't much like the thought of chasing after an enemy force that might outclass him instead of just outnumbering him. His odds of success were bleak enough already.

Still, whether he liked his odds or not, he needed to know what he was up against. And that meant getting a good look at the arrow's head, which had completely disappeared into the tree. If it had belonged to a goblin warrior, they would likely have hafted a goblin-made arrowhead onto it. As a rule, goblin smiths forged their arrowheads wider and heavier than elven ones, often with the addition of serrated edges that would further slow an arrow's flight. A goblin sent on a mission as important as kidnapping a human prince wouldn't risk missing a shot because he wasn't accustomed to his arrows' flight path.

Moranthus wrapped a hand around the arrow's shaft and gave it a hard tug, but it didn't budge. He tried again, using both hands, with the same result. It had gone in too deep for him to get it out the easy way.

"Want some help with that?" Gerrick's voice had a mocking tone that Moranthus didn't appreciate in the slightest. This wasn't the first time another man had mistaken his lithe build for a sign of weakness, and he doubted it would be the last. Still, if Gerrick could save him the time and effort of cutting the arrow out, he could make whatever mistaken assumptions he liked. And if Gerrick decided to press the issue later on, Moranthus could throw a punch hard enough to make him reconsider that assumption.

Moranthus let go of the arrow and took a step away from the tree. "You're welcome to try, but at this point, that arrow's not coming out without taking part of the tree with it."

Gerrick pushed past him and almost sent him stumbling into a grave. "It can't have gone in *that* far."

Moranthus scrambled to regain his balance, fighting the urge to give Gerrick a good shove toward the graves in retaliation. If Moranthus had fallen into that grave, he could easily have snapped an ankle and shattered their chances of catching up with Orthenn's kidnappers along with his bones. If Gerrick wanted to sulk over losing his prince, that was fine. Moranthus had done the same after losing his Patriarch. But letting his anger at Moranthus—and himself, if he had the capacity for self-reflection—cloud his judgment to the point he'd risk crippling his only guide through the Ghostwood was just stupid. Moranthus would've found himself facing a full exile or execution, if he'd tried anything like that in the wake of his Patriarch's death. And he'd had *much* more reason to act out over his loss.

"See for yourself," Moranthus replied. "If the shaft snaps on you and ends up in your eye, don't say I didn't warn you when you spend the rest of your life half-blind."

Gerrick let out a short huff of breath in response and gave the arrow a sharp, one-handed yank. Moranthus was almost relieved when the arrow stayed lodged in the tree. Even if Gerrick did manage to pull it free, at least he wouldn't get to make it look easy.

Gerrick readjusted his grip on the arrow and planted his foot against the tree's trunk for leverage. Careful to keep away from the loose, sandy earth at the graves' edges, Moranthus made his way to the more intact goblin's corpse in search of a blade he could use to cut the arrow out. He held the collar of his shirt over his nose and mouth to protect himself from the stench as he knelt beside the fallen goblin.

Whatever animal he'd fallen prey to seemed to have tired of goblin meat after it finished with his friend; it had eaten the better part of one of his legs, but left his torso, and the patchwork brigandine that covered it, almost unscathed. Either that, or Moranthus and Gerrick had scared the beast off when they arrived at the camp, and it still lurked among the trees somewhere nearby, watching them from the shadows.

A shiver ran down Moranthus's spine at the thought. He'd rather face an enemy goblin than a starving bear or wolf any day. Goblins could be reasoned with, and if that failed, they fought in a way he could understand and predict. They also wouldn't eat him if that fight didn't end in his favor.

The sooner he and Gerrick could put Orthenn's camp behind them, the better. If the creature that had unearthed the corpses didn't come back for the rest of its meal, something else would come along to finish what it had started. The scent of rotting meat never went unnoticed for long.

Moranthus cast a wary glance into the murky shadows between the trees closest to him before turning his attention back to the goblin. The goblin's sword had stayed in its scabbard through his burial and subsequent exhumation, but would make a poor tool for wood carving. He needed something smaller. A quick glance at the goblin's sword belt didn't reveal any daggers, but he would have carried at least one with him. He'd probably just worn it on his back.

The dagger strapped to the goblin's back slid free of its dirt-caked sheath easily enough, and its blade looked sturdy. Moranthus got to his feet, brushing the last of the dirt off the dagger's hilt. Its weight felt comforting in his hand when he turned around to find Gerrick staring at him, a deep frown etched into his face. The arrow remained lodged in its tree as firmly as ever.

"You're stealing from the dead." Gerrick let out a deep, resigned sigh. His eyes held the disapproval of a man accustomed to burying the dead's possessions along with them instead of passing them on to living men and women who could actually make use of them. Humans were touchy about corpses.

Moranthus knew there was no way of winning that argument. Better to distract Gerrick from it instead. "Good observation. Keep this up, and you might even notice that the grass is green, the sky is blue, and you've had a piece of jerky stuck between your teeth since last night. Or longer."

Gerrick raised a self-conscious hand halfway to his mouth, then froze for a moment before running it over his beard instead. "This isn't something to take lightly."

"Would you like me to carve into that tree with your dagger instead? Because I'm not ruining mine just because you don't like the thought of angering a man who's already dead."

Gerrick's frown deepened. But he remained silent as he stepped away from the tree, keeping himself as far from the open graves, and the corpses that had once occupied them, as possible.

"Stealing from the dead it is, then." Moranthus made his way back to the tree and set about cutting the arrow out of its trunk.

"We don't have time for this. You've got plenty of arrows already; why do you want this one so badly?"

"Because if I can get a good look at it, it might give us a better idea of what we're up against." Moranthus hoped that would be enough to satisfy Gerrick. He didn't intend to mention the possibility of Moonridge involvement in Orthenn's kidnapping, if he could avoid it. "If you want to make yourself useful in the meantime, see if the raiding party left any supplies behind." It wasn't likely, but it would keep Gerrick from asking any more questions Moranthus didn't want to answer.

"Fine," Gerrick replied.

Out of the corner of his eye, Moranthus watched him stalk across the camp until he moved out of Moranthus's sight. Even then, the sound of Gerrick's footsteps gave Moranthus a good idea of his location. Gerrick hadn't crossed Moranthus since he'd tried to steal Storm, but Moranthus still didn't trust him enough to leave him fully unattended.

Moranthus smiled to himself as he carved into the wood surrounding the arrow, careful to keep the dagger's blade clear of the arrow's shaft. After days of uncertainty and failure, he found a sense of comfort in facing a simple task he knew he could complete. Whatever he found when he got the arrow free, at least it would help to answer the questions swirling at the back of his mind.

He'd finally cut deep enough into the tree to reach the arrow's head when he heard Gerrick's footsteps come to an abrupt stop somewhere near the camp's opposite edge.

"Forget the arrow. We need to leave." Gerrick's voice was so low that Moranthus could barely hear it.

"No. The arrow's almost free now, and I'm not leaving before I've gotten a proper look at it." If the raiding party that took Orthenn had any elves with them, Moranthus *needed* to know about it.

"Moranthus. Leave it."

"Why?" Moranthus turned to face Gerrick.

Gerrick's face had gone white as fresh snow, and his eyes were fixed on something to Moranthus's right. He patted his sides with trembling hands, searching for a sword belt that wasn't there. Moranthus tightened his grip on the goblin's dagger as he followed Gerrick's gaze to the edge of the forest near the graves.

Not twenty paces away from him, sitting back on its haunches as it stared him down with dark, beady eyes, stood the largest brown bear Moranthus had ever seen. Even while sitting, it was almost as tall as he was, and easily twice as broad. The pale fur around its muzzle was streaked with blood, and several clumps of dirt clung to its forelegs. It must be the same animal that had dug up the goblin corpses, come back to finish its meal. With a snort, it drew itself up to its full height and let out a long, low growl.

Suddenly, Moranthus realized how poorly the goblin-made dagger fit in his hand. How much its blade had dulled after he'd put it to use as a carving knife. How long it had been since he'd faced a real fight against an opponent he wasn't certain he could defeat. And how pitifully few avenues of escape were available to him.

His best—no, his only—hope of leaving Orthenn's camp alive was to keep from provoking the bear any further. If it attacked him, even if he managed to get his sword out in time, he'd be lucky to survive its initial charge, let alone long enough to kill it. But it wouldn't have any reason to attack him unless he gave it one.

It was only a brown bear, after all. The Ghostwood hadn't changed that. Unlike Moonridge's great ice bears, which viewed elves as nothing more than unusually intelligent prey animals, it probably didn't want anything to do with the strange, two-legged creatures that occasionally ventured into its territory. It had probably only dug up the goblins because they were an easy way to put a bit more fat on its bones before it settled into its long, winter sleep. And if the full goblin's worth of meat it had eaten that day hadn't taken the edge off its hunger, it still had almost an entire corpse left that would make a much more appealing meal than a live elf the bear would have to catch, kill, and risk injuring itself for. He'd just need to get out of the camp before the bear finished with the corpse and had time to decide it wanted more.

Moranthus circled around the graves, until his back was toward the center of the camp and he could back away from the bear without cornering himself against any trees. If he could put enough distance between him and the bear, he didn't see any reason why it wouldn't let him collect Storm and Gerrick from the opposite side of the camp without a fuss.

The bear dropped onto all fours and roared as Moranthus took his first steps backward. Moranthus flinched, but kept his movements slow and steady. If he turned and ran, the bear would chase him, and he knew better than to think he had any chance of outrunning it.

Instead of the soft, sandy dirt that he expected, Moranthus's foot landed on something hard and round that slipped out from under him. He stumbled, risking a brief glance at the ground as he righted himself. A wooden bowl teetered on its side, as though mocking him for stumbling over a simple piece of cookware.

With a second, louder roar, the bear charged. Moranthus let go of the blunt, useless goblin dagger and let his hand drop to his sword. He wrapped his fingers in a death grip around its hilt, but forced himself to leave it in its scabbard. There was a chance that the charge was only a bluff. If it was, he couldn't risk doing anything that might change that. He held his ground and his breath. Locked eyes with the bear and watched it barrel toward him.

As he began to wonder if he'd made a mistake in not drawing his sword, the bear came to a stop, so close to Moranthus that he could almost reach out and touch it. Whether it had stopped out of fear or confusion, Moranthus didn't know and didn't trust himself to guess. For a moment, they just stared at each other. Moranthus could see himself reflected in the bear's dark, unreadable eyes, and wondered if this was what death looked like: one last glance at his own shortcomings that lasted just long enough for him to realize where he'd gone wrong and why it had killed him. It was almost beautiful.

But he wasn't dead yet, and he'd have plenty of time to reflect on his mistakes later. The bear tensed, no doubt readying itself to charge again. It wouldn't stop short of him a second time. In a single, fluid motion, Moranthus drew his sword and slashed at the bear's face.

The bear staggered backward with a startled bellow, bleeding from a gash across its nose. For a moment, it looked as though it would turn and retreat back into the woods, and Moranthus relaxed his grip on his sword.

Then, the bear stopped. It shook its head, tossing a fine mist of blood droplets into the air around it. Before Moranthus could ready his sword for another strike, it charged again, and he barely managed to throw himself out of its path.

Moranthus struck out at the bear as it barreled past him and opened a long, deep wound along its left flank. Dark blood oozed out of the cut, staining its fur a muddy shade of red. It opened its mouth in an enraged roar, exposing the long, sharp teeth that lined its jaws. Moranthus recoiled as its hot, rank breath rolled over him, enveloping him in the scent of rotting goblin flesh.

The bear raised its paw to swipe at him. Moranthus took a step backward, holding his sword out in front of him to keep it from lunging. The bear kept its unflinching gaze locked on Moranthus, but lowered its foreleg, digging its daggerlike claws into the ground. Slowly, it began to circle around Moranthus, its breath coming in harsh, ragged pants. Moranthus turned along with the bear, careful to keep the point of his sword between them. He felt a twinge of satisfaction at the way the bear favored its left leg, keeping its injured side facing away from Moranthus as it tried to work its way around him. However things played out, it wouldn't walk away from this encounter unscathed. It had tasted Moonridge steel and learned to fear its bite.

Still, with what seemed like every step, the bear edged closer to him, until it was almost within his striking range again. And until Moranthus was almost within reach of its claws. When Moranthus tried putting more distance between them with a step backward, it took another step forward, until it had pushed him back almost to the tree line at the camp's edge. Moranthus couldn't retreat any farther. There was no avoiding this fight. If he didn't take the initiative and attack the bear, it was only a matter of time until the bear attacked him.

Moranthus steeled himself against the possibility of the bear charging him as he readied his blade for another slash across its face. That wouldn't kill the bear but might stun it long enough for Moranthus to get himself into position to strike at its heart. He didn't like his chances of success, but it was the only plan he had.

The bear hesitated, casting a wary glance at Moranthus's sword. As Moranthus took a step toward it, a shrill whinny rang out from across the camp. He froze and turned toward Storm.

While he'd been focused on the bear, Gerrick had made a run for Storm. He held her bridle with one hand and groped blindly at her saddle with the other. The bastard was trying to steal her again.

Moranthus felt, rather than saw, the bear's first swipe at him when its paw slammed into his left side. And then the world went sideways.

He let go of his sword and held his arms out in a failed attempt to break his fall. His sleeve tore open as he slid across the ground. The immense strength behind the bear's paw, coupled with the force of his impact with the ground, knocked the air out of his lungs. When he came to a stop, it was all he could do to take in a series of shallow, wheezing gasps in an effort to regain his breath.

Still wheezing, he got his hands under him and pushed himself into a sitting position, opening his mouth in a silent scream at the swirling knot of pain the motion created beneath the left side of his rib cage. He kept still, blood frozen in his veins as he wondered whether the bear had torn something open inside him. But the pain subsided when he stopped moving, fading into a deep, but manageable, ache. The bear had just bruised him.

The bear plodded toward him with the practiced ease of a predator that had incapacitated its prey in the same manner countless times before. Blood still trickled down its left hind leg, leaving a thin, red trail behind. It stopped when it reached his sword, lowering its head to sniff at the blade.

With a snort, the bear swatted his sword. Moranthus watched as it skittered across the camp, only coming to a stop when its cross guard caught on the edge of a bedroll. He gritted his teeth against the pain in his side and tried to get his feet under him. If he could keep himself upright long enough to make a run for his sword…

Moranthus felt as though a dagger had been thrust into his side and twisted. He flopped onto his back with a whimper that would have sounded pathetic coming from a newborn fox kit, let alone an elf nearing his second century. Shaking from the agony even such a small movement caused him, he pushed himself up onto his elbows and met the bear's gaze as it approached him. If this was his death, he wouldn't face it lying down. In a distant corner of his mind, he hoped Storm would let Gerrick steal her this time. At least she'd get to live.

The bear stood over Moranthus, pinning his arms to his side by placing its forelegs on either side of his shoulders. He turned his head away from the concentrated puffs of its foul breath as it brought its face close to his and gave him an inquisitive sniff, as though it wanted to get an idea of how he tasted before it bit into him. After a moment that felt like a lifetime, the bear let out a satisfied huff and took a step backward, freeing Moranthus's arms enough for him to remove his dagger from its sheath. As the bear raised its paw to deliver a killing blow, Moranthus raised his dagger to his chest, readying himself to thrust it into the bear's throat when it shifted its weight forward and brought its paw down.

Instead, the bear staggered and lowered its paw to the ground in an effort to steady itself. For a moment, it swayed on its feet, a dull, unfocused look in its eyes, but it couldn't regain its balance and came crashing down on top of Moranthus. Its body gave one last, lingering shudder, then went still.

Moranthus craned his neck in an effort to see over the mountain of fur on top of him. He could just make out the shape of a sword hilt protruding from behind the bear's right shoulder.

"You all right?" Gerrick's voice, as rough and curt as ever, sounded as sweet as the spring's first rain to Moranthus's ears.

Moranthus couldn't suppress a brief spasm of laughter at the sheer absurdity of the question and paid for it with a flash of stabbing pain beneath his ribs. "As 'all right' as I can be, given the circumstances. Never been trapped under a nicer dead bear."

"Good. I'm useless at patching up wounds."

"You're not half bad at creating them though."

Gerrick replied with a grunt that sounded happy for a change and pulled his sword free. It slid out of the bear's corpse with a slick, sucking noise, followed by a scraping sound that Moranthus assumed was Gerrick wiping the blade clean.

"I don't suppose you'd be willing to help me out from under this?" Moranthus's voice came out sounding more strained than he'd have liked it to. Even if he'd had the strength to push the bear off, its corpse had pinned his right arm, his hand still clutching his dagger against his chest, leaving him only his left to work with. "I seem to be a bit stuck." He gave the bear an ineffectual shove with his left arm to prove his point.

Gerrick leaned forward over the bear's corpse. The corners of his mouth were upturned in a ghost of a smile that took years off his face. "You *are* stuck. I'll see what I can do."

Moranthus expected Gerrick to grab him under the shoulders and try to pull him out from under the bear. Instead, he stepped around the bear's corpse to stand at its side, knelt down, and shoved his full weight against it. The bear was easily twice Gerrick's size, but he rolled it off Moranthus as though it had been nothing more than an overenthusiastic hunting dog. His bulk didn't just come from the padding beneath his mail. That kind of strength would come in handy when they caught up with Orthenn and his captors.

With the bear out of the way, Gerrick got to his feet and dusted himself off. "Can you stand?"

Moranthus shoved his dagger back into its sheath and pushed into a sitting position, trying not to wince at the pain in his torso when he bent forward. Gerrick had seen him trapped under a bear. That was more than enough damage to his pride for one day. "I'll be fine. Just give me a moment."

Gerrick leaned down and reached toward him. "We don't have a moment. Give me your hand."

Moranthus glared up at him but couldn't put his heart into it. With a sigh, he grabbed hold of Gerrick's hand and let Gerrick pull him onto his feet, gritting his teeth against the searing pain that flared up in his left side.

Moranthus tore his hand out of Gerrick's as soon as he was certain he could hold himself upright. "If you're in that much of a hurry to get moving, you could have just taken Storm and let the bear finish me off, you know."

Gerrick shrugged. "I need you to lead me to Orthenn."

"I suppose I owe you my thanks, regardless."

"You do."

"Good. I'm glad that's settled."

Simultaneously, their gazes drifted to Gerrick's side, where his sword hung neatly in its scabbard. Gerrick rested a protective hand on its hilt and raised his eyes to meet Moranthus's in an unspoken challenge.

Moranthus held his gaze for a moment, then looked away. "Well, you have it back now. I may as well let you keep it. If I try to take it from you again, it's bound to end in at least one of our deaths. And that would just be unproductive, now wouldn't it?"

Eleven

"That arrow had better be worth all this." Gerrick knew he didn't sound as annoyed as he should. He didn't care. With the reassuring weight of his sword on his hip, he felt whole again. That was all that mattered.

Moranthus gave him a blank stare. His eyes were wide, and his hands trembled at his sides. Then, with a start, he replied, "Right. The arrow. It's worth it; just give me a moment."

Gerrick wanted to kick himself for reminding Moranthus about the damned arrow. If he'd kept his mouth shut, they could have just left it in its tree and moved on. Like they should have done in the first place. "Fine."

Moranthus crossed the camp with a slow, awkward gait, keeping his shoulders slightly hunched. The bear's claws had left long gouges in his leather jerkin, and a few bits of stuffing poked out from the padded jack beneath it. Altogether, he looked like a battered rag doll. Along the way, he stopped to pick up his sword and fell to his knees, clutching his side, when he bent down for it. Probably still feeling that bear slap. Gerrick hoped he hadn't lied when he said he was fine.

Moranthus got himself back onto his feet without Gerrick's help this time though. And without dropping his sword. He was tough, for someone so skinny. Gerrick couldn't deny that. He'd held his own against the bear pretty well too. Not a bad man to have at his side if he had to take on an entire goblin raiding party to save Orthenn's stubborn hide. He'd still have chosen Orthenn, or anyone else from their company, over Moranthus in a heartbeat, but until he got his brothers-in-arms back, Moranthus would do.

Gerrick followed after Moranthus in case the arrow was still too deep in the tree for him to pull it out. He didn't have enough patience left to sit through any more whittling. But it didn't take Moranthus long to get the arrow out. He really had almost gotten it free before the bear showed up. From what Gerrick could see, it didn't look like anything special. Definitely not worth almost getting both of them killed over.

After spending a good, long while puzzling over it, Moranthus dropped the arrow, then leaned against a tree with a sigh of relief. "Thank the skies," he said. "It's only goblins."

"Who else would have done this?"

Moranthus narrowed his eyes. "No one you need to worry about."

"That's not an answer."

"And?"

"After saving you from that bear, I deserve an answer." Moranthus was a bit flighty, but he was no fool. If something had him worried, Gerrick wanted to know about it.

Moranthus shook his head. "I swear, if you go back to accusing me of being a goblin spy after this…"

"I won't. Just tell me."

"The fletching on that arrow came from Moonridge. There was…" Moranthus looked away from Gerrick. "There was a chance the raiding party that took Orthenn had elven soldiers with them."

"How do you know they don't?"

"That's a goblin arrowhead if I've ever seen one." Moranthus nudged the arrow with the toe of his boot. "You can tell by the serrated edges. No self-respecting Moonridge archer would carry something like that in their quiver. I would know."

"How did a goblin archer get his hands on an elven arrow?"

"Your guess is as good as mine. They might have traded for it, stolen it… Skies above, one of their archers might have decided to keep it as a souvenir after someone shot them with it, for all I know." Moranthus sighed. "It's hard to believe it's just a coincidence though. Whatever this is"—Moranthus gestured to what was left of the camp—"goes deeper than just a kidnapping. And it's making fools of us both."

Gerrick shrugged. "So what if it is? We still need to get Orthenn back. That hasn't changed."

"I know. And I intend to see this rescue mission through to its end, whatever that may be. But if you aren't certain you want to pay the price for your prince's freedom, I won't force you to."

Gerrick scoffed. "If you think I'm going to turn my back on the oath I swore—"

Moranthus held up a hand. "Just hear me out. At this rate, we aren't likely to overtake the raiding party that took Orthenn until after they've reached the goblin territories. That's some harsh country at the best of times, and it'll only get harsher with winter setting in. I like the thought of having you at my back more than I like the thought of going it alone, but if you aren't willing to work with me, I'll be better off without you.

And once we do overtake the raiding party, assuming we even make it that far…"

"What?"

"I don't know. Maybe we'll get lucky, your soldier friends will be in fighting shape, and we can arrange a sneak attack of our own on their captors. But if that's not an option—and odds are, it won't be—our best chance at saving Orthenn is for you to take his place. And there's no telling what will happen to you once that raiding party, or their warlord, realizes you've cheated them out of Orthenn's ransom. Their warlord might try to ransom you back to your king anyway, but if they don't, or your king decides you aren't worth the cost… Well, spending the rest of your days in forced service to that warlord is the best you can hope for."

"What's the worst?"

"Death. And not a pretty one; they'll want to make an example of you."

"I see." Gerrick thought of his daughter, waiting for her papa to come home. Of the promise he made to her every time he followed Orthenn on a mission that as long as there was life left in his body, he wouldn't let anything take him away from her.

He'd always known, in the back of his mind, it was a promise he couldn't keep. That his service to Orthenn would cost him his life, or at least his life as he knew it, one day. But he'd always expected it would be a sudden thing. With only a moment's notice, he'd sacrifice himself for Orthenn's well-being without question. When he had time to think about it first, though…that made things hard. The thought of never seeing his daughter's sweet, gap-toothed smile again was almost more than he could bear.

But he didn't have a choice. He never had. Working as Orthenn's body double paid more than twice a normal soldier's stipend. It usually kept him closer to home, too, and with her mother dead, his daughter needed as much time with him as she could get. If he died, or was lost in any other way, in Orthenn's service, Orthenn would see to it that his daughter's needs were provided for in his absence. Orthenn's pride wouldn't let him do anything less. And if Gerrick abandoned Orthenn after letting him fall into goblin hands, there'd be no future in Dawn's Gate for him or his daughter. Better for him to condemn himself than condemn them both. His daughter was a smart girl. She'd understand when she got older.

"If your best plan is to trade me for Orthenn, what will you do if I decide I don't like the sound of it?" Gerrick asked.

"I'll think of something; that's what I do best." Moranthus shrugged. "And I'll send you on your way with the rest of your gear and half our store of supplies. Just follow the trail of marked trees out of the Ghostwood, and I'm sure you can find your own way home from there."

Gerrick ran a hand over his beard. Of course, Moranthus was determined not to make this easy on him. Damn elves and their twisted logic. "You're madder than a sack of cats."

Moranthus laughed, then winced and doubled over, clutching at his gut. "Maybe I am. But you did save my life earlier. It wouldn't be right for me to take yours away from you without at least warning you first." He grimaced as he pulled himself upright. His eyes had a warmth to them that Gerrick hadn't seen before though. "Also, you're armed now, and I'd rather not fight you at the moment."

"You won't need to. I'm going with you, and I'm getting Orthenn back. No matter the cost." Gerrick wanted to hate himself for saying it, but he knew it was the right thing to do. And that was the kind of example he wanted to set for his daughter, whether he was there to help her follow it or not.

"Good. I'm happy to have you with me." Moranthus pushed himself off the tree and extended an arm toward Gerrick. "Ready to put this camp behind us?"

Gerrick clasped Moranthus's forearm and gave it a shake. "I've been ready since we got here."

"I know." Moranthus raised an eyebrow at him. "If this ends in you trying to steal my horse again, I'm going to be very disappointed in you."

Twelve

Inside of a week, they reached the Ghostwood's western edge. The dense clusters of oaks and willows around them thinned, then disappeared. Tall shrubs and sparse grasses took their place, poking out like loose threads from a tapestry of dry, rocky soil. A wide river rolled through the jagged hills ahead of them, winding its way toward the horizon.

Moranthus had never seen this part of the goblin territories before. It had a harsh beauty to it that reminded him of Moonridge's uninhabited regions. But in spite of its inhospitable appearance, this part of the goblin territories *was* inhabited. Somewhere in the distance, a plume of smoke curled into the air, forming a gray stain against the pale blue sky.

"Think that's our raiding party?" Gerrick asked, gesturing toward the plume of smoke.

Moranthus squinted at it, craning his neck in an effort to get a better view of its source, but it was too far away for him to make out anything useful. "I doubt it," he replied. "They'd have no reason to stop and build a fire at this hour, and less reason to make one big enough to draw so much attention to themselves. It's probably coming from a settlement of some kind."

"Who'd want to settle in a place like this?"

"Goblins." Moranthus gave Gerrick a sidelong glance. "Not that they have much choice in the matter. Most of the goblin territories look like this, or worse. They've got plenty of settlements in the saltwater marshes along their western coast and the pine barrens up north too. Compared to those, this settlement's people are living in a fucking paradise."

"Didn't know your people cared so much about goblin living conditions. You're sure you didn't have a hand in them snatching Orthenn? They could probably use him to squeeze a fair bit of land out of his father."

"Don't be ridiculous." Moranthus aimed a frustrated glare at Gerrick. He thought they'd moved past Gerrick accusing him of working with goblins. "As a rule, we don't care. Skies above, *I* don't care. I just had the dubious privilege of accompanying my Patriarch on a diplomatic visit to one of the northern warlords a few years before..." Before Moranthus lost everything. He swallowed the lump that formed in his throat at the memory of that visit. It hadn't lasted long, and his Patriarch had spent most of his waking hours renegotiating the terms of a decades-old peace treaty between Moonridge and Clan Stoneheart, the goblin territories' largest northern clan. Moranthus had seen the exhausting frustration of those negotiations in his Patriarch's tired eyes each night when he retired to the guest chamber they'd shared. But in the end, his Patriarch had maintained the peace between Moonridge and Clan Stoneheart. Until his daughter reneged on his hard-won treaty after the coup.

Moranthus shook his head. Now wasn't the time for dwelling on the past. "It doesn't matter when it happened. The point is, I've been here before, and I've seen enough of this place to know what it's like. I don't agree with them kidnapping your prince and harassing your borders—the same way plenty of their northern clans do to elves in Moonridge, might I add—but I can understand why they do it. That's all."

Gerrick winced. "Fair enough."

"I hope you're finished doubting my intentions, then. It's a little late for you to turn back at this point, so I'm afraid you're stuck with me. I suggest you find a way to make your peace with that."

"I have." Gerrick didn't meet Moranthus's eyes. "We should get moving. We're losing daylight."

Moranthus took another look at the plume of smoke. "It may not be our raiding party, but that settlement's still worth a look. Odds are, the raiding party passed through there to resupply themselves. It wouldn't hurt us to do the same, and if we're careful about asking around, we might be able to get an idea of where they're headed."

"You're sure that's safe? People are bound to get suspicious if a couple outsiders start acting too interested in one of their raiding parties."

"And what makes you so certain they'll know we're outsiders? I won't look any more out of place here than I do back home." Moranthus's hand drifted to his hair. His half-exile status made him an outcast in Moonridge, but in the goblin territories, it wasn't anything out of the ordinary. Almost every elf living there was either a Moonridge exile or a descendant of one. And their numbers had only gone up since his Matriarch had taken Moonridge's throne. Moranthus was lucky she'd only sentenced him to half-exile; most of his former Patriarch's supporters were either fully exiled or dead by now. He couldn't mask the bitterness in his voice as he added, "If anything, I'll fit in better here than I do back home."

"I won't. My people don't just set our criminals loose on our neighbors' land, like yours do. We put them in prisons or send them to the headsman's block," Gerrick said, as though exile wasn't an equivalent punishment to death or imprisonment. And as though Moonridge didn't have prisons and executioners to dispose of its criminals who weren't worthy of a razor. But trying to convince Gerrick of that would cost them time they couldn't afford to lose.

"Only the ones you can catch." Moranthus smirked. "Trust me; you'd hardly be the first human to give goblin living a try."

"How do we explain why we're traveling together?"

"If anyone asks, we tell them we're a couple of sellswords who got hired for the same job a while back and decided to travel together for a bit of extra safety on the road. This"— Moranthus hooked a finger under Gerrick's tabard and gave it a tug—"will need to come off, of course, but once that's taken care of, no one should have any reason to doubt us."

"You're not wearing anything that would look out of place on a sellsword?" Gerrick cast a skeptical glance at Moranthus.

"Not particularly. My gear's a bit on the pricier side of believable, I suppose, but so is yours. Discretion is a crucial part of a duskblade's job. Wearing anything that could easily identify me would be counterproductive."

"You're a poor choice to send on a rescue mission, then."

Moranthus shrugged. "That depends on how you look at it. My order specializes in retrieving things. More often than not, those things are in the hands of parties with a vested interest in them *not* being retrieved, or are actively trying not to be retrieved. I'd say that describes your prince quite nicely at present. Wouldn't you?"

"Orthenn is not a 'thing.'"

"For the purposes of this discussion, he is."

"He's a thing you lost because your fool of a Matriarch couldn't be bothered to make you look trustworthy, then."

"Would he have listened to me if I *had* looked trustworthy, or would he have sent you home in his place anyway?" From what little Moranthus had seen of him, Orthenn seemed to have more honor than sense. Whether he'd trusted Moranthus or not, Orthenn should've known better than to stay in his camp after an enemy scout had tracked him there. Moranthus doubted Orthenn would've given one of his father's messengers a warmer reception than Orthenn had given him.

"That's not the point."

"Isn't it though?"

Gerrick was silent for a moment. Glancing skyward, he let out a long sigh—the closest he was likely to come to conceding Moranthus's point—before replying, "Your Matriarch still should've given you something to identify yourself by."

"And your king should've kept a tighter rein on his son, your prince should've taken that goblin scout more seriously, you should've dropped your prince act as soon as you realized I wasn't taking you to the goblin territories, and I should've made damn sure I had the right man before leaving your prince's camp. We could stand here and argue all day over whose fault this is, but that's not going to bring us any closer to getting your prince home and saving both our necks, now is it?"

Gerrick nodded. "You're sure that visiting that settlement will help us?"

"If we can find out which warlord that raiding party serves and how much land they're sitting on, it'll give us a better idea of their numbers and how well they'll be armed." Moranthus cast a tired glance at Storm's saddlebags. "And we really should replenish our supplies if we can. Our food stores are thinner than I'd like them to be, and there won't be much forage in these parts."

"Let's get it over with, then." Gerrick loosened his sword belt and yanked the edges of his tabard out from under it but hesitated before removing it. Just as Moranthus began to wonder if he'd lost his nerve, he pulled the tabard over his head in a single, sharp movement, like it was an old bandage stuck to a scabbed-over wound, and shoved it into Moranthus's hands. His uniform must be important to him. Moranthus wondered if he would've had the same difficulty setting a uniform aside if he had one. Probably not. He knew where his loyalties lay; he didn't need a symbolic piece of clothing to remind him.

"It's nice to see you're being reasonable for a change." Moranthus rolled up Gerrick's tabard and tucked it into one of Storm's saddlebags. With that out of sight, no one would recognize Gerrick's allegiance to Dawn's Gate just by looking at him. But there was no overlooking Gerrick's resemblance to Orthenn, no matter what he was wearing.

Moranthus let out a frustrated sigh. "This isn't good enough. Anyone who saw Orthenn pass through that settlement is going to realize the two of you are damn near identical. That's going to be a problem."

"What do you want me to do about it? I can't take my face off."

"No, but we can do something about your hair."

"You want me to shave it off?"

"Of course not." Moranthus shuddered at the thought. He wouldn't wish that on anyone. Shaving was hardly a disguise anyway; Gerrick showing more of his face would just make it obvious that his resemblance to Orthenn went deeper than his beard. "I've got something better in mind."

Moranthus led Gerrick to the riverbank and fished a small, leather pouch of charcoal powder out of his pack. Gerrick eyed him with distrust as he shook its contents onto a flat rock and mixed them with a few drops of river water to make a thick, black paste.

"I always carry a bit of this with me on missions," Moranthus said in an effort to alleviate Gerrick's misgivings. "It comes in handy when I need to not look like myself for a while."

"What is it?"

"Charcoal. It makes a decent hair dye, and it's easy to wash out once it's served its purpose."

"You're sure that's enough to keep people from noticing I look like Orthenn?"

"It'll have to be. No one's going to pick up on the resemblance just by taking a quick glance at you, at least." Moranthus shrugged. "Now, I need you to wet your hair and beard for me."

Gerrick did as he was told, wincing as he splashed water on his hair and face. "Damn, that's cold," he muttered.

The river certainly wasn't warm, but Moranthus hadn't thought it was anything worth complaining over when he'd dipped his hands into it earlier. If this was too cold for Gerrick, Moranthus didn't know how he planned to weather the winter snows ahead of them. But he kept his concerns to himself as he worked the charcoal mixture into Gerrick's hair and beard. Once the sandy-blond color had darkened to a grayish black, Moranthus stepped back to admire his work.

If he didn't know better, the change would be enough to keep him from picking up on Gerrick's resemblance to Orthenn. In addition to obscuring his hair color, darkening Gerrick's hair had further set him apart from Orthenn by making his eyes look more vibrant. Moranthus hadn't noticed how blue they were before. It was almost enough to distract him from the stony frown that seemed to be Gerrick's attempt at a neutral expression.

Gerrick studied his reflection in the river while Moranthus washed the excess charcoal off his hands. "It actually worked," he murmured. Moranthus tried not to take offense at the note of surprise in his voice.

"Of course, it did." Moranthus took one last, long look at Gerrick, then nodded to himself. "You look just nondescript enough for this to work. Posture's a bit too good for a sellsword, but no one will be looking at you close enough to notice that. Would it kill you to try to smile though?"

Gerrick's frown deepened. "It might."

"Then could you at least cut back on the scowling? Keep that up, and someone's bound to think you're looking for a fight. And if that happens, I won't be bailing you out."

"I'm willing to take that risk." Gerrick's face remained as stony as ever as he followed Moranthus toward the smoke curling over the horizon.

Thirteen

On the surface, the goblin settlement didn't look like much. It had a weathered stone wall built around it with a pair of goblin sentries perched atop its open gate. Each seemed more interested in the game of dice they'd set up between them than his work, and they barely glanced down as Gerrick and Moranthus passed through the gate beneath them. That kind of carelessness would have earned them a few lashes, at least, in Dawn's Gate, but Gerrick could hardly blame them. Inside the settlement, he didn't see much worth guarding.

The settlement's shops and houses were small and widely spaced, built of mismatched stones that never stretched much taller than he was before ending in shabby, thatched roofs. Some of them didn't even reach Gerrick's full height; he would've had to hunch over to fit inside them. Here and there, stray pigs rooted through the muck, searching for a few last morsels of food before winter struck and the ground froze over. Unwashed children chased each other through the unpaved streets, their playful shrieks and laughter filling the air with a warmth that took the edge off the cold sting of late autumn. Most of them were goblin, but there were a handful of elves and humans mixed in. Gerrick wondered if they'd all still get along so easily when they grew up.

Near the settlement's center stood its largest building. Built of the same stone as the homes around it, it didn't stand much taller than they did but was easily as wide and long as four or five houses put together. A large, wooden sign rose out of the muddy ground in front of it. Gerrick couldn't see any words in its design, but judging by the stylized bed and hearth painted on it, it had to be an inn. Its roof looked new, compared to the others Gerrick had seen, and the thick plume of smoke curling out of its chimney promised a roaring fire inside. Gerrick rubbed his cold, chapped hands together, his mouth watering at the warm, heady scent of something stewing over a fire that wafted out from under the door.

A stable, filled with an odd mix of horses and large boar, leaned against the inn's side. Moranthus left Gerrick standing by the inn's door while he led his horse to the stable and hailed a goblin stable boy who sat, dozing, on a pile of hay in an empty stall. The stable boy was small, even by goblin standards—when he stretched himself to his full height, he was barely as tall as Moranthus's shoulder—but he carried himself like a man twice his size while the two of them argued over the price of keeping Storm there for the night. Gerrick couldn't make out much of their conversation, but by the sound of the bits and pieces he could pick up, the stable boy won.

Moranthus walked back to Gerrick, carrying Gerrick's pack and one of his saddlebags in his arms. "She'd better be grateful for this," he said, shaking his head.

"She's a horse. Horses don't understand gratitude." Gerrick took his pack from Moranthus and slung it over his shoulder.

"That kind of attitude is why you're stuck walking everywhere, you know. Storm is smarter than you give her credit for. She knew enough to let you take your sword back from her, didn't she?"

"She was tied to a tree. What could she have done to stop me?" Gerrick frowned. Moranthus needed to stop treating that animal like she was a person. That kind of thinking would ruin her if he wasn't careful.

"She still could've kicked you if she'd had a mind to. And you were close enough to bite. You'd never have gotten near her saddle if she wanted to keep you away from it."

Gerrick couldn't argue with him there. Storm had nearly trampled him when he'd tried to steal her. She was loyal to her master; he couldn't deny her that. But that didn't make her anything special. She knew who kept her fed and sheltered. That's all there was to it. "Then she's earned a night under a roof whether she's grateful for it or not. So have we. Stop fussing over the horse so we can go inside and get ourselves tended to."

"It's hardly fussing. If you knew the price he was demanding—"

"If it was that high, you shouldn't have paid it. Stay out here if you want; I'm going inside." Gerrick didn't know why he'd bothered waiting for Moranthus in the first place. Or why he'd wasted so much time bickering with him over a damned horse when he had a fire and a hot bowl of stew calling his name. Without looking to see if Moranthus had followed him, Gerrick put a hand on the inn's door and pushed his way inside.

He relaxed his shoulders in a happy sigh at the wave of heat that rolled over him as he stepped over the inn's threshold. The common room's central fire filled it with a warm, dim glow. A tall, makeshift counter grew out of the back wall at an awkward angle, separating the kitchen door from the rest of the room. An elf woman—probably the inn's publican—stood behind it, resting her chin on her hand as she slumped over a ledger.

Rough-hewn wooden tables and chairs were strewn across the rest of the common room's straw-covered wood floor, crammed so close together there was hardly enough space to pass between them. Most were taken by large, rowdy groups of local farmers and shopkeeps, with a few smaller, rowdier clumps of soldier-looking types mixed in. Like the children outside, most of them were goblin, but there were enough elves and humans among them that Gerrick didn't look out of place.

Still, Gerrick felt out of place as he crossed the room with an awkward, hurried gait, too conscious of the way he walked to do it normally. He tried not to make eye contact with anyone he passed on his way to the counter and tried harder not to think of how many border villages they might have raided. How many homes they might have burned, how much human blood they might have spilled… Gerrick wondered how much of this settlement—how much of the inn he was standing in—had been built on the spoils of those raids. Orthenn would never have set foot in a place like this without causing enough commotion to wake the dead. If his captors had brought him here, they'd moved on long ago. Maybe too long ago to pick up their trail.

The weight of a hand on his shoulder—squeezing hard enough so he could feel it through his mail and the quilted doublet beneath it—put an end to that line of thinking. Gerrick shrugged the hand off and turned on his heel, ready for a fight, only to find Moranthus staring back at him with his eyebrows raised and his mouth set in a worried frown.

"You all right there?" Moranthus asked.

"I'm fine."

"You might want to let go of your sword, then." Moranthus nodded toward the woman at the counter. "Walk up to that counter with a hand on your weapon, and you'll be lucky if the worst she does is call the guards on you."

With a start, Gerrick let his hand fall from the hilt of his sword. He hadn't realized he'd been gripping it. "Nervous habit," he muttered. He didn't owe Moranthus even that much of an explanation; he just didn't want Moranthus pestering him about it later.

"Ever considered taking up nail-biting instead? It's bad for your teeth, but you won't accidentally start any fights that way."

"We can't all be as unflappable as you are."

"Trust me, I'm flapped on the inside."

Gerrick just stared at him.

Moranthus shook his head as he pushed his way past Gerrick. "That was a joke. Your face won't break if you smile, I promise."

"Why do you care if I'm smiling?"

"Because you always being so on edge is starting to set me on edge." Moranthus didn't so much as look at Gerrick as he sauntered over to the counter. "So you'll either need to put a stop to it or find a better way to hide it. Your choice."

With a frustrated sigh, Gerrick followed after him. If Moranthus really was on edge, he hid it well. Anyone in that inn would've killed him if they knew why he was there, and he carried himself like he owned the place. Either he was a fool, or he knew something Gerrick didn't. Gerrick guessed he'd have to wait to see what condition they were in when they left the inn to know which.

The publican perked up the moment she noticed Moranthus was headed her way. She stood up straight and ran her hands over her close-cropped fuzz of black hair. Gerrick wondered why she'd chopped it off so close to winter. Elves didn't feel the cold the same way humans did, but she could still use something to shield those ears of hers from the wind. She could probably use something to shield all of her from the wind, really. She looked thin, even for an elf. Thin enough that her faded dress hung a bit loose on her where the ties of her stained apron didn't cinch it in. And the bags under her eyes gave her a tired look.

Somehow, she managed to look pretty in spite of all that. Her violet cheeks had a rosy glow to them, and her eyes had a shine that the bags underneath them couldn't dim. She had a nice smile, too, even if she'd only put it on for Moranthus's benefit. Gerrick hoped Moranthus didn't get taken in by it. She was probably only after his coin.

Moranthus didn't seem to realize he'd caught her eye. He tensed up when he noticed her watching him and only gave her a small half smile in return as he walked up to her counter. Gerrick wondered why it was her, and not the room full of potentially hostile armed men, that gave him pause.

"What brings you here this evening?" the publican asked.

"My friend and I are looking for lodging for the night. I don't suppose you have anything available?" Moranthus cast a worried glance at the almost-full common room.

The publican fixed Gerrick with a wide-eyed stare for a moment, like she hadn't noticed him until then. Her smile faded into a confused frown. With a shake of her head, she turned back to Moranthus. "We *are* quite full at the moment—end of the year's raiding season and all that; you know how it goes—but we can still fit you in. There's only one bed left, I'm afraid"—she cast an apologetic glance at Gerrick—"but it's in a private room. It'll cost you more than a shared room, of course, but those are all quite full."

"That's fine. We'll take the room. I think we're both determined to get ourselves a hot meal and a roof over our heads, whatever it costs us." Moranthus reached into his saddlebag and pulled out a coin purse that looked like it had seen better days. He set it down on the counter, a sheepish grin on his face. "I might need some help working out the exchange rate on this though. It's been a while since I've dealt with crescents, and this is the first time he's even seen them."

Gerrick had another look at the common room while they worked out a price. It wasn't a sure thing, but he thought he could pick out an empty table or two among the crowd. They'd at least have a place to sit once Moranthus had paid for their stay. Gerrick hoped they weren't getting cheated.

He turned his attention back to the counter when it sounded like Moranthus and the publican had worked things out. The publican swept a handful of silver coins, struck with an elaborate crescent-moon design, into a pocket of her apron. She placed a key on the counter in their place as she said, "I'm sorry we can't offer you a proper bath here, but I'll see to it that the washbasin in your room gets filled. And there's a slow spot in the river about a half a mile down the road if you're interested."

Moranthus pocketed the key. "That's nice of you to offer, but I'm afraid the only way this one"—he elbowed Gerrick in the ribs—"bathes himself is when someone's there to shove him into the water. And, well, he's a bit too solid for me to manage that most days."

Gerrick glared at him. If Moranthus wanted to get friendly with the publican, Gerrick was happy to leave him to it. If he planned to do it at Gerrick's expense, though, Gerrick wouldn't sit through much more.

The publican's lips twitched in the beginnings of a smile, and she let out a small snort of laughter. Then her eyes flicked to Gerrick, and she clapped a hand over her mouth. "Skies above, I'm so sorry. I shouldn't have—"

"It's all right. He said it, not you." Gerrick sighed. "He's an ass. At this point, there's no fixing him. I'm used to him."

"Most people find me charming, you know," Moranthus replied. "And I'm not the one frightening innocent publicans. Are you certain *I'm* the ass here?"

"I am. You started this."

Moranthus turned to the publican with a helpless shrug. "You see what I have to put up with? The man has no sense of humor. At least you get to wash your hands of him after tonight. I'm stuck with him all day, every day."

The publican raised an eyebrow at him, but her eyes were laughing. "All right, what are you *really* after here? No one's this friendly with me unless they want something in return." She patted her pocket. "And it's too late to weasel a cheaper room out of me. We don't offer refunds; my employer's very strict about that."

Moranthus put his hands up in mock surrender. "You've caught me. We're trying to find steady work before winter sets in, and I was hoping you'd know if any warlords are looking to hire a couple more sets of hands."

The publican's face fell. "Of course. I'm sure most of them are this time of year, but I couldn't give you any names." She gestured to a scar-faced goblin soldier seated in the far corner of the room. "You might want to talk to him though. He came in a few days ago with a raiding party that took some losses trying to keep their prisoners in line. I can't imagine that his warlord wouldn't want to replace them."

Moranthus placed a few more coins on the counter. "Would you mind bringing him another drink, then, and telling him I sent it?"

"Not a problem." The publican tucked the coins into a different pocket than the others. "I'll get your food out to you, too, once you've found seats for yourselves."

"Thank you for all your help. We'll be sure to stay here again the next time our path leads us here." Moranthus gave the publican a warm smile.

The publican smiled back at him and leaned forward across her counter. Her voice went low as she replied, "Good. I'll be looking forward to it."

Moranthus furrowed his brow as he led Gerrick to an empty table near the goblin the publican had pointed out. Gerrick didn't know whether he was acting or genuinely didn't realize that the publican was interested in him. No; he *had* to be acting. No one was that dense.

A long silence passed between them after they'd settled in at their table. On the road, that wouldn't have bothered Gerrick. He'd never seen the point in talking just to fill space. Most nights, he appreciated that Moranthus was happy to leave well enough alone. But keeping quiet when everyone around them was half shouting a conversation felt wrong. It made him feel like they stuck out in the crowd. No matter which way he turned, he felt like someone was staring at the back of his head, suspicious of why they were so quiet. He wondered what was taking the publican so long with their food. She might not have thought much of him, but she'd seemed eager enough for a chance to get closer to Moranthus.

"You're a lucky man." Gerrick startled himself by saying it out loud.

"What makes you say that?" Moranthus gave him the same confused look he'd given the publican. Maybe he really was that dense.

"Didn't you see the way that girl was looking at you? You've got an admirer."

"Oh. So she's not suspicious of us. Good."

"A girl like that takes an interest in you, and that's all you can think about?"

Moranthus shrugged. "I'm not interested in her. There's nothing else for me to think about."

Gerrick shook his head. "If she's not pretty enough for you, you're going to spend the rest of your life as a very lonely man."

"That's not what I meant. I'm sure she's very attractive; I'm just not interested in women in general. 'Pretty' doesn't do anything for me. Never has, never will." Moranthus laughed. "Give me a nice set of shoulders and a strong jawline any day."

Gerrick stared at Moranthus. He must have misunderstood him. These things happened. Gerrick knew that. But they weren't the sort of thing a man admitted in a crowded inn. Or to another man who was hardly more than a stranger. During his training, more than a few of his fellow recruits had struck up friendships that involved an eyebrow-raising amount of time spent skulking about in little-used rooms and dark corners. He'd heard that some had even kept at it once their training was over. So long as they didn't make a show of it, the worst that usually came of it was a bit of teasing and people keeping their distance from them while bathing. After all, it wasn't their fault they'd been born wanting other men the way they should've wanted women any more than it was a cripple's fault he'd been born with his deformities.

But it didn't make sense for them to flaunt that interest in men any more than it would've made sense for a cripple to flaunt his deformities. Liking men didn't make them anything special; every soldier in Dawn's Gate had probably had… urges during his training. When a group of young men spent months living practically on top of each other without a woman in sight, it was only natural for some of them to get a bit confused about what they wanted. But Gerrick had gotten over his confusion and found himself a woman, and he was better off for it. Moranthus would be better off if he moved on to liking women too.

And Moranthus was one of the last men Gerrick would've suspected of…*that*. Yes, he wore his hair long and had a bit of a feminine look to him. But so did all elf men, and most of them still liked women. Looks aside, there was nothing womanly about the way he acted. The man had held his own against a damned bear, and he'd snatched Gerrick out of Orthenn's camp as easily as if Gerrick had been a fresh-faced recruit armed with a wooden training sword. If he hadn't rescued the wrong Orthenn, Moranthus would've done better at Gerrick's job than Gerrick had.

"Skies above." Moranthus pinched the bridge of his nose like he was trying to fend off a headache. "That's right; you're human. I take it you're still burning people because you don't like the way they fuck in Dawn's Gate? How wonderfully backward of you."

"We're not 'backward.' No one's been burned for that in over a century," Gerrick snapped. Burning people as a punishment for that sort of thing had fallen out of favor decades before it was outlawed too. If that was what Moranthus thought of Dawn's Gate, he was the backward one. "The worst anyone could do to you without seeing the inside of a prison cell is insulting you or giving you a nasty look. That's nothing to complain about." He'd sat through his own share of insults and raised eyebrows on account of raising his daughter on his own. It was nothing a man couldn't learn to live with.

"Should I expect insults and nasty looks from you from now on? Or are you the sort who'd end up seeing the inside of a prison cell?"

Gerrick flinched at the venom in Moranthus's voice. "I'm not the sort who'd do any of that. I couldn't care less about who you're sleeping with, so long as you're helping me find… You know who we're trying to find. I've got better things to worry about." He cast a wary glance around the room. Out of the corner of his eye, he could see the publican pushing her way through the kitchen door. He hoped that meant she was on her way to their table. She'd be a welcome distraction from whatever he'd just started with Moranthus. He'd wanted to find something simple they could talk about. How had it gone so wrong?

"Would you still have better things to worry about than who I'm sleeping with if I couldn't help you find him?"

"Does that matter?"

"It does if you want me to keep helping you find him." Moranthus crossed his arms over his chest and leaned back in his chair. "I don't have the patience for being treated like a plague bearer for skies-know-how-long until we've accomplished what we came here to do."

Gerrick didn't say anything for a moment. He didn't know how he felt about Moranthus liking men. To the best of his knowledge, Moranthus was the first man he knew by name who…had that preference. But he'd never been one to judge a man for the way he lived his life. If he ever started sticking his nose where it didn't belong, it would be over something more important than whether or not Moranthus had the right amount of interest in pretty publicans. "I already said I don't care. It's your life. You can share your bed with whomever you want. Just don't try to make me a part of it."

Moranthus uncrossed his arms. "I suppose that's the best I can hope for from you. It's not as though you could think much less of me than you already do, at least."

"I don't think badly of you." Gerrick didn't particularly like Moranthus, but he was decent enough. Gerrick had been civil to Moranthus since their run-in with the bear. He wasn't sure what more Moranthus wanted from him.

Moranthus opened his mouth to say something, then snapped it shut again when the publican set two bowls of stew and two tankards of ale on the table between them. Gerrick didn't know how she'd managed to carry all that through the common room without spilling anything.

"My apologies if it's burned. You got here near the bottom of the pot, I'm afraid," she said. "I'll be getting a drink to…your friend over there in just a moment."

"Thank you." Moranthus smiled at her, but his eyes were on the scar-faced goblin at the next table.

The publican smiled back and leaned against their table. "Is there anything else you'll be needing tonight?"

"We've got all we need, thanks," Gerrick replied.

The publican's smile faded, and she shot an irritated glance at Gerrick. Gerrick wondered what he'd done to upset her. And why she'd taken such a liking to Moranthus in the first place. It must have had something to do with Moranthus's looks. He was tall, and his face was pleasant enough to look at when his mouth wasn't twisted into one of those smirks of his. And he had more than enough confidence. He was charming, too, when he had a mind to be. Gerrick could see his appeal. If that was the sort of thing he was interested in. But Gerrick liked to think he wasn't half bad to look at, either, and she'd looked at him like he'd insulted her mother when all he'd done was answer a question. Elves had relations—friendly and romantic—with humans and goblins often enough. Gerrick being human wouldn't be enough to put her off; there had to be something more to it.

"All right, then." The publican's eyes went soft again as she put a hand on Moranthus's shoulder. "You know where to find me if that changes."

With a start, Moranthus's gaze snapped back to her. "Of course," he replied. His voice and smile had a strained quality to them.

The publican stood beside their table a moment longer, worrying the edge of her apron between her fingers as she stared at Moranthus's hair. She let out a long, shaky breath, then said, "I'm sorry. I know I shouldn't ask, but how long have you…?" She ran her hands over the sides of her head.

Moranthus's expression softened. "A little over ten years now."

"That long?" The publican's brow furrowed, and she ran a hand over her own close-cropped hair. "Why have you kept doing that to yourself?"

"I'm not ashamed of what I am. I don't regret backing Ryllorin over Ilendra. If I had to, I'd do it all over again. And if this is the cost of that loyalty, I'm happy to pay it."

The publican shook her head. "You had a choice though. You didn't need to go into exile. If you'd stayed and tried to get on her good side, you could be home instead of…here."

Moranthus laughed. "I was never going to get on Ilendra's good side. I was too close to her father for that. I could see which way the wind was blowing, and I decided I was better off getting out of there before she got around to making a full exile of me. Or just saved herself the trouble and killed me, outright—you know how she is. Never looked back."

Moranthus covered it with a long drink of ale, but Gerrick still caught a glimpse of the pensive frown his face had fallen into. It matched the look he'd worn after the bear had attacked them in the Ghostwood better than the easy, unreadable smirk he'd worn while he'd lied his way into Orthenn's camp and while he'd charmed the publican into pointing them toward the scar-faced goblin. Gerrick wondered if Moranthus had been more honest than he'd intended when he said he didn't regret siding with his old Patriarch when his Patriarch's bastard daughter took over.

"You really don't regret it?" The publican gave Moranthus an awed look. If he wanted to make her lose interest in him, he was going about it the wrong way.

Moranthus set his tankard of ale on the table but kept his hands wrapped protectively around it. He'd gotten his smirk back. "I really don't. I'd rather be treated as an equal out here than as a pile of refuse back home. There's nothing to be gained by lingering somewhere you know you're not wanted."

"So, it *does* get easier once you've lived this way long enough." The publican sighed, her shoulders slumping in relief. Her hand shook as she rested it on their table.

Moranthus raised his eyebrows. He sounded concerned as he asked, "Are you all right?"

"No. But I will be." The publican steadied herself, then turned away from them. "Thank you," she murmured, and made her way back to the kitchen.

"I thought you weren't interested in her," Gerrick said once she was out of earshot.

Moranthus blinked at him. "I'm not."

"What did you say all that for, then?"

Moranthus ran a hand over his hair. "Exile is a hard life. She needed comforting, and I knew what she needed to hear." A sad smile flickered across his face. "And I suppose she reminded me a little of my old apprentice. I did my share of cheering her up, while I was training her. It must've become a habit at some point."

"Oh." Gerrick couldn't hide his surprise at that. Moranthus didn't look anywhere near old enough to have finished training an apprentice. He hardly looked old enough to have finished *being* an apprentice. Gerrick supposed it wasn't impossible though. Moranthus was an elf; they were all older than they looked. "That was…decent of you."

"Thank you." Moranthus's voice had a sarcastic edge to it. With a frustrated shake of his head, he started into his bowl of stew, shoveling it into his mouth like he thought someone was going to take it away from him. Occasionally, he glanced up at the scar-faced goblin and the kitchen door the publican had vanished through.

Before starting into his own stew, Gerrick took a better look at the goblin. He was broadly built, with his shirt hanging open over a bandaged but muscular chest. The gray-green skin of his face was marred by a long, jagged scar across his hooked nose and a series of smaller scratches over his left eye. One of his drooping, pointed ears was missing most of its upper half. The other was pierced with several rings that jingled against one another every time he moved his head. His thin lips were curled into a lopsided grin that balanced out his mismatched ears and made him look like a battered, old tomcat patrolling his territory.

Gerrick knew his type. To him, each of his scars marked a time he'd lived and someone else hadn't. And he had enough of them that, by this point, he probably thought he was invincible and had the skill to prove it to anyone who challenged him. If the rest of his raiding party was the same, it was no wonder they'd taken Orthenn's entire company with so few losses. Their warlord had sent his best men after them.

If the goblin's injuries bothered him, it didn't show as the buxom goblin woman under his arm rested her head on his chest. She'd pulled her hair back into a loose bun, with curled tendrils hanging free on either side of the sharp angles of her pale green face. She laughed at everything he said, but it sounded forced. Every time he stroked her hair, her face fell into a frown as she tucked the strands of hair he'd pulled loose back into her bun. And even as she leaned against his chest, she kept herself rigid, touching him as little as possible.

The goblin didn't seem to notice. He just looked happy to have a woman under his arm. Gerrick didn't know how Moranthus planned to pull him away from her long enough to get anything useful out of him.

Gerrick looked back at Moranthus, who was still busy with his stew. "You're sure you can get his attention?" he asked.

Moranthus set his spoon down, swallowed his latest mouthful of stew, and cast a longing glance at his half-full bowl before he replied, "I don't see why I couldn't. If nothing else, he'll want to know why I bought him a drink. That should be enough to get him talking."

"What about his girl?"

"She doesn't look half as interested in him as he is in her. If he does anything else to annoy her, odds are she'll leave him. Besides, he looks like the kind of man who likes having his ego stroked. Why would he settle for one arm ornament when he could have two?"

The kitchen door opened, and the publican began weaving her way through the common room again, a tankard of ale in her hands. Whatever Moranthus was planning, he'd have to do it fast. "You're sure about that?" Gerrick asked.

Moranthus pushed his bowl of stew away and sat up straighter when he caught sight of the publican. He undid the ties at the neck of his shirt and let it fall open, then unfastened a leather cord that held a pendant around his neck and shoved it into a pocket in his jerkin. "Trust me. I know what I'm doing."

"What if he doesn't like men?"

"Then he'll tell me he's not interested, and we'll laugh it off as a misunderstanding." Moranthus shrugged. "Goblins aren't touchy about that sort of thing like you humans are. He won't be offended."

The scar-faced goblin and the woman under his arm didn't pay any mind to the publican approaching their table until she set a tankard of ale in front of them. The goblin gave her a questioning look, then raised an eyebrow in interest when she shrugged and pointed him toward Moranthus. The woman under his arm stiffened and lifted her head off his chest, narrowing her eyes into a glare as the publican walked back to her counter.

The goblin gave her a reassuring pat on the shoulder, but kept his eyes on Moranthus as he rested his free hand on the tankard of ale Moranthus had sent him. "What's this about?" he asked, raising his voice to make himself heard over the din of the crowded common room.

Moranthus turned to face the goblin, leaning against their table in a way that made his shirt fall farther open. "You seem like an interesting man. I was hoping I might have a word with you."

"Really?" The goblin raked his eyes over Moranthus in a way that would've made Gerrick's skin crawl, if he were in

Moranthus's place. "What're you wanting to have a word with me about?"

"Anything, really. I was planning to ask if your warlord is hiring, but at this point, I'll settle for anything that gets me away from him"—he jerked his thumb toward Gerrick—"for a while. I've seen enough of that stony face to last me a lifetime. I swear, I've had better conversations with walls."

The goblin laughed. "I believe it. That's humans for you; doesn't matter how long they've been here, you'll never get all the Dawn's Gate out of them. Damn shame."

"I couldn't have said it better myself."

"Then I can't just leave you there, can I?" The goblin spared Gerrick a glance. "He the jealous type?"

"If he wants me that way, he should've done something about it a long time ago."

"That's his loss, then. Why don't you come sit here for a while, and we'll talk more about how interesting I am?" The goblin scooted closer to the woman under his arm and patted the empty space on the bench next to him. "There's always room for one more."

The woman sniffed. "Says you." With that, she lifted his arm off her shoulder like it was a dead rat, swung herself off his bench in a whirl of skirts, and sat at the next table over. A moment later, she was under another man's arm.

Moranthus dropped the key to their room on their table as he got to his feet. "I'll be back later tonight. Don't wait up on my account." With an apologetic smile, he picked up his tankard of ale and moved to the scar-faced goblin's table.

The goblin cast a rueful glance after his girl, then shrugged and put his arm around Moranthus's waist. Moranthus leaned against him, smiling like a fox in a hen house, and Gerrick tried to reconcile the sight of Moranthus letting another man make a woman of him so easily with his memory of

Moranthus staring down a bear without flinching. When the goblin caught Gerrick staring, he raised an eyebrow at him in a silent challenge. Gerrick looked away, his face burning with a shame he didn't understand. As he turned his attention back to his bowl of stew, he could just barely hear the goblin say, with a low, satisfied chuckle, "You'd better be worth what you just cost me there, friend."

The sound of the common room drowned out Moranthus's reply. Gerrick didn't bother trying to pick up anything past that. He'd heard enough from them already. If Moranthus learned anything important, he'd tell Gerrick about it later. The details of *how* he learned it weren't Gerrick's business.

Fourteen

"You'd better be worth what you just cost me there, friend." The scar-faced goblin—Scars would do for a name until Moranthus had something else to call him by—chuckled warmly as he wrapped a possessive arm around Moranthus's waist. Moranthus breathed an internal sigh of relief when Scars didn't try to call his girl back to him. If she'd stayed, she would've complicated things between him and Scars. His exclusive interest in men made him somewhat of an oddity among his people—most elves had at least some flexibility in their sexual preferences; living for several centuries made it difficult to see the world in such rigid absolutes—but there was no changing it.

"I certainly intend to be." With a smile, Moranthus leaned in close to Scars. It had been over ten years since someone had so openly taken an interest in him. Ever since the coup, the best he could hope for were a few shared, furtive glances followed by a hurried, unsatisfying coupling in a darkened alley. If he was lucky. It was nice to know he was still desirable underneath his half-exile status.

And Moranthus could certainly do worse for company than Scars. He was tall, by goblin standards, and nicely built. The mangled ruin of his left ear made Moranthus wince every time he looked at it, but the rest of his scars didn't detract from his appearance. If anything, they gave him a rakish charm that made him all the more appealing.

Scars let out a low grunt of approval and tightened his arm around Moranthus's waist. The pressure on Moranthus's midsection aggravated the deep bruise that his encounter with the bear had left behind, and he couldn't stop a sharp yelp from escaping him as a flash of pain raced up his left side.

Scars let go of him. "You all right there?"

"I'm fine." Moranthus laughed sheepishly as the pain subsided. If he let Scars think he was too delicate to follow through on what he'd started, Scars would cut his losses and move on to someone else long before Moranthus could get any information out of him. "I had a run-in with a bear a few days ago, and I'm still smarting a bit."

"That where you got this from?" Scars ran a hand over the gouges in Moranthus's jerkin.

"Not just those." In response to his companion's questioning look, Moranthus undid the fastenings on the front of his jerkin, shrugged out of the jerkin and the padded jack he wore beneath it, and pulled his shirt off over his head to reveal the large, yellowed bruise that covered most of his left side. The display earned him more than one appreciative glance from the inn's other patrons. Good. Now that Scars knew he wasn't the only interested party in the room, it'd be easier for Moranthus to keep his attention. Moranthus ran a finger along the bruise's dark purple outline. "If you look at it just right, you can almost see the paw-print."

Scars let out a long, low whistle. "Nice." He put his arm around Moranthus's waist—lower, this time, to stay clear of the bruise—and rested his hand on Moranthus's thigh. "So, you got a name you'd like to share with me, or am I calling you bear-killer for the rest of the evening?"

"I certainly wouldn't object to that, but I think Moranthus will do."

"Gralnag. Pleasure to make your acquaintance."

"Now that introductions are out of the way, can I talk you into telling me where this"—Moranthus rested a gentle hand on the bandages covering Gralnag's chest—"came from?"

"Not much to tell." Gralnag's shrug was indifferent, but the way his eyes lit up and the corners of his mouth turned upward into a confident smirk at the question told a different story. "Took some prisoners in a raid. They got a bit rowdy, and I caught a sword in the chest getting 'em back in line. Been holed up here the past couple days waiting for it to heal up enough to get myself home."

Moranthus couldn't afford to show any outward interest in the prisoners Gralnag had mentioned, or he'd never get the information he needed out of Gralnag. His best bet was to keep Gralnag talking about himself and wait for Gralnag to stumble into offering something useful in his own time. "The rest of your party just left you here after an injury like that?"

"It looks worse than it is. I got lucky; bastard didn't hit anything vital. Nothing else they could've done with me anyway. I'm not much use to them like this, and they couldn't dawdle here on my behalf. Winter's setting in, and they need to get those prisoners home to our warlord without freezing 'em. You know how humans are in the cold."

Moranthus nodded his agreement. "The one I'm running with starts shivering the moment summer ends, I swear. I couldn't find a better way to keep track of the seasons if I tried."

Moranthus cast a furtive glance at the table where he'd left Gerrick and was relieved to find it empty. He'd already made more jokes at Gerrick's expense than he probably should have; it wouldn't be fair of him to keep at it while Gerrick was still in earshot. Even if Gerrick had reacted to Moranthus's preference for male company with a look somewhere between disgust and pity, as though Moranthus had just vomited on his boots.

But, whether Moranthus was being fair to Gerrick or not, the burst of laughter he'd drawn from Gralnag gave him an excuse for wearing the triumphant grin that had worked its way onto his face. Gralnag's raiding party *had* to be the same one that had kidnapped Orthenn and his men; if their prisoners were any less valuable than a prince and his personal guard, those prisoners wouldn't still be alive after a show of rebellion that had badly wounded one of their captors. Still, they were moving faster than Moranthus had expected, if they'd reached this settlement days ahead of him and Gerrick. They must have riding boar with them—enough to carry both themselves and Orthenn's company. Whoever their warlord was, they had a not-insignificant amount of wealth at their disposal.

Gralnag gave Moranthus's thigh a light squeeze that snapped his wandering mind back to the task at hand. "Sounds to me like you've been wasting your time on that friend of yours for too long. It's good you're moving on to something better."

"For now, at least." Moranthus forced a sullen expression onto his face and a forlorn note into his voice.

"Don't be like that." Gralnag nuzzled at Moranthus's neck, sending a pleasant shiver down his spine. "You said you want to know if my warlord's hiring, right? I can tell you he is. And I can tell you you're just the sort of thing he'd want to bring into the clan. He might even find a place for your human friend if you're not ready to leave him behind just yet."

Moranthus looped an arm around Gralnag's shoulder and lazily traced a finger over the line where Gralnag's bandages met the bare skin of his chest. "That's quite the opportunity. I'd be a fool not to act on it. Who would I be working for, and where can I find him?"

"Knurlath, of Clan Stoneheart. His territory's about as far north as you can settle without freezing to death. Unless you're damn near immune to the cold like you elves are anyway."

Moranthus couldn't stop himself from tensing. He hadn't expected to hear *that* name again. Knurlath was the same warlord he'd visited with his Patriarch a few years before the coup. Moranthus was surprised he was still alive. The average goblin counted himself lucky if he lived to see forty, and Knurlath was well into his sixties now. Moranthus wondered how he'd kept himself in control of his clan for so long, when—if Gralnag was anything to go by—that clan had no shortage of younger, battle-hardened warriors for him to pass his title on to. Or to take his title from him by force if they decided he'd held on to it for too long.

"Looks like you're already familiar with him." Gralnag raised an eyebrow at him.

Moranthus shrugged. "All of Moonridge is familiar with Clan Stoneheart, and Knurlath's had control of it for longer than any of his predecessors. Patriarch Ryllorin's treaty with your clan kept raiding parties out of Moonridge's western settlements for years, until Matriarch Ilendra reneged on it. That's a hard thing to forget."

"That it is." Gralnag moved his hand to Moranthus's hip and started rubbing slow circles with his thumb just above the waistband of Moranthus's trousers. "But you didn't come over here just to talk business, did you? I've got myself a private room, courtesy of Knurlath's interest in speeding my recovery. It'd be a shame not to use it to its full potential while I'm here."

"That was generous of him."

"Knurlath's a generous man. And, just between you and me, the old man hasn't been feeling quite himself lately. Healers are saying he's picked up a wasting sickness and he might not last the winter. Assuming they're right... Well, you're looking at his logical successor. He's got every reason to want me back at his side as soon as I can get there."

Moranthus tucked that bit of information away for later. His Matriarch would want to hear about it if he ever made it back to Moonridge. "I'll have to be careful with you, then. I'd hate for you to have to keep him waiting on my account."

"Don't you worry about that. You're nothing I can't handle." Gralnag flashed a wide, confident grin at Moranthus that, under different circumstances, would've made his heart melt. It still might have made his heart melt if Moranthus hadn't thought back to the small, gruff smile he'd won from Gerrick after their encounter with the bear and found that Gralnag's smile looked exaggerated and insincere in comparison.

Moranthus turned away from that line of thinking before he could reach its logical conclusion; nothing but heartache lay at the end of *that* road. But he still felt a twinge of disappointment as he followed Gralnag to his room. Nothing he couldn't move past by focusing on the way Gralnag's warm, rough hand felt on the small of his back, but that didn't change the fact that he shouldn't have had to move past it to begin with.

He had nothing to be disappointed about; Gralnag had told him everything he needed to know—more than he needed to know, in fact—and he was steps away from the first proper lay he'd had in years. What did it matter if Gralnag's friendly, open demeanor was just a front to get him into bed? Moranthus's interest in Gralnag and willingness to play along with Gralnag's self-aggrandizement were equally insincere. This wasn't about sincerity. It was about getting an attractive stranger into bed, sending him on his way after you'd had your fun with him, and bragging about it later. If circumstances allowed, and the attractive stranger in question was particularly good in bed, maybe you'd repeat the process a few times before going your separate ways. Before Ryllorin, Moranthus had happily spent over a century doing exactly this sort of thing. His work didn't leave him with enough spare time to pursue anything more serious. It had never bothered him then, and he shouldn't let it bother him now. So he *wouldn't* let it bother him now.

To prove his point, he leaned down and pulled Gralnag into a long, hard kiss the moment Gralnag shut the door to his room behind them. Let himself drift on the faint taste of ale on Gralnag's lips and the jolt of Gralnag grabbing his ass until they broke apart and Gralnag gave him a shove backward toward the rough-hewn bed on the other side of the room. Let the momentum from that shove push him onward when Gralnag sat beside him on the bed and kissed him again, harder, as he ran his hands over the bare skin of Moranthus's chest. Lost himself in the thrill of just being *touched*, slipping his own hands under Gralnag's shirt to explore the broad, muscled plane of Gralnag's back and marveling at the contrast between warm skin and rough linen bandage he found there.

Screwed his eyes shut and tried to ignore the nervous knot in his gut when one of Gralnag's hands drifted to his hair. Felt panic rising like bile in the back of his throat as that hand started loosening the tie that held his braid together.

Moranthus caught hold of Gralnag's wrist and tried to guide Gralnag's hand away from his hair. "Don't."

"Why not?" Gralnag's hand stayed where it was.

Because that braid was a marker of everything Moranthus was and everything he'd accomplished. Without it, he was more than naked—he was no one and nothing, utterly vulnerable and exposed to anyone who saw him in that state. He hadn't let his hair down for anyone since Ryllorin. But Gralnag was a goblin, accustomed to interacting with exiled elves who'd long since lost their ties to Moonridge. He couldn't have known that. "My people don't take letting our hair down lightly. I'm… not ready to do that with you. I'm sorry."

Gralnag pursed his lips into a disapproving frown, but he let his hand drop and kept it clear of Moranthus's hair when Moranthus let go of his wrist. "It's fine. You're not living with your people anymore though. You should've made your peace with that by now."

"I know." Moranthus gave Gralnag an apologetic kiss. He'd ruined the night for both of them. They'd never quite make it back to the same intensity they'd started with; they'd been at an awkward standstill for too long. "Let me make it up to you?"

Gralnag shrugged. "Why not?"

As a compromise, Moranthus let Gralnag wrap his braid around his hand while he pleasured Gralnag with his mouth. He was almost grateful when Gralnag only shoved a half-hearted hand down the front of his trousers in return; it saved him from having to feign any more enthusiasm than he actually felt. It was better than spending a night alone with his right hand, at least. At this point, that was all he could ask for.

After, Moranthus only stayed long enough to avoid causing offense before gathering his things and leaving Gralnag's room. He hoped that Gerrick was still awake. He had the beginnings of a plan stirring in his mind, and he needed to talk through its finer points with Gerrick before they left the inn in the morning.

Fifteen

Once he'd shut the door to the room he and Moranthus had rented and cut himself off from the sounds of the common room, Gerrick's frustration with Moranthus began to fade. In its place, he just felt…tired. He'd sat at a table next to one of Orthenn's kidnappers, looked the man in the eye, and there hadn't been a thing he could do about it. He hadn't done anything without Moranthus's help since he and Moranthus had reached the goblin territories. Moranthus had led them to the settlement, put a roof over Gerrick's head for the first time in weeks, and while Gerrick sat and sulked in their room, he was charming Orthenn's whereabouts out of a goblin who hadn't given Gerrick a second glance. Gerrick wouldn't be of any use to anyone until Moranthus could trade his freedom for Orthenn's.

The room was small and spare. Its walls were built from the same bare stone as the rest of the inn. The rough, wood planks of its floor were decorated with only a small, threadbare rug woven in a pattern that had long since faded. There were no windows to let in light from outside, but an oil lamp burned on a small wooden table beside the washbasin against the back wall, casting a faint, soft glow over the room. The only other piece of furniture in the room was the bed pressed against its right wall, covered by a blanket as worn and faded as the rug.

It reminded Gerrick of the barracks he'd lived in during his training. The bed was larger than the narrow bunk he'd been assigned to, and he wouldn't be sharing the room with dozens of other recruits, but it had the same austere feeling. It was a fine place to spend a night after he'd spent weeks sleeping on the ground, but he couldn't imagine living in a place like that again.

He dropped his pack on the floor, kicked off his boots, and sat on the bed with a long sigh. His shoulders felt light and free when he pulled his mail hauberk off, and he rolled them in satisfaction as he set it on top of his pack. For the first time since Moranthus had taken him from Orthenn's camp, he had a chance to reach inside his shirt and pull out the silver locket, engraved on the outside with the daisy that had given his daughter her name, that he wore around his neck.

But this was also his first real chance to see to the upkeep of his gear since Moranthus had taken him from Orthenn's camp. With a journey deeper into the goblin territories ahead of him, and no tabard to shield his hauberk from the elements, this had to come first. Gerrick sighed, let go of the locket, and set about cleaning and oiling his sword and mail.

Gerrick's mind wandered while his hands were busy with the long, thoughtless task he'd set them to. He had a hard time ignoring the uneasy feeling that formed in his gut at the thought of Moranthus and the scar-faced goblin spending so much time together. In the time Gerrick had known him, Moranthus hadn't had a single kind word to say about his Matriarch. From the way he'd talked about her with the publican, it sounded like he outright hated the woman. Moranthus didn't seem too attached to Moonridge, either, from what little he'd said about his homeland. He didn't have a shred of the dogged loyalty Gerrick would've expected from a man in his line of work.

If the goblin put much effort into talking up his warlord—and Moranthus had been eager enough to cozy up to him that it *wouldn't* take much—Gerrick had an uncomfortably easy time imagining Moranthus genuinely turning his back on Moonridge. And if Moranthus gave up on going back to Moonridge, it wouldn't mean anything good for Gerrick. The best he could hope for was for Moranthus to leave him stranded at the inn, without supplies or a guide. Otherwise, he'd end up as a hostage again, given to the goblin's warlord as a way for Moranthus to prove his worth.

Even if Moranthus didn't turn on Gerrick, there was a risk of him slipping up and the goblin figuring out what Moranthus really wanted from him. Gerrick trusted Moranthus to hold his own against the goblin easily enough—he was better armed, had a longer reach, and probably had decades more experience—but if things came to a fight between them, Moranthus would have every able-bodied man in that common room to contend with too. He'd never win against those odds. And once the goblin and his friends had finished with Moranthus, they'd come looking for Gerrick.

Gerrick's hands began to shake as he finished oiling his mail and let it fall to the floor. He should've stayed in the common room. At least then he'd see it with his own eyes and have a chance to intervene if things went wrong, instead of sitting pretty and fretting like a woman whose husband had gone off to war. There wasn't any point in going back to the common room now though. If something was going to go wrong, chances were it already had.

His hands shook worse as he let them drift back to his locket. He flipped it open and held the small sketch of his little Daisy close to his face, studying it as though he hadn't memorized every last detail. The sketch was only a few months old, but Daisy had already started to outgrow her resemblance to it when he'd left home. She'd lost one of the front teeth in her sketch's smile, and her hair had taken on more of a curl. If Gerrick ever made it home to her, he wondered how much more she'd have changed.

He snapped the locket shut again when he heard the door scrape open and barely had time to tuck it back under his shirt before Moranthus sauntered into the room and flopped onto the bed beside him. His shirt collar hung halfway off his shoulder, and his hair was about the only part of him that didn't look disheveled. He'd done exactly what he'd set out to do, and now he'd come back to gloat about it. Probably had the time of his life while he was at it too. Gerrick scowled and wondered why he'd bothered worrying about him in the first place.

"Looks like he was eager enough to get you into his bed. What were you so keen on coming back here for?" Gerrick asked.

Moranthus sat up straighter and pulled his shirt collar back into place. "Him being eager to get me into his bed doesn't mean I was eager to stay in it. I didn't get anything out of him I couldn't have done to myself. I suppose I would've had to sit on my arm until my hand went numb to get quite the same effect, but it would've saved my jaw some effort."

Gerrick didn't have anything to say to that.

Moranthus laughed. "What? Was that too much for your delicate Dawn's Gate sensibilities? I didn't particularly enjoy his company out of bed, either, if that's a more palatable explanation for you." The corners of his mouth dropped into a frown. "He just had something we needed, and that was the easiest way to get close to him; I'm lucky things worked out between us as well as they did."

Gerrick cleared his throat. "Can we talk about something else?"

"All right. What's in that locket of yours?"

So he'd seen it. Of course, he'd seen it. If there was one thing Moranthus was good at, it was finding new ways to get under Gerrick's skin. "Nothing you need to know about."

Moranthus lightly elbowed his ribs. "Why not? There's no shame in you having a girl back home."

Gerrick sighed. "It's got nothing to do with 'a girl.' It's a sketch of my daughter. That's all."

"Your wife's not worth a locket?"

"My daughter's mother is dead. We were never married." Gerrick clenched his jaw and waited for the scornful laughter that always followed. The taunts over how he'd never rightly know if his daughter was even his—as though that mattered, after he'd spent the better part of the last six years raising her as his own. How could she not be, when he was the only father she'd ever known? The only *parent* she'd ever known. But that was never enough to stop the taunting, when he and her mother had gone their separate ways months before she was born, and he hadn't even known Daisy existed until she was almost a year old.

He might never have known she existed if her mother hadn't slipped up arresting a cutpurse and paid for her mistake by catching a dagger between her ribs. City guards were supposed to be safer than soldiers; that was why they let women join them. She wouldn't have expected to die so young in her line of work. If she'd had her way, she would've raised Daisy into adulthood without saying so much as a word about her to Gerrick.

Gerrick would've married her to spare her the shame of raising a fatherless child if she'd told him about Daisy. They hadn't loved each other, but they'd liked each other well enough; they could've put up with each other long enough to raise a child. She hadn't needed to raise Daisy on her own—she must have known that, or she wouldn't have used her dying words to get Daisy sent to him—but she'd done it anyway.

"Wouldn't most men have just handed her off to someone else or put her in an orphanage where you come from?"

"Yes." Gerrick had thought about it, more than once. Daisy had spent most of her waking hours crying during the weeks it had taken her to warm up to him. He'd been driven to tears himself a few times by the sleepless nights he'd spent trying, and failing, to comfort her. But he could never bring himself to go through with giving her up. Daisy was his responsibility. He wouldn't run from that; he owed her mother at least that much.

"You really aren't like them, then." Moranthus's voice was low and soft. "I'm sorry I assumed you were. That was unworthy of me."

Gerrick stared at him. "You're not going to laugh? Tell me she's probably not mine?"

"Why would I laugh at you for that? There's nothing wrong with raising your child, and if you've raised her, she's yours." Moranthus's brow furrowed. "Do you really think I'm that heartless?"

Gerrick wanted to like Moranthus for that. He did a good job of hiding it, but he had the makings of a good man somewhere inside him. Gerrick felt the beginnings of a small, grateful smile warm his face. But it had come on too fast and too easily for him to trust it. He kept his mouth set in a frown as he replied, "You were quick enough to have a laugh at my expense with that new goblin friend of yours."

Moranthus gave Gerrick a tired look. "You didn't actually believe any of that, did you?"

"I did."

"You shouldn't have. I'll swear on whatever you'd like that anything unflattering I said about you goes double for him."

"Walls are twice as interesting to talk to as he is?"

"Walls don't leave you wishing for older, better days at the end of the night. Let's leave it at that."

Gerrick pretended not to notice the tired, defeated tone of Moranthus's voice. He didn't have time to waste on comforting Moranthus over whatever had gone wrong between him and the goblin. He needed to know what Moranthus had learned about where the raiding party was taking Orthenn. "Did you at least get anything useful out of him?"

Moranthus bit his lower lip and looked away from him.

"Then this was a waste of our time." Gerrick ran a frustrated hand over his beard. "I hope getting away from me for an hour or two was worth it."

"It had nothing to do with wanting to get away from you. Stop being an ass about this because I'm done trying to justify myself to you," Moranthus said through gritted teeth. "And it wasn't…" He bit his lower lip again.

"It wasn't what?" Gerrick fought the urge to grab Moranthus's shoulders and give him a good shake. If Moranthus had learned something—anything—from what he'd done with the goblin, Gerrick deserved to know. Finding a weakness in that raiding party was the only way he'd ever see Daisy again.

"Nothing. Forget I said anything." Moranthus took a deep breath and let it out in a long, slow sigh. "You shouldn't have agreed to do this in the first place. Nothing I learned from him changes that."

"What do you mean?"

"If you take Orthenn's place, you'll be orphaning your daughter. If I'd known that, I would have gone on without you. Why didn't you say something earlier, when there was still time for you to turn back?"

"Why do you care? It's no business of yours."

"I care because I know what it's like to be orphaned. I wouldn't wish that on anyone." Moranthus's voice wavered.

"Whatever you hope your daughter will gain from you sacrificing yourself for your prince, I can promise you she'll spend the rest of her life wishing you'd come home to her instead."

Gerrick clenched his jaw. Whether he was orphaned or not, Moranthus was wrong to butt into Gerrick's life like this. And he didn't know enough about Gerrick or Daisy to justify his acting like he knew what was best for them. Telling Moranthus about Daisy had been a mistake. "I *will* come home to her. Orthenn will pester his father into ransoming me back. It might take a while, but he'll do it. I trust him."

"You don't understand." Moranthus shook his head. "He won't get a chance to."

"Why not?"

"I did learn something, talking to Gralnag."

"Who?"

"The 'goblin friend' you're making such a fuss about. I know who he works for, and I know how to get to his stronghold. If we don't drag our feet, we might even be able to get there before the rest of his raiding party does. They'll be staying off the roads to keep their prisoners safe from bandits. Not a bad idea in these parts, but they won't be getting anywhere fast that way."

For the first time since he'd left Orthenn's camp, Gerrick didn't feel helpless. He had a clear path forward and something useful to do at the end of it. Gerrick let out a breath he hadn't known he was holding in. There was still hope. For Orthenn, for him, and for his daughter. "Why didn't you tell me this to start with?"

Moranthus sighed. "Because I know his warlord. Knurlath's a fair-minded sort and about as honest a goblin as you're likely to find. If we tell him that you're the real Orthenn and you'll willingly become his prisoner if he lets the rest of your men go free, he'll respect that. Probably enough to accept your offer."

"Good! The fewer men Orthenn's father has to ransom back after this, the better." Gerrick didn't see why Moranthus had been so determined to keep this from him. He'd already agreed to trade himself for Orthenn. Getting a chance to save the rest of his brothers-in-arms along with Orthenn just proved that he'd made the right decision.

"He won't be ransoming *anyone* back if you go through with this, Gerrick."

"Yes, he will. If we can do this, I'll be a hero. If he doesn't ransom me back after that, he'll dishonor himself in the eyes of his people. He can't afford that."

"It's got nothing to do with his honor. There won't be enough of you left to ransom back once Knurlath's through with you. I told you, he's a very fair-minded man. Which means he'll also be a very angry man when he finds out you're not the real Orthenn. Nothing your king can offer him would be enough to save you. Knurlath would weaken himself in the eyes of his clan if he let you go unpunished. And the only punishment that means anything in this part of the world is death."

Gerrick's heart sank. "I see."

"Can you also see why you can't go through with this, then?" Moranthus stared into Gerrick's eyes, unblinking. "Think of your daughter."

"I am thinking of my daughter. That's why I need to go through with this. If this is how I die, it's a good death. I won't run from it." Gerrick swallowed the lump that had formed in his throat and tried to ignore how heavy his locket felt. It *was* a good death. And nothing he hadn't signed on for when he started working as Orthenn's body double.

Moranthus set his jaw, but nodded his agreement. "Fine. It's your choice, not mine. But you'll have no one to blame for that death but yourself. Don't try to hold me responsible for your mistakes."

"This isn't a mistake. If you're done telling me what to do with my life, I'm going to bed." Gerrick got to his feet, then remembered he and Moranthus were sharing a bed. He stiffened and cast a wary glance at Moranthus.

Moranthus glared at him. "If sharing a bed is going to be a problem for you, you're the one sleeping on the floor. This didn't bother you before you knew I like men; it shouldn't bother you now." He swung his legs up onto the bed and leaned back against its headboard to prove his point.

"That isn't…" Gerrick trailed off into a sigh. Knowing Moranthus was—the way he was—didn't help things, but it wasn't the only reason he'd balked at the thought of sharing a bed with Moranthus. It wasn't even the main reason. "It isn't just because you like men. You wouldn't want to sleep next to a man who's leading you to your death either." The words came out harsher than he'd meant them to.

Moranthus tensed. His voice was cold, and he had a wounded look in his eyes as he muttered, "Never mind that it's a death I just tried to talk you out of."

Gerrick pretended not to hear him as he spread his bedroll out on the floor. Somewhere at the back of his mind, he knew he should apologize. He wasn't being fair. They both knew that. Setting things right between them would only get harder the longer he put it off. But he was tired and he'd had his fill of talking.

Once he'd made himself as comfortable as he could on his bedroll, he heard Moranthus mutter a terse "idiot" under his breath. A moment later, the bed's blanket landed on top of him. Gerrick didn't complain about Moranthus throwing it at him. It was warm. That was all that mattered.

Sixteen

That night, Moranthus's dreams carried him back to the winding streets of Lower Aurora. The sun had just begun to crawl its way over the horizon, bathing the time-worn cobblestones beneath his feet and the faded, old shopfronts around him in a hazy, pink glow. Most of the city still slept. Down at the docks, the fishermen had long since rowed out in pursuit of their day's catch, and the smell of baking bread filled the air, but the streets around him were empty and draped in a heavy veil of silence. His footsteps echoed as he wandered in search of something important. He couldn't remember what it was or why he needed to find it, but he knew that if he just kept walking, his feet would carry him to it sooner or later, and he'd recognize it when he saw it.

He wasn't surprised when his feet carried him to the run-down street near the bottom of Lower Aurora where he'd grown up, always bathed in darkness by the shadows of Upper Aurora on one side or the towering city wall on the other. He also wasn't surprised to see his childhood home still standing instead of the brothel that had taken its place after it was burned to the ground. Half the homes in Lower Aurora were burned along with it in an effort to purge Aurora of the plague that had ravaged its lower districts before it could reach the upper city. It was a drastic measure, but a successful one. The plague claimed only a handful of lives in Upper Aurora, while there wasn't a single elf in Lower Aurora who hadn't lost at least one relative to its deadly clutches.

As if in response to Moranthus's thoughts, the world began to shift around him, the entire street twisting from a fond memory to the cold, unfamiliar slum it had grown into. Moranthus shook his head to clear his mind, and his childhood home snapped back into place. This was what he'd been looking for, after all. He knew that now. And he couldn't let it slip away from him until he remembered why he'd gone looking for it.

A plume of smoke curled out of his childhood home's chimney. If Moranthus stopped to peer through the cracks in the wooden shutters over its window, there was no doubt in his mind that he'd see his parents, and himself, huddled around their hearth like they always did on cold winter mornings. Maybe that was why he'd come here.

The moment he stopped walking, the front door swung open, and his mother stepped through it. Not the withered, pock-marked corpse he'd last seen her as, after she'd succumbed to the plague, but the tall, wiry woman who'd carried him on her back all through the city while she picked up clothes for the wash. She'd taken more care while weaving her red hair into a simple commoner's braid than most nobles did with theirs, and her mouth was downturned in the worried frown she'd often worn when she thought Moranthus and his father couldn't see her.

Instead of disappearing, the way it usually did when she noticed Moranthus, her frown only deepened. Her gray eyes narrowed, and she shut the door tight behind her as she asked, "What do you want?"

"Nothing," he replied, shrinking under her gaze as if he were still a child and she'd caught him misbehaving. "I'm just… It's so good to see you again."

His mother shook her head. "I'm sorry, but I don't know you. You…you need to leave. Now."

She must not recognize him. How could she recognize him when he'd been a child the last time they'd seen each other? But she'd know who he was once he told her. She had to. Moranthus smiled and took a step toward her. "Yes, you do. It's me, Moranthus. Your son."

"No. You can't be." His mother's eyes went wide with fear. "Don't come any closer!"

"But I am. Please, just hear me out." Moranthus took another step toward her.

His mother flattened herself against the door and screamed.

Moranthus reached out to comfort her but recoiled when he saw himself reflected in her eyes. Where he should have had a face, there was only a black, gaping void.

Seventeen

Moranthus woke with the strangled beginnings of a terrified cry. He sat bolt upright, clutching at his chest in an effort to slow the frenzied pounding of his heartbeat. The room was cold, cold enough that he almost regretted tossing his blanket onto Gerrick earlier, but his shirt was soaked through with sweat, clinging to his shaking body like a second skin.

He couldn't remember the last time he'd dreamed about his parents—either of them. And in the dreams about them he could remember, he'd never seen either of their faces so clearly. Why had he gotten his first glimpse of his mother's face in over a century just so he could watch it contort in horror at the sight of what he'd become?

It must have had something to do with Gerrick. He'd just dropped the fact that he had a daughter on Moranthus, after all, as though that detail didn't dramatically alter the circumstances under which Gerrick would be sacrificing himself. Moranthus couldn't think of anything else that could've wormed its way so deep into his mind. He cast a wary glance at the floor beside the bed, hoping he hadn't made enough noise to wake Gerrick. He didn't have the energy or presence of mind to explain what had given him such a fright without slipping back into the argument they'd ended last night with. In the gloom, he could just make out a mound of blankets, rising and falling with the slow, even pattern of Gerrick's breathing. Never before had Moranthus taken such comfort in the sound of another man's snores.

Moranthus shook his head. No man should've been able to sleep that soundly, knowing that he'd soon make an orphan of his child. And if Gerrick was really that eager to wash his hands of his daughter, he should never have tried to raise her on his own to begin with. Taking her mother's place for so long, only to tear himself away from her as soon as an opportunity presented itself, was just cruel. He would've been kinder to abandon her from the start, before she had a chance to grow attached to him.

Not that Moranthus cared. He had no reason to care. What was some human girl he'd never so much as laid eyes on to him? Nothing. And Gerrick…Gerrick was a complication on Moranthus's way to grabbing Orthenn and leveraging him into a journey home. Nothing more. And certainly nothing worth losing sleep over.

But Gerrick had sent him spiraling into a nightmare all the same. A nightmare that Moranthus had a sinking feeling he'd slip right back into if he fell asleep again. He needed to clear his head.

He shucked off his sweat-soaked shirt, hanging it on a bedpost as he swung his legs over the side of the bed and shoved his feet into his boots. It had to be near dawn. Not a bad time to have a look at that slow spot in the river the publican had mentioned. It had been long enough since he'd last had a chance to bathe, and the morning's chill would see to it that he had the solitude he needed to give his hair a good wash. And to give the sides of his head a desperately needed shave while he was at it, as much as it pained him to do it. The water was going to be cold, even for him. Any human or goblin stupid enough to try bathing in those conditions would risk freezing themselves on their way home, and any elf with the same idea as Moranthus would understand that Moranthus attending to his hair was a private matter and stay a respectful distance away from him.

If he kept things quick, he could make it back to the inn before Gerrick woke up to find him gone and had another chance to assume the worst of him. Moranthus supposed that was more of a reason not to keep things quick, really. Letting Gerrick have some time to himself to wonder if Moranthus had finally had enough and decided to abandon him would serve him right.

The slow current crawling along the river's bank wrapped around Moranthus like a lover's embrace as he lowered himself into the clear, shallow water. He inhaled a sharp, gasping breath at the sudden chill, the beginnings of a shiver running down his spine, but he forced himself to stay submerged until he'd adjusted to the river's temperature. The sun had just begun to creep over the horizon, casting a pale, orange glow over the world around him. Soon enough, its warmth would follow its light. He'd bathed in much colder places than this; he'd be fine. Skies above, he'd spent his childhood getting dunked in his mother's iced-over wash bucket whenever he was fool enough to get himself dirty during winter. Compared to that, this was nothing. And while he waited for the sun to make the river's temperature more tolerable, the icy water would keep him from thinking of anything else. Just the way he wanted it.

The blissful daybreak silence around him lasted long enough for him to scrub off the lingering grime from his journey through the Ghostwood and work all the knots out of his hair for the first time in weeks. Even the grim task of shaving the sides of his head couldn't break through the sense of calm that settled over him. This was likely to be the last shave he ever gave himself, after all. Once he'd rescued Orthenn, his time as a half-exile would be over. He left his hair down while he sat on the riverbank, dangling his feet in the water while he waited for it to dry. The skin on the soles of his feet would be wrinkly and tender during his walk back to the inn, but the last few moments of clarity it bought him were well worth it.

All he needed to do was deliver Gerrick to Knurlath's stronghold, and soon enough, he'd be dipping his feet into a Moonridge stream. Compared to everything they'd faced so far, it was simple. Moranthus rubbed a nervous thumb over the worn etchings of the cameo of his Patriarch that hung around his neck from a long leather cord. For the first time since he'd realized that Gerrick wasn't Orthenn, he felt victory was within his grasp. So why, now that the perfect plan had all but fallen into his lap, was he so reluctant to go through with it?

He scoured the farthest reaches of his mind, trying to find the source of his newfound uncertainty. But no matter how desperately he searched for another, better reason, all he could think of was Gerrick. It didn't make sense; there was no meaningful distinction between Gerrick and any other man, or woman, he'd tracked down and dragged off to similar fates. He'd even grown to like some of them more than he liked Gerrick in the short time he'd known them, and he'd put their lives in the hands of his Patriarch's justice all the same. They'd all had families, and some had bombarded him with tear-streaked stories of the children they'd left behind in a last-ditch plea for Moranthus to show them the mercy their Patriarch wouldn't.

He supposed that was the problem, really. Gerrick hadn't offered Moranthus a glimpse into his life because he wanted to save himself; he'd waited for Moranthus to ask for it, and even then he'd said as little as possible. He'd never tried to escape his duty to Orthenn, either, and never tried to fight Moranthus once he knew they shared the same goal. And when he'd had the chance to rid himself of Moranthus, when the easiest thing he could have done was run away and let that bear finish Moranthus off, he'd decided to put himself at risk to save Moranthus's life instead.

Moranthus couldn't remember the last time someone had stuck their neck out for him like that. Not since he'd lost his parents anyway. And even in his half-exile state, when his shame had been shaved into his hair for anyone to see, Gerrick had never looked at Moranthus like he was anything less than Gerrick's equal. It was a shame for a man like that to be wasted in service to a fool of a prince. Gerrick deserved better.

Moranthus smiled sadly and raised the cameo of his fallen Patriarch—no, of *Ryllorin*—to his lips. He hadn't been so different from Gerrick, really. They were both driven by an unwavering loyalty to their respective homelands and an unflinching desire to do right by their people. And they'd both struggled to reconcile that loyalty with their love for their children. That had been the death of Ryllorin. If things went according to plan, it would also be the death of Gerrick.

But Gerrick *wasn't* Ryllorin. Moranthus had grown so desperate for affection that he'd drawn a false equivalence between Ryllorin and the first man who hadn't recoiled at the sight of him since Ryllorin's death. That was all. He couldn't let himself turn away from what he needed to do just because he'd deluded himself into seeing a few superficial similarities between Gerrick and Ryllorin.

It was because of Ryllorin that he had to move forward with sacrificing Gerrick for a prince who didn't deserve his loyalty, after all. Regardless of Moranthus's thoughts on the matter, Ryllorin's daughter, Ilendra, had asserted herself as his rightful successor, and Ryllorin had accepted that in the end. Serving Ilendra was the same as serving Ryllorin. Moranthus wouldn't deny Ryllorin his dying wish by letting himself forget that. He *couldn't* forget, when he'd watched Ryllorin acknowledge Ilendra as Moonridge's new Matriarch with his own eyes. And then he'd watched Ryllorin die.

It had been a lazy, summer evening in Aurora. Moranthus and Ryllorin lay together on Ryllorin's bed, still naked from when Ryllorin had called Moranthus into his bedchamber earlier that day and, foregoing their usual foreplay, all but commanded Moranthus—in much more eloquent terms—to fuck him into his mattress.

Moranthus was still halfway on top of Ryllorin. He'd buried his face in the crook of Ryllorin's neck, breathing him in as Ryllorin rubbed slow circles on the small of his back with a warm, soft hand. Moranthus lived for moments like these, when Ryllorin didn't have to be his Patriarch, didn't have to play the refined, born nobleman to his coarse, up-jumped commoner, didn't belong to anyone but him...and had enough time to spare that it didn't all have to come to an end the moment the sex was over. They'd been together like this more than usual as of late. Ryllorin was deeply troubled over a series of rumors that had surfaced regarding his daughter, and Moranthus's presence seemed to comfort him.

The sun's dying light filtered in through the large picture window set into the western wall of Ryllorin's bedchamber, casting a warm, golden glow over everything in the room. The cavernous fireplace, flanked on either side by hulking ice bear statues carved from pristine white marble, that occupied the wall opposite Ryllorin's vast four-poster bed sat empty and cold in the summer heat. Plush, richly colored rugs covered much of the chamber's polished stone floor, and elaborate tapestries adorned its walls. The walls themselves were carved and subtly painted to resemble a glacier illuminated by the aurora that had given Moonridge's capital its name.

Moranthus always felt out of place among so much finery, but Ryllorin—even in the disheveled state their lovemaking had left him in—looked like a natural outgrowth of the opulence that surrounded them. The bright, cold white of his unbound hair stood in sharp contrast to the duller, warmer white of the linens beneath them. His dark amethyst eyes sparkled in the sunlight, and the corners of his mouth were upturned in a soft, contented smile that smoothed the fine worry lines that his five centuries of life had etched into his brow. He had the blue-tinged violet skin typical of Moonridge's nobility, kept soft and unblemished by a life spent almost entirely behind castle walls. Even the slight paunch his belly had settled into in recent years only added to his beauty in Moranthus's eyes. A man like that could've had anyone he wanted in his bed. And still, he'd chosen Moranthus. Moranthus had had some forty-odd years to get used to it, but the thought still left him breathless and giddy.

Moranthus pressed his lips to the underside of Ryllorin's jaw. "You're so fucking beautiful. Better than the aurora on a cloudless night. Better than the sun and the moon and the stars put together." He punctuated each sentence with another kiss. "I love you."

By then, Moranthus knew better than to expect Ryllorin to say it back to him, and Ryllorin wouldn't have fooled either of them if he had. Still, the words were enough to make Ryllorin's breath catch in his throat. "Mora..." he murmured, his voice heavy and thick with affection as he ran his fingers through Moranthus's unbound hair. It wasn't what Moranthus dreamed of on the lonely nights when his work took him away from Aurora. But it was enough.

Anything else Ryllorin might have said was lost when a hard, sharp knock sounded against his door. Moranthus reluctantly shifted his weight off Ryllorin, but Ryllorin locked his arm around Moranthus's back to keep him close.

"I gave distinct orders that I wasn't to be disturbed," Ryllorin muttered. He took a deep breath that he let out in a long, frustrated sigh before he called out, "I am currently indisposed; unless this is a matter of the utmost urgency, I'm afraid it will have to wait until morning. Leave a note on my desk, and I'll attend to it at my earliest convenience."

Another knock answered him, hard enough to rattle the door in its frame. Ryllorin started and tightened his arm around Moranthus for a moment, then let go of him.

"I suppose I'd best see what this is about." Ryllorin got out of bed and began combing his fingers through his hair. He gave Moranthus a gentle kiss as he added, "You're welcome to stay here if you'd like. I don't expect I'll be gone long."

Moranthus smiled and nodded as he rolled onto the warm indentation Ryllorin's body had left in the mattress. "I'll be here when you get back."

To whoever was on the other side of his door, Ryllorin called out, "I'll be with you in just a moment! Until then, I must insist that you refrain from assaulting my door any further, or I will be forced to interpret it as a display of aggression and respond accordingly."

Ryllorin had just begun weaving his hair into his eleven-strand Patriarch's braid when his door flew open and crashed against the wall, its lower hinge torn completely out of the doorframe. Ryllorin froze, the beginnings of his braid slowly unwinding as he stared, wide-eyed, at the door. Moranthus scrambled into a sitting position, his eyes scanning the room in a frantic search for his right boot and the dagger he kept hidden inside it.

A heavily armored woman strode through the door, a scuffed dent in the toe of one polished steel sabaton from where she'd kicked the door in. A long-handled axe hung at her side, its blade notched from recent use. She had Ryllorin's eyes and coloring, and her face would be a good match for his if her expression wasn't so severe. Her jet-black hair, pulled harshly away from her face in a tight braid, set them apart even farther. The cut of her armor and the steel-blue ribbon woven into her nine-strand noblewoman's braid marked her as a high-ranking war-bear. She carried a helmet with a visor engraved to resemble the snarling jaws of a bear under her right arm, and her left hand rested on the back of a young ice bear that padded dutifully along at her side. The bear was hardly more than a cub, but his shoulders were already the same height as his master's waist. Full-grown, he'd be almost as tall as she was. The intricate harness he wore, weighted down at regular intervals with sandbags that sank into his thick coat of white fur, looked comical now, but in a few years' time he'd be wearing a saddle and armor as his master rode him into battle.

Ilendra. She was the youngest of Ryllorin's three children, born to the first lover Ryllorin had taken after his consort died giving birth to their second son. In spite of her illegitimate status, Ryllorin had always favored her, though their relationship had grown somewhat strained after Ryllorin had ended his involvement with her mother and taken Moranthus as a lover shortly afterward. Strained, but never broken until, a few weeks earlier, Ilendra had fled Aurora amid allegations that she was plotting to overthrow her father and usurp the elder of his two legitimate sons as the heir to Moonridge's throne. She should have been leagues away from Aurora, either finding a way to prove her innocence or trying to rally enough support for a full-scale civil war. Instead, she'd come home.

A pair of tall, bulky frostguards—who should have kept Ilendra far away from her father, or at least died trying—followed her into the room, their faces obscured by the featureless visors of their slate-gray armor. Even with his dagger, Moranthus was no match for all three of them—four, if he counted Ilendra's half-grown bear. He probably wouldn't even last long enough to buy Ryllorin time to escape. And he *didn't* have his dagger. He was utterly exposed and defenseless, help-less to do anything but sit and watch as Ilendra did whatever she'd come here to do.

Ilendra cast a disdainful glance at Ryllorin. She gestured at one of the frostguards. "Give him something to cover himself with. He has an urgent matter of state to attend to—the last of his career, if I'm not mistaken. He'll want to comport himself with the dignity that such a momentous occasion deserves."

The frostguard nodded and unhurriedly approached Ryllorin, stopping along the way to pick up a simple white dressing gown that lay discarded on the floor. He shoved the dressing gown into Ryllorin's trembling hands, then nodded toward Moranthus. "What about him?" the frostguard asked, his nasal voice deepened and distorted by his helmet.

Moranthus's heartbeat quickened. If he was allowed to dress himself, he'd have a chance to get to his dagger. If he could get it out of his boot and thrown before Ilendra and her frost-guards caught on, he'd have a clear shot at Ilendra's unprotected throat. Her frostguards would kill him for that, and Ryllorin would never forgive him if they didn't, but Ryllorin would be alive and safe. That was all that mattered.

Ilendra wrinkled her nose in disgust as she replied, "He stays as he is. And *where* he is. I don't want him to interfere. If he moves, kill him."

"Yes, Matriarch." The frostguard unsheathed his sword and held its blade against Moranthus's neck. Moranthus shuddered at the feeling of cold, sharpened steel against his skin.

"Ilendra." Ryllorin shrugged into his dressing gown and tied it shut with a remarkable level of composure. He kept his voice firm and even as he said, "Please, let Moranthus go. There's no need to involve him in this."

"If you didn't want him involved in this, then you shouldn't have set my mother aside for a piece of trash you plucked out of the gutter."

Ryllorin's voice softened. "I regret that my separation from your mother still causes you such pain. Had I known that my actions would trouble you so deeply, perhaps I would have acted differently." He began the process of braiding his hair again.

"Leave it. You'll have no need for a braid soon enough." Ilendra's voice was sharp and cold. "The time for apologies has passed, Father. Your reign as Patriarch has made Moonridge weak. I have no reason to believe that your sons are capable of reversing the damage you have done. Our neighbors laugh at us and encroach upon our borders as we shrink back from them in the name of peace. For the good of our people, I have no choice but to remove you from your throne and place the burden of Moonridge's rule upon my own shoulders."

Ryllorin shook his head and let his hands fall to his sides. "Peace has not weakened us, Ilendra. For the first time in centuries, our western villages aren't burning at the hands of goblin raiding parties, and we aren't warring with Dawn's Gate over our farmlands in the south. Don't be so quick to cast that aside."

"The cost of your peace is too high. Our enemies have forgotten that they are prodding a sleeping bear. When the moment comes, that bear must be ready to awaken."

"Moonridge can ill afford to waste lives on such aggression. Not two centuries have passed since the plague; our populace is still diminished. We must take care not to diminish it further."

"And how did you respond to that diminishment? By welcoming your father's exiles with open arms. Welcoming the human and goblin customs they adopted in their absence along with them. Filling Moonridge with their exile-born children, who were raised not knowing what it means to be an elf and find our ways to be utterly foreign." Ilendra's voice rose in volume and intensity with each word. "They are making humans and goblins of us all, and you have stood by and done nothing!"

Unflinching, Ryllorin replied, "And yet, your concern over such things is a very human one."

Ilendra recoiled as though she'd been struck. Her mouth hung open, jaw silently working as she tried, and failed, to form a counterargument. Finally, her mouth snapped shut, her eyes shining with cold fury.

"I did not come here to debate philosophy with you, Father. Let us not lose sight of our true purpose here," Ilendra said through gritted teeth. She handed her helmet to the frostguard who'd remained at her side, slid a razor out of a pouch on her belt, and tossed the razor to the floor at Ryllorin's feet. "Your life in Moonridge is at its end. Make your choice: death or exile."

Ryllorin picked up the razor and turned it over in his hands. "Is there truly no way I can dissuade you from this course of action?"

"There is not."

"Very well, then." Ryllorin's face betrayed no expression as he eased the razor's blade out of its handle and raised it to his throat.

Ilendra's eyes widened. "You're certain you wouldn't prefer exile? In time, I might be persuaded to allow your return to Moonridge. You have knowledge I could make use of once you've proven that your acceptance of my rule is genuine."

A sad smile flickered over Ryllorin's face. "If this is what my life has come to, then I have nothing left to live for. I wish you all the best, Matriarch, and I truly hope that your methods prove to be more effective than my own."

The words were a knife in Moranthus's heart. Watching Ryllorin drag the razor across his neck ripped his heart's battered remains out of his chest. A choked sob tore itself from Moranthus's throat as Ryllorin's blood dyed the front of his dressing gown a vibrant red, and Ryllorin's lifeless body crumpled to the floor. The frostguard's blade against his neck stopped him from doing anything more.

The bear at Ilendra's side enthusiastically sniffed at the coppery scent of blood in the air and took an eager step toward Ryllorin.

"No." Ilendra's voice wavered as she dug her fingers into the fur on his back. When the bear looked up at her with a soft, confused cry, her expression softened and she moved her hand to scratch behind his ears. "We'll find you something better to eat later."

The bear didn't show any further interest in Ryllorin as he followed Ilendra to his corpse. With a wave, Ilendra dismissed the frostguard holding a sword to Moranthus's throat. "You may release him," she said. "He poses no further threat to my purposes."

The frostguard pressed the edge of his sword against Moranthus's skin just hard enough to draw blood. Moranthus held his breath to keep it from cutting any deeper.

"Are you certain you wouldn't like him killed, Matriarch?" the frostguard asked, an eager note in his low, nasal voice. "I'd be happy to dispose of him for you. I can't imagine you have much use for your father's old bedwarmer, after all."

Ilendra gave the frostguard a withering look. "That decision is not yours to make. I am no murderer. You *will* release him. Do not make me repeat myself a second time."

"Yes, Matriarch. My apologies." The frostguard sheathed his sword and made his way back to the door, nudging Ryllorin's corpse out of his path with his foot as though Ryllorin was just another of the pieces of discarded clothing that still lay on the floor.

Moranthus supposed he could make a move for his dagger now. But there wasn't anything to be gained by that anymore. He was too late; Ryllorin was gone. He'd died almost within arm's reach of Moranthus, and Moranthus hadn't been able to lift a finger to stop it from happening. He swallowed another sob that threatened to form in his throat. Blinked away the tears prickling at his eyes.

Ilendra's eyes looked tired, and there was no joy in her expression as she reached down to pry the razor from Ryllorin's hand. "Your Patriarch is dead." She dropped the razor still slick with Ryllorin's blood onto the bed beside Moranthus. "You may accept me as your new Matriarch, or you may face the same choice he did."

Moranthus stared down at the razor. For a moment, he considered wrapping his fingers around its handle and letting his own lifeless body join Ryllorin's on the floor. Ilendra had done nothing to deserve his loyalty, and compared to a lifetime of servitude to a woman who'd caused the death of the only man he'd ever loved, death seemed like a mercy. But that wasn't what Ryllorin would have wanted. He'd used his dying words to acknowledge Ilendra as Moonridge's new Matriarch; if he'd lived, he would have expected Moranthus to show her the same respect. Moranthus had always trusted Ryllorin's judgment while Ryllorin was alive, and Ryllorin had never led him astray. He wouldn't disrespect Ryllorin's memory by questioning his judgment after his death. "I am at your service, Matriarch."

"And I accept that service." Moranthus could feel the disappointment in Ilendra's voice as she cast a baleful glance at him. She hadn't wanted him murdered, but she clearly wasn't happy he was alive. "But in light of your...intimate involvement with my predecessor, I have no choice but to sentence you to half-exile until you have proven yourself worthy of my trust. Mark yourself as such, then clean up this mess. I expect my new quarters to be in livable condition before nightfall."

The sound of heavy footsteps behind Moranthus pulled him free of his bloodstained memory. Moranthus's hand flew to the hilt of the dagger he'd kept beside him on the riverbank as a precaution—and apparently a necessary one—and he leapt to his feet, twisting around to face whoever had approached him.

"Calm down. It's only me." Gerrick stood behind him, fully dressed and fully armed and with what looked like Moranthus's shirt slung over his shoulder. His charcoal-darkened hair was already returning to its usual shade of sandy blond. They couldn't afford to linger in the settlement much longer.

Moranthus lowered his dagger. "It never hurts to be on your guard in a place like this."

"Then you shouldn't be wandering around..." Gerrick cleared his throat, and his voice took on a strained quality as he continued, "You shouldn't be out here naked." He tossed Moranthus's shirt at him.

Moranthus caught it and slung it over his own shoulder. "What are you, my mother?"

Gerrick scoffed. "This is the stupidest way you could give yourself frostbite. I'm stopping you."

"Elves don't get frostbite. Everyone knows that."

"You should still wear a shirt. And trousers." Gerrick cast an interested glance at Moranthus's unbound hair.

"Do you mind?" Moranthus snapped.

Gerrick averted his eyes. "Odd time to grow a sense of shame," he muttered.

Moranthus bit back a retort as he let his dagger fall to the ground and ran his fingers through his hair, hurriedly separating it into the strands that would form his braid. Out of the corner of his eye, he could see Gerrick's brow furrow in confusion. He'd probably expected Moranthus to dress himself first, as though his body was something to be ashamed of, when he was infinitely more exposed without the braid that served as a marker of everything he was.

Only once his hair was tied back in a neat, secure braid did Moranthus set about getting his clothes back on. His trousers were still a bit damp from the hasty wash he'd given them, but Gerrick's face had gone a shade of red that rivaled Moranthus's hair, and he preferred soggy clothing to the thought of starting an argument with Gerrick about the circumstances under which nudity was acceptable. And humans wondered why the rest of the world assumed they were all sexually repressed.

"If this is such a problem for you, you had no reason to come looking for me, you know," Moranthus said as he pulled his shirt over his head and put his dagger back into its sheath.

"I was worried."

"About what? That I'd suddenly changed my mind, fallen madly in love with last night's bad idea, and run off to start a new life with him without bringing so much as my shirt with me?"

"That you'd decided to leave me behind." Gerrick scowled. "You seemed set on not bringing me with you last night."

"Well, I didn't leave you behind." Moranthus ran a self-conscious hand over his hair to ensure his braid didn't have any loose strands and he hadn't missed any spots when he'd shaved the sides of his head. "You said it yourself: you wanting to get yourself killed is no business of mine. I won't get in your way."

"Thank you." Gerrick's expression softened as he cast another glance at Moranthus's hair. "Your hair means a lot to you, doesn't it?"

"It does."

"And you keeping part of it shaved like that has something to do with your Matriarch?"

Moranthus shot him an irritated glare. "Yes."

"What does it mean?"

"Why do you want to know? You've never taken an interest in this before now."

"We've got a long way left to travel together. And you're the last friendly face I'll see before…" Gerrick let out a deep, heavy sigh. "Before the end. I should know you better than I do."

Moranthus knew he should rebuff Gerrick's interest in him and set them back to the safe, cold tolerance they'd settled into before the bear. They'd both be better off that way. But Moranthus stood to benefit from Gerrick's sacrifice just as much as Orthenn did. If getting better acquainted with Moranthus would make that sacrifice easier on Gerrick, then Moranthus owed him at least that much. Gerrick certainly could have chosen a less sensitive subject to start with, but at least it would spare them any further awkward misunderstandings over his hair. "The braid is a marker of my rank and occupation. I had to shave part of it off after Matriarch Ilendra took the throne. I was…closer to her father than she was comfortable with, and she felt that made me untrustworthy. Until she decides I've earned her trust, I'm stuck like this as a marker of my probationary status."

"Is that why you hate her so much?"

"I don't…" Moranthus let his voice trail off, surprised at how difficult it was to say the words out loud. He swallowed, then tried again. "I don't hate her. She just…isn't her father."

"Why keep working for her, then? She killed him."

"She didn't kill him; he took his own life. She just put the razor in his hand." Moranthus shut his eyes against the image of Ryllorin's lifeless body. "And he supported her becoming Matriarch in the end. If he had that much faith in her, then it's only right of me to show her the same loyalty as her father."

"That's a lot of loyalty for a dead man."

"He was…special. He had this way of seeing the best in people. Making them think they could be more than they were. He was the kind of man who'd pluck a scrawny little thief out of the gutter and give him a chance to make something of himself." Moranthus sighed, his lips quirking into a sad smile at the memory of the man who, in his heart, would never stop being his Patriarch. "I swear, when the light hit him just right, the man fucking glittered."

Gerrick's gaze drifted to Moranthus's cameo of Ryllorin. "Is that his face on your pendant?"

Moranthus nodded. "It is."

"So, the two of you were—" Gerrick's brow furrowed. His voice sounded strained when he finally continued. "—in love?"

Moranthus laughed. "Oh, he didn't love me. I think he loved that I was in love with him, but that's not the same thing."

Gerrick stared at him. "That didn't bother you?"

"I was too infatuated with him for it to bother me when we were together. And when it did start to bother me, he was already gone, so it didn't matter anymore."

"Sounds like you could've done better."

"Maybe I didn't want better." Moranthus shrugged and forced his voice into a light, effortless tone. If he let Gerrick press *that* matter any further, they'd be stuck on the riverbank all day. "We should get back to the inn. We've wasted too much time here already."

Eighteen

Gray clouds filled the sky as Gerrick followed Moranthus back to the inn. By the time they'd collected their things and Storm, a light rain had begun to fall. When they came to a stop at a shop near the settlement's gate, the rain turned to a wet snowfall. Gerrick hoped it would let up soon, or he and Moranthus had a long, miserable day on the road ahead of them.

Moranthus cast a wary glance at the sky before tying his horse to a hitching rail in front of the shop. "Will you be all right waiting in this while I buy supplies?"

"Why can't I go in with you?" Moranthus had never had any qualms about keeping Gerrick close to him before. Gerrick didn't know why he'd decided to start now.

"I'd rather no one else got a close look at you before we leave here; it could mean trouble for us later on. You have the kind of face that draws attention."

"Why? I'm not the only human in this settlement."

"You being human isn't the problem." Moranthus shook his head. "It's your expression, your features, the way you carry yourself…"

"Why is that a problem?" Gerrick winced at the defensive note in his voice. He sounded like a petulant child.

"Because you have a very noble bearing. That…isn't something you see very often. Even among *real* nobility." Moranthus gave him a wry smile. "There's a reason you make such a convincing double of your prince."

"Thank you?" Gerrick wasn't sure if Moranthus had meant that as a compliment, but he didn't know how else to respond. "But I don't see why that means I have to stay outside."

Moranthus sighed. "Because if the shopkeep sees you acting like a stiff-necked nobleman when you're *supposed* to be a common sellsword, they're going to remember that. Maybe enough to make it a conversation topic the next time they go drinking with their friends at the inn. And if Gralnag overhears that conversation and starts asking questions, he's sharp enough to make a connection between us and Orthenn. I'd rather that didn't happen, and I'm sure you feel the same."

"That didn't stop you from bringing me into the inn last night."

"You're less conspicuous in a crowded inn than you are in an empty shop." Moranthus cast a glance at Gerrick's hair, lips pursed in a worried frown. "You also looked less like yourself last night; the charcoal's wearing off now. I'm not taking any more risks with you." His tone left no room for argument.

"All right. I'll wait here for you." Gerrick couldn't deny that Moranthus had a point. Getting out of the snow for a while wasn't worth jeopardizing their chances of rescuing Orthenn. "Just be quick about it. It's too cold to be standing around like this."

"Thank you. I won't be long." Moranthus clapped Gerrick on the shoulder before he turned and vanished behind the thick blanket that hung like a curtain over the shop's open doorway.

Gerrick pulled his woolen cloak closer around his shoulders and leaned against the hitching rail. He tried to make himself look inconspicuous by keeping his eyes on the ground and making a show of readjusting Storm's tack whenever someone passed by. It seemed to work. No one cast more than a passing glance in his direction as they hurried along their way. They didn't want to be out in this weather any more than he did.

But a weather-beaten man wearing what looked like an aged, battered version of Gerrick's own mail hauberk and armed with a notched sword of human make caught Gerrick's attention. And held Gerrick's attention, when Gerrick realized that the man's face looked familiar, though he couldn't quite place it. Their eyes met, and Gerrick remembered where he knew the man from. Too late, he looked away.

The man hailed Gerrick with a shout.

Gerrick tensed but pretended not to hear him.

Undeterred, the man approached him and made himself comfortable leaning against the hitching rail beside Gerrick. The years hadn't been kind to him, but Gerrick would've known that broad, flat face and greasy brown hair anywhere.

His name was Willem. They'd reported to Kingstone, Dawn's Gate's capital, to start training as soldiers at around the same time. Gerrick had been assigned to the bunk next to Willem's in the city barracks. Gerrick, at least, had hoped they might become friends, until their initial conversation revealed that they had almost nothing in common. Gerrick had grown up on a farm near the Ghostwood and joined the army in the hopes of protecting people like his family from goblin attacks. Willem, born and raised in Kingstone, came from a long line of soldiers and had only joined the army to keep his father from disowning him. The lack of common ground between them had sparked an initial dislike that flared into a heated rivalry as their training progressed. That rivalry might still be going if Gerrick's path hadn't led him into Orthenn's service. And if Willem's hadn't somehow led him to the goblin territories.

Willem gave Gerrick a nudge with his elbow. "All right," he said in a gravelly voice that had had a higher pitch the last time Gerrick heard it. "Tell me where I know you from."

Gerrick put off answering Willem as long as he could. Tried to think of what Moranthus would do in his position. Finally, in as gruff a voice as he could manage, he replied, "Can't say I know you from anywhere." With a shrug, he checked the girth on Storm's saddle for at least the fifth time. She flicked an ear in annoyance, but played along with his act.

"Bullshit." Willem grabbed Gerrick by the shoulder and brought their faces close together. "I know faces. Yours isn't new, but I damn well haven't seen it around these parts before. Help me remember, will you?"

Gerrick fought to keep his expression blank as he stared into Willem's pale green eyes. "Shove off. I already said I don't know you. You must have me confused with someone else."

Willem's eyes narrowed. He took hold of Gerrick's cloak and pulled it off one shoulder, then jabbed a finger into Gerrick's mail hauberk. "That's Dawn's Gate mail, if I've ever seen it. Looks like it's in fairly new condition too. You're a deserter, aren't you?"

Gerrick bristled at the accusation. Before he could stop himself, he swatted Willem's hand away and yanked his cloak back into place. "It takes one to know one, Willem."

Willem's expression darkened. He took a step backward, hands curling into fists at his sides. "So, you *do* know me."

Gerrick felt the blood drain from his face. Dug his nails into the hitching rail behind him to ground himself. Tried to ignore his heart pounding in his chest as he tried to think of an explanation that wouldn't give him away. "We trained together. In Dawn's Gate. Never talked much though. I didn't remember until just now," he offered, hoping he'd changed enough over the years to keep Willem from putting a name to his face.

Willem's eyes widened in recognition, an incredulous look on his face. "No. You can't be." He leaned in closer to Gerrick, eyes narrowed in a squint. Then, his lips curled into a sneer that made Gerrick's stomach turn. "Or *can* you?"

"I can't be what?"

"Like you don't know." Willem let out a cold, humorless laugh. "Looks like perfect little toy soldier Gerrick went and deserted. Who'd have thought you had it in you?"

Gerrick glared at him. "I wouldn't have pegged you for a deserter either. What makes me any different?"

Willem's sneer turned to a scowl. "What makes you different?" He grabbed Gerrick's cloak again and pulled him close. "You want me to tell you what makes you *fucking* different?" he asked, his voice rising in volume with every word.

Gerrick kept still and silent, the hair on the back of his neck standing on end at the half-mad look in Willem's eyes.

"You getting plucked out from the rest of us for a cushy castle job is why you're different," Willem continued. "You know what happened to me on my first assignment? What's probably happened to half the men we trained with by now? Why I'm hiring on with goblin warlords out here instead of making my father proud by holding a command post—the command post *you* walked away from because you were too good to go out and fight like the rest of us?

"I'll tell you what happened. We got stationed in a little village near the Ghostwood. They'd had some trouble with goblin raids, but nothing too serious, they told us. Nothing our training hadn't readied us for. The plan was for us to go out there, get some experience in the field, and come home heroes when raiding parties stopped hitting that village and went looking for easier targets. It should've been easy. We never expected…" Willem loosened his grip on Gerrick's cloak, the mad look in his eyes fading to something between sadness and resignation.

"What didn't you expect?" Gerrick asked. His face was flushed from the warm puffs of Willem's breath, and his back ached from the awkward position Willem had forced him into, but he didn't want to risk moving. Not until Willem's mood was less volatile.

"We didn't expect to be slaughtered like cattle. We clashed with a small band of goblins during our first week there. They broke and ran before we'd finished off half their number, so I didn't see any harm in chasing the stragglers back to the Ghostwood.

"But the moment the trees closed in around us, something changed. Everything went quiet as the grave, like we were the only living things in there. Then they hit us—them and the rest of their raiding party. They had us pinned in on all sides, and there were more than twice as many of them as we followed in. More than we stood any chance against. We lost two or three men before we even knew what was happening. It only got worse from there. For every goblin we cut down, there was another to take his place, and they weren't panicked and half-blind from the darkness like we were.

"I was the only man left standing when it ended. Their leader gave me a choice. He said I could surrender, and he'd let me join up with them or go crawling back to the village and tell them how I'd failed. Or I could keep fighting and he'd kill me like he killed the rest of my men. I…" Willem's voice cracked. "I didn't want to die, and I couldn't bear the shame of facing those villagers after losing my entire company, so I took him up on his offer. Been working for Clan Boarblood under Warlord Zalgron ever since."

"Willem, I…" Gerrick gently pried Willem's hand off his cloak. He hadn't liked Willem while they'd trained together, and he didn't like Willem now, but no man deserved to live through something like that. "I'm sorry. I never knew—"

"Don't tell me you're sorry," Willem spat, snatching his hand back like Gerrick's touch had burned him. "I'm not. I made my choice, and I've lived with it like a man should. There wasn't any life for me in Dawn's Gate after a failure like that, and you know it. Better scraping together a living for myself out here than going home in disgrace and tarnishing my hero father's reputation. I have a *reason* to be here." Willem gave Gerrick a calculating look, a cold glint in his eyes. "But I'm not sure about you."

Gerrick shrugged. "I have my reasons."

Willem scoffed. "What *reasons* does a pampered royal guardsman have for running away from his soft castle life?" Willem leaned in close and lowered his voice to a near whisper. "And how does a man like that end up anywhere near the goblin territories?"

"I was Prince Orthenn's bodyguard, not a royal guardsman," Gerrick replied. "And princes travel, the same as the rest of us."

"Not near the Ghostwood, they don't. Unless…" Willem rested a hand on the hilt of his sword. "What scheme did your prince drag you into, Gerrick?"

Gerrick's hand dropped to the hilt of his own sword. He stammered, "I— I'm not—"

"Is this man bothering you, Gerrick?" Moranthus's voice rang out from behind him. His tone had a warm, playful note to it that made Gerrick relax his posture in spite of himself. "I told you hanging on to that old gear of yours would bring us nothing but trouble."

Moranthus's voice seemed to have the same effect on Willem. He let go of his sword, and some of the intensity left his gaze as he turned it toward Moranthus.

Gerrick kept his hand on his sword but allowed himself a glance over his shoulder to see what Moranthus was doing.

Moranthus stood just outside the shop's door, one hand on his hip and an exasperated look on his face. His posture looked relaxed, as always. The only sign that Willem's presence concerned him were the armload of small bags and parcels scattered around his feet, as though he'd set them down in a hurry.

"You're welcome to explain what has the two of you so agitated whenever you'd like," Moranthus continued. He strode over to them and gave Willem a withering look. "Either of you."

"It's nothing," Gerrick replied. "Just a misunderstanding."

"Is it?" Moranthus kept his eyes fixed on Willem. "It looked like it was serious enough for weapons to be involved, from where I was standing."

Willem glared at him but took a few steps back from Gerrick. "Why is it any of your business what Gerrick gets up to?"

Moranthus didn't flinch. "I happen to be invested in his well-being, and I'd like to be certain you aren't a threat to him. Is that not enough?"

"What are you, his lover?" Willem gave him a derisive snort.

Moranthus's eyes narrowed. "If I am, is that going to be a problem for you?"

Willem's gaze shifted from Moranthus to Gerrick, then back to Moranthus, his expression a mix of confusion and disgust. Gerrick felt his face flush red. He'd seen that look on Willem's face before.

It had happened toward the end of their training. Gerrick had had trouble sleeping one night, so he'd left his bunk and let himself out into the practice yard for a bit of after-hours training. It hadn't been exactly allowed, but sneaking out of bed to work on his swordsmanship wasn't much of an offense. He'd never seen an officer punish a recruit for taking on extra work, and he doubted they'd start tonight. His class of recruits had only just been allowed to switch to blunted steel blades instead of the wooden swords they'd been using for most of their training, after all. He'd needed the extra time to adjust to the change.

Just as he'd gotten centered and fallen into a familiar rhythm of thrusts, blocks, and parries against an imaginary opponent, he heard a snort of laughter behind him. Startled, he whirled around to find Willem leaning against a weapon rack, a sneer on his face.

"Would you look at that," Willem scoffed. "Even when he goes sneaking off after hours, perfect little toy soldier Gerrick's just trying to find new ways to show the rest of us up."

"I'm not trying to show anyone up," Gerrick replied, suddenly feeling more than ready for a good night's sleep. "I just wanted to get some more practice in."

"Since when do *you* need more practice? Our officers already think you're fucking perfect. What's the point?"

"The point is not getting killed when our training's done and we get sent into real fights. I don't care about impressing our officers. I care about protecting Dawn's Gate. Maybe our officers would think better of you if you felt the same." Gerrick realized the words were a mistake the moment they left his mouth. But it was too late to take them back.

Willem ground his teeth, a scowl etched deep into his face. "So, me sleeping through the night means I don't care about protecting Dawn's Gate?" He grabbed a practice sword off the weapon rack. "Maybe I should join you, then."

"You don't have to do that, Willem. You know that isn't what I meant."

Willem advanced on him, sword at the ready. "Then what did you mean? You're an expert on earning our officers' favor, aren't you? Why don't you be a good sword brother and keep telling me what I'm doing wrong?"

"No. I'm not doing this with you tonight. Give it a rest." Gerrick kept his sword lowered and his sword arm relaxed. Willem was looking for a fight, not a sparring session. Gerrick knew better than to give it to him.

"Why not?" Willem took another step forward and struck Gerrick on the arm with the flat of his blade. "Afraid you'll lose?"

"No." Gerrick stepped backward. "I'm afraid one of us will get hurt."

"Don't think you can handle a few bruises? What happened to getting ready for real fights?" Willem hit him again, harder.

Without thinking, Gerrick slashed at Willem with his own blade.

Willem blocked his strike, a wolfish grin on his face. "That's better. Maybe you can actually hit me next time."

"There's no 'maybe' about it." Gerrick broke free of Willem's block and gave him the fight he wanted.

Within moments, Gerrick had Willem disarmed. Before he could declare his victory, Willem tackled him to the ground. Gerrick lost his grip on his sword, and they grappled in the dirt, their training forgotten in favor of releasing years of frustration and resentment.

Willem flinging a handful of dirt in Gerrick's face settled the matter. While Gerrick blinked the grit from his eyes, Willem pinned him to the ground. Their limbs were hopelessly tangled together, and their faces were only inches apart. Gerrick struggled against his grip, but he couldn't break free.

"Just give up," Willem snarled.

With a sigh, Gerrick relented. "Fine. You've won. Now get off me."

Gerrick tried to pull free, but Willem held him fast. "Not so above it all now, are you, Gerrick?" He let out a harsh, panting laugh and pressed their foreheads together. "How does it feel?"

It felt better than it should. Gerrick shuddered at the sudden closeness, a wave of heat rolling over him in spite of the cold night air around them. A sudden desire to tilt his head back, so their lips were pressed together instead of their foreheads, came over him. As if in agreement, his cock stiffened.

Dread gnawed at his gut. There was no doubt Willem could feel it, pressed up against him like he was. Worse, Gerrick could feel Willem's cock—every bit as hard as his own—pressed against his thigh. And that only made his own situation worse.

Willem pushed himself off Gerrick, his expression blank. Their eyes met. Gerrick couldn't look away. Couldn't find the words to dismiss what had just happened—words that would make it safe and not real. Willem's blank expression gave way to a look of shock and disgust, and Gerrick braced himself for Willem's inevitable angry outburst.

Instead, Willem shoved him into the ground and got to his feet. "Dirty faggot," he spat, then stormed off, tugging his shirt down to cover the bulge in his trousers.

Ashamed, Gerrick snuck out of the barracks and paid a visit to Edith, a guardswoman-in-training who'd made a pass at him the last time he visited Kingstone on leave. That visit earned him a week of scrubbing privies and a public dressing-down from his commanding officer when he got caught sneaking back into the barracks the next morning. Months later, it earned him a daughter.

He wasn't sure where that sparring session had taken Willem.

Willem's easy acceptance of Moranthus's claim brought back Gerrick's old shame. But he didn't correct Willem's mistake. Or feel angry with Moranthus for playing into it. Gerrick was just relieved that Willem's attention was safely off him and his reasons for being in the goblin territories. Whatever Moranthus's plan was, it was working. And letting Willem think he liked men was better than letting Willem know the truth.

Willem finally shifted his attention back to Gerrick. "What happened?" he sputtered. "You mean to tell me you abandoned your honor, your prince, and your country just because you picked up a taste for elf dick?"

Gerrick shifted uncomfortably, unable to meet Willem's eyes. "I… I suppose that's…"

"He didn't abandon anything. We met in a tavern while he was accompanying Prince Orthenn on a visit to a fortress near the Wintersbreath, and I helped him come to terms with some truths about himself that he was having a hard time accepting. After that, he decided he'd had his fill of being told it was shameful to be the way he was, so he resigned from his post as Orthenn's guard and followed me here so we could find a less judgmental home for ourselves." Moranthus tousled Gerrick's hair. "Isn't that right?"

Gerrick nodded. "More or less."

"No." Willem shook his head. "I don't believe it. He was at the top of our class—our officers' golden boy—and you're telling me that all along he was some simpering, limp-wristed boy lover?"

Moranthus gave him a sidelong glance. "Why in the skies would a man's sexual preferences have any bearing on his skill as a fighter?"

"Like you don't know." Willem gave Moranthus a sidelong glance of his own.

"As a matter of fact, I don't." Moranthus took a step closer to Willem. "Please, enlighten me." The light, friendly tone of his voice only made him sound more threatening.

Willem stood his ground. Squaring his shoulders, he drew himself up to his full height—and came up a good half a head shorter than Moranthus in spite of his efforts—before replying, "Looking at another man as a lover instead of a friend or brother-in-arms is a woman's way of thinking. And that makes you soft. You can't play a woman's role in bed and still be a man on the battlefield." Willem cast an appraising glance at Moranthus, lips curled into a sneer. "I know *you* don't look like much of a man. I'm surprised a twig like you can even lift a sword."

The way Moranthus's jaw clenched at that remark made Gerrick wince. This was going too far. Someone needed to stop them before it went any farther.

Gerrick pushed himself off the hitching rail. "Willem, don't—"

"I have no objection to him speaking his mind," Moranthus interjected. "That manner of thinking is hardly surprising, coming from someone like him." He took another step closer to Willem. "In fact, if I didn't know better, I'd assume that his fixation on your sexual preferences stems from him having some doubts about his own."

Willem's fist connected with Moranthus's face with a solid *thud.* Moranthus let out a small, pained grunt and staggered backward, a stunned look in his eyes.

Gerrick grabbed Willem's arm before he could try anything else. "Let it go, Willem. This is wrong."

Willem wrenched his arm free and gave Gerrick a hard shove. "Get your hands off me, faggot."

Moranthus's expression hardened as Willem advanced on him. He neatly ducked out of the way of Willem's second swing and drove a knee up into Willem's gut. Willem doubled over, clutching his midsection, and Moranthus rammed his elbow into Willem's face as Willem pitched forward.

Willem fell to the ground, covering his face with his hands. Blood streamed from between his fingers. Moranthus glared down at Willem, gingerly raising a hand to his left eye. The eye was already starting to swell shut.

"If I'm simpering and limp-wristed, I'm not sure what this makes you," Moranthus said.

Willem pushed himself onto his knees and wiped the blood trickling from his nose on the back of his hand. "I'll show you limp-wristed," he muttered, fumbling at one of his boots.

"Will you, now?" Moranthus raised an eyebrow. "If you're going to hit me again, you could at least do it hard enough to—"

With a shout, Willem drew a dagger from his boot and lunged at Moranthus. Moranthus caught his wrist, stopping the blade mere inches away from his chest, and twisted it until something popped.

Willem dropped the dagger, mouth open in a silent scream of pain. Moranthus let go of his wrist and snatched the dagger out of the air. Before Gerrick could make sense of what was happening, Moranthus grabbed Willem's hair in one hand, wrenching his head back, and pressed the dagger against Willem's throat with the other.

Moranthus leaned in close to Willem and said, through gritted teeth, "Give me one good reason why I shouldn't kill you where you stand."

Willem started trembling, clutching his wounded wrist close to his chest with his good hand. His mouth opened and closed, but no sound came out.

"That's what I thought." Moranthus adjusted his grip on the dagger.

Gerrick put a hand on Moranthus's shoulder. "Don't."

"And why shouldn't I?" Moranthus asked. "It's exactly what he would've done to me if I hadn't stopped him."

"I know," Gerrick replied. "And he was wrong to do it. But if you kill him now, you're no better than he is."

Moranthus tensed. "Maybe I'm not better than he is."

"You are. I know that. And so do you." Gerrick tightened his grip on Moranthus's shoulder. "Let him go. Please."

Moranthus sighed, then let go of Willem's hair and lowered the dagger. "Looks like I'm feeling merciful today. Lucky you. You'd do well to make sure our paths don't cross again. I won't be as forgiving next time." His lips curled into a chilling smile. "My thanks for the new dagger."

Without a word, Willem turned on his heel and ran, disappearing behind the nearest row of houses.

Gerrick let go of Moranthus's shoulder, hands shaking slightly from relief. "Thank you."

Moranthus gave him a hard look. "If this comes back to bite us on the ass later…" He shook his head. "Never mind. Let's get back on the road before we run into any more acquaintances of yours."

Nineteen

"Moranthus?" Gerrick's voice startled Moranthus out of the comfortable doze he'd settled into and put an end to a day-long stretch of near silence.

Moranthus pushed himself up off his bedroll and opened his eyes, squinting in the light of their small campfire. He would've liked to put more distance between them and the settlement before stopping for the night, but they'd happened across a rocky outcropping that offered shelter from the wind and snow just before sundown, and Moranthus knew better than to waste an opportunity for a comfortable night's rest. Skies only knew how long it would be until they found another halfway decent campsite.

Gerrick sat across the campfire from him, bedroll still unopened and a troubled look on his face. That didn't bode well for the conversation ahead of him. Moranthus was hardly in a comforting mood, but it was too late for him to pretend he hadn't heard Gerrick. He supposed he might as well get this over with.

"What?" Moranthus asked, not bothering to soften his rough, irritated tone.

Gerrick winced. "You're still angry with me for stopping you from killing Willem. Aren't you?"

Moranthus sighed. "I'm not angry with you." Maybe he should be, but he wasn't. If anything, he was angry with himself.

He had no excuse for allowing the confrontation with Willem to escalate as far as it had. Skies above, he'd intervened with the intention of avoiding bloodshed, not causing it. But he'd let himself get angry, and that had made him careless. Dangerously careless. And he was lucky the only thing it had cost him was a blackened eye. Willem had come within inches of putting a knife in Moranthus's heart. If Moranthus had reacted any slower, he'd be dead. All because of a few snide remarks about his sexual preferences from a stranger whose opinion should have meant less than nothing to him.

Gerrick didn't look convinced. "For a man who isn't angry, you're certainly acting like you are."

Moranthus could see how he'd given Gerrick that impression. He'd gone the entire day without speaking a word more than was strictly necessary, and the few words he had said were brusque and cold. Not because Moranthus was angry with Gerrick, but because nipping any attempts at a drawn-out conversation in the bud had stopped him from starting into a tirade against Gerrick that Gerrick had done nothing to deserve.

It was completely unfair of him—and he knew that—but as hard as he tried, Moranthus couldn't stop himself from interpreting Gerrick's insistence on sparing Willem's life as a display of approval for everything Willem had said and done. How could he not, when, during their stay at the inn, Gerrick had expressed a gentler version of the same disgust that had driven Willem's actions?

But Gerrick had gone out of his way to keep things civil between them instead of hurling insults, and he hadn't attacked Moranthus for being what he was. He'd been understanding—sympathetic, even—after finding out about Moranthus's involvement with Ryllorin. And after Willem punched Moranthus, Gerrick told Willem he was wrong and tried to stop Willem from attacking Moranthus a second time. That should weigh more heavily than a few disapproving looks and a reluctance to share a bed with Moranthus. It would, if Moranthus could just set his feelings aside and be reasonable about this. But reasonability was a hard thing to come by where Gerrick was concerned.

"I'm not angry with you," Moranthus said, more for his own benefit than Gerrick's. "That being said, I *would* like to know why you were so adamant about sparing the life of a man who'd just pulled a knife on me."

"Fair enough." Gerrick drew his knees up to his chest and stared into the fire. "I don't know how much of it you overheard, but Willem told me how he ended up in the goblin territories. He's…had a hard life these past few years. I pity him."

"From what I understand, you haven't had an easy life, yourself, and I've never seen you display any murderous tendencies. Or any inclinations toward betraying your homeland and running off to the goblin territories, for that matter."

"Compared to Willem, I *do* have it easy. He lost his entire company to a goblin raiding party and came close to dying with them. If I hadn't gotten hired on as Orthenn's body double…" Gerrick shifted in obvious discomfort. "It could just as easily have been me in his place. I can't know if I would've handled it any better than he did. Maybe I'd have picked desertion over death too."

Moranthus raised a skeptical eyebrow. That hardly sounded like the Gerrick he knew. "Really? I thought deserters deserved a prison sentence or a visit to a headsman, the same as any other criminal. Or is that only the case for the ones you don't know personally?"

"That's not what I meant. Desertion *is* a crime, and crimes should be punished. But…"

"But what?"

Gerrick sighed. "Maybe your people aren't wrong to use exile as a punishment. If there's no place for a man in his homeland, maybe he should have the right to find a place for himself somewhere else. It's kinder than an execution or a life in prison if a man's crimes haven't harmed anyone."

Moranthus snorted. "Exile isn't a kindness. When we're given a choice, it's not uncommon for elves to choose death over a life in exile. Trust me."

"Why? Exile's a lighter sentence, isn't it?"

"Hardly. Death is painful, but more or less instantaneous. Spending centuries cut off from your homeland and your people might not hurt as much, but that hurt never stops." Moranthus knew that from personal experience. "If anything, it's probably more painful in the end."

Gerrick's eyes drifted to Moranthus's hair, and Moranthus cringed as a look of understanding dawned on Gerrick's face. "I shouldn't have spoken of it so lightly. You know what it's like better than I do."

Moranthus's hand drifted to his braid. "That's one way of putting it. At least your friend Willem seems to be enjoying his exile well enough. I'm sure you're very happy for him."

"He's not my friend. And I'm not happy for him." Gerrick ran a hand over his beard, a tired look in his eyes. "Willem was wrong to attack you. The way he spoke to you was wrong too. But did he really deserve to die for that? You saw the way he ran off. He's learned his lesson. He won't do it again."

"If he wasn't ready to die, he shouldn't have drawn his weapon." Moranthus shrugged. "And I'm less concerned about whether he tries something like that again than I am about what's going to happen if he starts running his mouth around the wrong people."

Gerrick's brow furrowed. "What do you mean?"

"He knows who you are, doesn't he? And he knows you were working as Orthenn's guard. I doubt he'll be eager to discuss his encounter with us after losing a fight so badly, but if he's pressed about it in the company of, say, a certain goblin soldier who was involved in Orthenn's kidnapping…"

Gerrick buried his face in his hands, stifling a long, low groan. "I'm a fool. What was I thinking?"

Moranthus's frustration dissipated at the anguished sound of Gerrick's voice. He was being harsher with Gerrick than he needed to, and instead of pushing back, Gerrick had quietly accepted it. The same way he'd accepted it back at the inn. Moranthus lowered his gaze to the ground, grateful that Gerrick couldn't see the embarrassed blush that had crept onto his face. He was making an ass of himself. And he needed to stop before he took things too far.

"You were thinking you didn't want to see a familiar face killed in front of you," Moranthus replied. "There's nothing foolish about that."

"That's no excuse. Why did you let me talk you out of it?"

"You said you thought I was better than that. It's…been a long time since anyone had that much faith in me. I didn't want to prove you wrong." Though painful to admit, Moranthus owed Gerrick an honest answer. Once he'd gotten over his initial distrust of Moranthus, Gerrick had always been honest with him. That was probably why Moranthus cared so much about Gerrick's opinion of him; Gerrick wouldn't have said Moranthus was a better man than Willem if he hadn't meant it.

Gerrick looked up at Moranthus. "It was really that import-ant to you?"

"I suppose it was." It was important enough to make Moranthus forget the potential consequences of letting Willem go until Willem was beyond his reach anyway. "Which makes me the fool, doesn't it?"

"You might be." Gerrick nodded. "But you're also a good man."

Moranthus's breath left him in a contented huff. "I don't know if I'd go *that* far. But thank you." He gave Gerrick a wry smile. "We've drifted far off subject though, haven't we? I assume you weren't trying to get my attention just so you could ask if I was angry with you."

"There was something else," Gerrick replied. "But there's no need to go back to it. It was nothing important."

"Are you certain of that? Whatever it was, you seemed quite concerned about it."

"I wasn't concerned about anything. Just..." Gerrick wouldn't meet Moranthus's eyes. "Why did you tell Willem we were lovers?"

Because, as Ryllorin had never tired of saying, Moranthus was incapable of being subtle about what he wanted when it came to matters of the heart. But that wasn't what Gerrick wanted to hear. "I needed a valid reason for caring about you, and playing along with his assumptions saved me the trouble of inventing a different explanation."

"You could have just told him we were friends."

"I could have. But friends let friends fight their own battles in this part of the world. He wouldn't have taken that as an excuse."

"It might've stopped your fight from happening."

"I doubt it. From the way he was acting, he would've taken any excuse to start a fight. I just gave him a reason more convenient than the truth." Moranthus tossed another piece of wood into the fire, grateful for the small degree of separation between him and Gerrick that the flames offered. If he'd known it would cause this much tension between them, Moranthus would've thought twice before sharing his sexual preferences with Gerrick. "But I apologize if I offended you. It wasn't my intention to make you feel uncomfortable."

"I'm not offended. Just don't do it again if you can avoid it." Gerrick held his hands out toward the fire, an unreadable expression on his face. "You weren't serious, were you? When you said that Willem only got so angry over you liking men because he likes men too?"

"Oh, I was *very* serious. And very correct." Moranthus raised a hand to his injured eye, wincing at the swollen flesh and dull, throbbing ache he found there. "He wouldn't have given me this if the accusation wasn't true."

Gerrick gave him an incredulous look. "You're sure there wasn't another reason?"

"None that I can think of. Why does that surprise you?"

"He just doesn't seem like the type."

Moranthus bit back a groan and braced himself for a repetition of Willem's insinuations about him. He really should have just pretended he was asleep. "And why would that be?"

"He's never had a kind view of people like you. The things he said today were mild compared to what he was like back when I knew him."

"Denial is a powerful thing, Gerrick. When a man is that determined to show he's disgusted by something, he's usually trying to convince himself more than anyone else." That kind of self-loathing would have been pitiable if it hadn't come uncomfortably close to costing Moranthus his life.

"But he's never acted like he likes other men. There's nothing womanly about him."

"So you agree with that 'woman's role in bed' nonsense? Wonderful."

"I didn't mean it like that," Gerrick said, practically tripping over the words in his haste to get them out. "Just…there'd have to be *something* different about him if he liked men. Wouldn't there? That sort of thing must have an effect on a man."

"It does. And that effect is an attraction to other men. Nothing more." Moranthus shook his head. It was frustrating to watch a grown man struggle with a concept that every child in Moonridge had no difficulty grasping, but at least Gerrick's questions seemed more curious than judgmental. Gerrick deserved some credit for that. "You do realize that for every one of us playing a woman's role in bed, there's another playing a man's role, correct? Where do they fit into all this?"

"I…suppose that's not unmanly of them."

"And what if I were to tell you that it's not uncommon for people like me to be perfectly comfortable playing both roles?"

Gerrick was silent for a moment, then shrugged, a helpless look on his face. "I don't know. That makes things complicated. All of this is complicated. How can you act like it's such an easy thing to understand?"

"Because it *is* easy to understand. You're just getting caught up in the details and making it more complex than it needs to be. If you can stop fixating on whether or not an attraction to men is inherently womanly, everything becomes much simpler. I promise."

"I wish I could," Gerrick replied. "But I can't think of it the same way you can. Things are different in Dawn's Gate. Maybe you elves don't have to worry over what's manly and what isn't, but I do. It isn't something I can let go of."

"I understand." Moranthus tried not to sound disappointed. Gerrick was right; Dawn's Gate and Moonridge *were* different, and there was nothing wrong with Gerrick abiding by his homeland's customs. Gerrick had heard him out, at least. That was more than most humans would do.

"But that doesn't change what I said earlier," Gerrick said, an earnest look in his eyes. "It *was* wrong of Willem to attack you and say the things he did. Not everyone in Dawn's Gate is like that. *Most* people in Dawn's Gate aren't like that. I'd never hurt you for being what you are. I don't know if you believe me, but…"

"I believe you. I know you aren't like Willem. I wouldn't have kept you with me this long if you were." Moranthus gave Gerrick a reassuring smile. Gerrick's words weren't an apology or a statement of approval, but they weren't an attempt to justify Willem's actions either. And there was no doubt in Moranthus's mind that Gerrick meant them. That was all he had any right to ask for.

"Thank you." Gerrick's sigh of relief was more than enough to soothe any lingering sense of frustration Moranthus felt.

Whatever Gerrick thought of Moranthus, he was still the first person in ten years to have anything good to say about him; Moranthus wouldn't let himself forget that over a few hurt feelings. He was better than that.

Twenty

Gerrick spent the better part of a month following Moranthus north until the scraggly shrubs around them turned to a sparse scattering of pine trees and the crisp air of late autumn gave way to the icy claws of winter. The change in season brought with it a harsh, bitter wind that cut through Gerrick's sturdy wool cloak and the layers of armor and clothing beneath it as though they were thin as a lady's nightgown.

During the day, he could ignore the chill as long as he pushed himself into as fast a walk as he could manage. He needed to push himself that hard to keep pace with Moranthus's longer strides anyway. But the nights… The nights were a blur of curling into himself at the edge of a campfire that did next to nothing to keep the cold—and his shakes—at bay and clenching his jaw to stop his teeth from chattering.

If he'd been traveling with any man but Moranthus, Gerrick would've taken up huddling against him to share body heat. But things had felt strange between them since the inn. If Moranthus held that night against Gerrick, he didn't show it, but he had a grimness to him that hadn't been there before. Gerrick couldn't shake the feeling it had something to do with him.

He couldn't rightly suggest sleeping closer to each other when he still hadn't figured out how to apologize for the way he'd thrown away Moranthus's first offer to share a bed with him, either. And Moranthus hadn't offered again. He didn't even seem to notice the cold, wrapped up in that heavy, fur-lined cloak of his. Snug as a fox in his den, even if he'd lost a bit of his smirk. Gerrick wouldn't be getting any warmth from him unless he asked for it. Shivering through the nights seemed like a safer bet. So that's what he did.

The pines around them grew thicker as the days wore on, until the barren hills around them were obscured by a wall of trees on either side of the road. Moranthus had started complaining about stagnant air after the trees had grown too dense for either of them to see past them, but Gerrick was happy to be rid of the wind.

The trees were filled with a small army of squirrels though. The damned things let out a near-constant stream of chittering as they raced along the tree branches and rustled through the underbrush. Occasionally, the ragged cries of a murder of crows who'd been too fool to fly somewhere warmer would cut through the air. It caught Gerrick off his guard and gave him a start that sent his hand flying to the hilt of his sword. Every time. It was enough to make him miss the Ghostwood's unnerving silence.

Two days into the forest, something changed. As the evening began to fade into night, Gerrick realized that he couldn't hear a single crow, and he couldn't remember the last time he *had* heard one. Even the squirrels—and their damnable chittering—seemed to have vanished. But in spite of the conspicuous nothing surrounding them, he couldn't shake the feeling they weren't alone.

"I don't like this," Moranthus muttered under his breath. He'd noticed it too. At some point—Gerrick couldn't have said exactly when—he'd taken his bow out of the bag he carried it in. And he held it like he expected to find a use for it.

Gerrick nodded his agreement and put a hand on the hilt of his sword.

As they rounded a corner in the road, they found their path blocked by not one, but two fallen trees. One tree was a coincidence. Two was a trap. It might not have been laid for them, but they'd still walked right into it. Bandits weren't choosy; they wouldn't let an opportunity like this pass them by.

Gerrick drew his sword. Out of the corner of his eye, he saw Moranthus nock an arrow onto his bowstring and felt a small sense of comfort. Whatever came next, he wasn't facing it alone.

"What's our plan?" Gerrick asked, his voice little more than a whisper.

An arrow whistled past his ear and lodged itself in a nearby tree.

Moranthus whipped around and loosed his own arrow in the direction the shot had come from. Gerrick couldn't see what he'd aimed for, but a solid *thud* and pained scream confirmed he'd hit his target.

"Try not to die," Moranthus shouted to make himself heard over the noise. He gave Storm a slap on the flank that sent her galloping into the trees to the right of them, straight past two men rushing at them from the cover of the forest. Hoods covered most of their faces, but they didn't have much height to them and they carried serrated blades. Goblins.

One broke off from his companion to run after the horse, but the other kept coming, sword raised as a ragged cry tore its way out of his throat. Gerrick raised his sword to block the blow, the scream of steel meeting steel ringing in his ears.

Small as he was, the goblin was strong. Gerrick would have his hands full with this one. Anything coming at them from the left was Moranthus's problem.

The goblin broke free of Gerrick's block and ducked under his counterattack. With a quick, sharp kick to the back of Gerrick's knees, he knocked Gerrick off his feet. Gerrick's breath left him when he hit the ground, and he gasped as he struggled to fill his lungs again. In a heartbeat, the goblin was standing over Gerrick, sword held high in both hands, the tip of its blade pointed down over Gerrick's heart.

Gerrick rolled out of its path, still wheezing to regain his breath. The blade slid, harmless, along the shoulder of his mail and lodged itself in the ground. As the goblin struggled to pull it free, Gerrick got to his knees and thrust his own sword through a gap in the goblin's brigandine just under his arm.

The goblin drew in a sharp, gurgling breath, then flopped to the ground, limp as a rag doll, when Gerrick pulled his sword free of his body. The goblin clutched at his wound as his blood spilled into a growing pool on the ground beneath him, his dying gasps tearing through the still air around them. His hood had fallen back at some point during their scuffle, and his glassy eyes locked on to Gerrick's, his face contorted into a mask of pain.

But it wasn't a man's eyes Gerrick looked into. Gerrick's cry of triumph died on his lips. He'd just killed a woman. A young one, too, from the look of her. There was no honor in that.

Gerrick got to his feet and wiped her blood from his sword. He set his mouth in a grim line. Man or not, she was a goblin. And she'd chosen this death for herself when she'd chosen a life of banditry. But women had no place in battle, even as skulking bandits. No self-respecting man would dishonor himself by accepting a woman as his opponent. It wasn't right. What kind of place was the goblin territories to allow even its women to be pushed into the harshness of a warrior's life? Not even a warrior's life—the life of a bandit, without even a warrior's honor or hope of a future. If her father still lived, Gerrick hoped he met a messier end than she did. A man who'd so utterly failed to provide for his daughter deserved nothing less.

"Are you all right?" Moranthus's voice sounded strained, and his breathing was ragged.

"I'm fine." With a weary sigh, Gerrick turned to face Moranthus. "I just wasn't expecting…" His tongue and heart were too heavy to say the words out loud.

"You weren't expecting what?" Moranthus tilted his head in confusion. His right shirtsleeve was torn open and stained with blood from a shallow cut in his arm. Two dead goblins lay on the ground nearby, one with an arrow through his neck and the other stabbed through the heart with his own dagger.

"There are women with them." Gerrick shook his head. "They shouldn't have women with them."

"Why shouldn't they? She put up as good a fight as any of them by the look of it."

She had. But that wasn't the point. "A girl her age should be safe behind city walls. She should be starting a family somewhere, not…" Not bleeding out in the dirt. Not dying like a dog for whatever bandit scum had talked her into joining up with his gang. Not making the man who'd killed her ache for the daughter he'd left back home.

"Keeping weapons out of the hands of half your population because you think they'd be better off raising children is a luxury the rest of the world can't afford, Gerrick." Moranthus put a hand on his shoulder. "This isn't Dawn's Gate."

Gerrick shrugged his hand off. Of course, he didn't understand. Elves were as quick to send their women into battle as goblins were; they'd even let their Matriarch play at soldiering for a while if the rumors were true. But if all of Moonridge was as inhospitable as the northern goblin territories, maybe the elves were right to let their women take up arms. Maybe the goblins were too.

Gerrick didn't want to think about it any longer. "Think that was all of them?"

"No." Moranthus cast a wary glance at the forest around them. "The rest are probably just regrouping. We need to move before they come up with a better strategy."

"What about your horse?" Wherever she'd run off to, she'd taken most of their supplies with her. They wouldn't get far without her.

Moranthus pursed his lips in a worried frown. "She'll find her way back to us. Or we'll find her. This isn't the first time we've gotten separated. She should be fine."

Gerrick wasn't convinced, but he let Moranthus grab him by the arm and lead him into the trees in the same direction Storm had taken. Moranthus stuck to following her trail at first. They might even have caught up with her if they hadn't had to abandon the path she'd cleared through the underbrush when they heard the shouts and heavy footfalls of the rest of the bandit gang behind them. Gerrick could hear their leader's orders not to leave him and Moranthus alive.

After that, Gerrick didn't think even Moranthus knew where he was leading them. He just took off running into the forest, and Gerrick didn't see any choice but to chase after him. Every time he looked over his shoulder, he could see the glow of torches in the forest around them. No matter how fast they ran, it didn't seem to put any distance between them and their pursuers. They needed a place to hide.

The last of the day's light had long since faded when Moranthus came to a stop near a dense clump of trees. The soil around them had worn away, and their exposed roots formed a large hollow at their base. In the pale moonlight, Gerrick could just see Moranthus disappear into the hollow, then reach his arm out and beckon for Gerrick to follow him.

The hollow's dirt floor was hard and cold beneath him as he sat beside Moranthus under its low ceiling. It was large enough to hold the two of them, but too small to leave any space between them. No matter which way Gerrick leaned against the root wall behind him, he could feel Moranthus pressed against his side.

But Gerrick didn't want to pull away. Instead, he had to fight himself to keep from leaning even closer to Moranthus and the warmth he gave off. The moment he'd stopped running, the frosty night air had chilled him to the bone and set his teeth chattering too hard for him to clench his jaw into silence. He'd started shivering, too, bad enough that he was afraid it would start shaking the trees above them. Moranthus must have noticed. He couldn't *not* notice, when he was all but sitting on Gerrick's lap.

"You're cold," Moranthus murmured. He didn't even pretend to phrase it as a question.

Gerrick ignored him. If Moranthus could endure the cold, so could he.

Moranthus sighed, then undid the clasp holding his cloak around his shoulders. He scooted closer to Gerrick as he shrugged out of the cloak, until he *was* partly sitting on Gerrick's lap, or close enough that it made no difference.

"What are you doing?" Gerrick hissed, his words slurred by the chattering of his teeth.

"Making sure you don't freeze to death." Moranthus threw his cloak over both of them like a blanket and wrapped an arm around Gerrick's shoulders. "You're welcome."

Every protest Gerrick thought of didn't make it past his lips. Not when he already felt his shivers easing and warmth flowing back into his limbs. His entire body screamed for him to just give in, and he didn't have the strength to fight himself any longer.

With a long, shuddering sigh, he slumped against Moranthus, soaking up as much of Moranthus's warmth as he could. In spite of the shivers that still wracked his body and the shouts of the bandits still hunting them, his eyelids grew heavy, and he let sleep claim him. If Moranthus's shoulder made a better pillow than it should and he felt more at peace with Moranthus's arms wrapped around him than he'd care to admit, he was too comfortable to care. Too exhausted to waste the last of his waking thoughts trying to make sense of it.

Gerrick woke up, alone, to the bright light of midmorning shining through the gaps in the roots above him. He couldn't hear any sign of their pursuers, but the damned squirrels had come back in full force to make up for it. A thin, glittering layer of snow had fallen on the ground outside the hollow, and his breath formed frosty clouds in the winter air, but inside the hollow, he felt warm. Warmer than he'd felt in weeks.

When he sat up and found Moranthus's cloak securely fastened around his shoulders, he realized that his own cloak had vanished. Moranthus must've swapped them during the night. Of course, he had. Moranthus had to have everything his own way, whether Gerrick agreed to it or not.

He didn't have any problem with the cloak itself. It sat a bit high on his shoulders, and when he stood up, he knew it would be a bit long on him, but other than that, the fit wasn't terrible. He couldn't deny that it kept him a far sight warmer than the one Moranthus had stolen off him.

But men were supposed to keep themselves warm. Begging a man's cloak off him because you hadn't dressed for the weather was fine for a woman, but Gerrick was no woman. No matter how hard Moranthus had tried to make one of him.

Moranthus sat just outside the hollow, skinning a pair of squirrels and wearing Gerrick's cloak like it was the most natural thing in the world. The sight of his cloak hanging, a bit loose, on Moranthus's shoulders put a warm flutter in Gerrick's chest.

When their eyes met, Moranthus raised a hand—still holding a half-skinned squirrel—in a small, short wave. "Good. You're awake. I was starting to worry you'd frozen while I was away."

Gerrick didn't have the patience for whatever game he was trying to play. "You stole my cloak."

"I'm not sure it qualifies as stealing when I left you mine in return. Which is significantly more valuable than yours in this kind of weather, might I add. If anything, you're stealing from me."

"Why?"

"Why what? If you're wondering about the squirrels, they're dinner if we don't catch up with Storm and get our supplies back by the end of the day."

"Not the squirrels." Gerrick ran a frustrated hand over his beard. "Why did you give me your cloak? I didn't ask for it."

Moranthus shrugged. "It was weighing me down too much. If you want this one back, you're going to have to take it off me. And I won't be letting it go without a fight." His lips curled into that insufferable smirk he used every time he thought he'd won an argument. "I certainly wouldn't mind if you gave it a try though."

Gerrick crossed his arms over his chest and fought to keep his frustration from showing on his face. "Fine. Keep it." He could suffer the insult to his pride if it kept him from freezing. Just like he could ignore that the cloak smelled overwhelmingly and inescapably of Moranthus, especially when he had the hood up. And the equally inescapable fact that the scent gave him a strange sense of comfort.

"Good. I'm glad you decided to listen to reason on this."

A long silence settled over them as Moranthus finished with the squirrels. But for the first time since the inn, that silence didn't feel awkward. Gerrick wanted to keep it that way. Wherever it led them.

Before he could talk himself out of it, he said, "About…what happened at the inn. I said things I shouldn't have. Things I didn't mean. There's nothing wrong with you liking men, and I don't think any less of you for it. I just…" His voice trailed off before he could wrap his tongue around a full apology. He'd never been much good with words. That was half the reason things hadn't worked between him and Edith.

Moranthus wiped the last of the squirrels' blood from his dagger and turned to look at him, one eyebrow raised. He watched Gerrick for a moment, like he was waiting for something, then let out an exasperated laugh. His lips quirked into a smile that warmed his eyes as he replied, "It's all right. That snow's already melted; don't waste your time worrying about it now. Just don't do it again, and I'll assume you've gotten over your misgivings about me, whatever they may have been."

"Thanks." Gerrick didn't dwell on the laugh at his expense. Moranthus had understood him. That was what mattered.

"Any time." Moranthus sheathed his dagger and got to his feet. "Are you ready to get moving?"

"I am." Moranthus's cloak felt more comfortable around Gerrick's shoulders as he followed after Moranthus. He knew better than to let himself wonder why.

Storm turned up late in the evening, after they reached the forest's northern edge. She took off galloping toward them the moment she saw them without so much as a whistle from Moranthus. She stopped, ears pinned back, to sniff at Gerrick's cloak when she reached Moranthus, then gave him an affectionate headbutt that came close to knocking him off his feet.

Moranthus's face broke into a wide, lopsided smile as he wrapped his arms around her neck, burying his face in her mane. "Thank the skies you're all right," he murmured.

Gerrick couldn't help but smile at seeing her alive and unharmed too. She was a good, sturdy horse and loyal as a dog to her master. It would've been a shame to lose her to bandits who'd probably just slaughter her for meat. Gerrick was tempted to try giving her a pat on the nose until he noticed her saddlebags were missing. "She's all right, but we aren't. She lost all our gear."

"She didn't lose it. Someone stole it off her." Moranthus held up the remains of one of the cords that had attached his horse's saddlebags to her saddle. "This was cut, not torn."

"Whatever happened to our gear, it's still gone. We aren't going to last long without our food stores."

Moranthus let out an exasperated sigh. "It's not as bad as all that. If you're so worried about starving, go find us some firewood. We have squirrels to cook."

In the end, Gerrick couldn't deny that Moranthus was right. The squirrels didn't make much of a meal, but they were better than nothing. And the bandit who'd cut the saddlebags from Storm's saddle had left their bedrolls alone, so at least they wouldn't be sleeping on the ground. He tried to keep that in mind as he fished his locket out from under his shirt.

He didn't like looking at it when Moranthus could see him—he didn't want Moranthus calling him soft or thinking he was having second thoughts about trading himself for Orthenn—but after their brush with death yesterday, he needed the sense of comfort it would give him more than he worried what Moranthus thought of him.

The moment Gerrick flipped his locket open, Moranthus looked up from running a whetstone along the blade of his dagger. "What's she like?" he asked.

Gerrick didn't look up from his locket as he replied, "Who?"

"Your daughter." Moranthus gave Gerrick a playful nudge with his elbow. "Who else?"

Gerrick wasn't sure how to answer. Other than Aldous, Moranthus was the first man Gerrick had fought alongside who'd asked about his daughter as anything more than a new way to poke fun at him for raising her on his own. "What do you want to know?"

"Anything, really. She seems quite important to you for someone you never talk about. If you're at such a loss over this, why not start with her name?"

"Daisy. She's…a little over six years old now. Acts about the same as any other child her age. She's always busy with some new game of hers and gets herself into trouble as fast as I can get her out of it. Wears through clothes faster than she can grow into them." Gerrick shook his head. "I don't know why I keep buying them too big for her. There's no point."

"Does she look like you or take more after her mother?"

Daisy was a sturdy little thing, with blue eyes and pale blonde hair that was growing darker as she got older. Just like her mother. And just like Gerrick when he had been a child. "Both. She's got her mother's curly hair, but everything else could have come from either of us."

"She has her mother's smile, too, I hope?" Moranthus's eyes were shining with some joke only he understood.

"What's that supposed to mean?"

"Only that you're the most stone-faced man I've met in almost two centuries. That's quite the accomplishment."

"I'm not stone-faced." Gerrick caught himself in a scowl that proved Moranthus's point. He tried to keep his face pleasantly neutral instead.

"Yes, you are. I could count on one hand the times I've seen you smile since I met you. And still have fingers left over."

"I haven't had much to smile about. That's all."

"Fair enough." Moranthus didn't look convinced. "Who takes care of her while you're away?"

"She stays with Aldous's wife and children."

"Should I know that name?"

"He's another of Orthenn's soldiers. The one with the graying hair and the long mustache."

Moranthus gave him a vacant nod that made it clear he didn't have the faintest idea who Gerrick was talking about.

"Gralnag didn't mention anything about the rest of Orthenn's company when the two of you were…talking, did he?"

Moranthus shook his head. "I'm sorry. I didn't ask. He didn't say anything about killing anyone, but…"

Gerrick felt a twinge of guilt as Moranthus's voice trailed off. He'd hardly spared a thought for the rest of his company since he'd found out Orthenn was captured. Soldiering was dangerous work. Serving under a prince didn't change that. His brothers-in-arms knew that as well as he did. And Orthenn was the most valuable man in his company; his brothers-in-arms would've focused on him, too, if they were in Gerrick's position.

Still, that was no excuse for letting himself forget that Orthenn wasn't the only man he was trying to save. There was no denying that Gerrick's position as Orthenn's body double was the only reason he wasn't captured—or killed—along with his brothers-in-arms either. He was lucky. But if he and Moranthus didn't reach Knurlath's stronghold in time, his brothers-in-arms wouldn't be. *Aldous* wouldn't be, and he'd leave more fatherless children behind than Gerrick would, if he didn't come home from this.

"But he also didn't say he hadn't killed anyone," Gerrick said. Avoiding the words didn't make them any less true. Better to get them out, and be done with it.

"He didn't. But there's nothing we can do about it now. Even if you've lost part of your company, it's better to focus on saving what's left of them than dwelling on the ones who are beyond saving, isn't it?"

"I know. Just… It could just as easily have been me in their place. I've been traveling freely with you all these weeks, while they've been prisoners. It's not right."

"You aren't traveling with me for the fun of it. We're doing everything we can to get them home in one piece. Don't let yourself forget that." Moranthus gave him a sympathetic look, a reassuring smile on his face. He pulled Gerrick's cloak closer around his shoulders, its dull-gray fabric standing in stark contrast to his vibrant coloring, and Gerrick was struck by how beautiful he was.

The realization caught Gerrick off guard. This couldn't be happening to him. Moranthus and Gerrick were both men, and men weren't supposed to have those kinds of thoughts about other men. Gerrick *didn't* have those kinds of thoughts about other men; he'd rid himself of that problem years ago. He shook his head, trying to force the thought back into whatever dark, caged corner of his mind it had crawled out of. But there was no escaping it now that it had broken free. Moranthus *was* beautiful.

It was the way his eyes shone like gold in the firelight. The way his braid had loosened over the past two days, softening the angles of his face with the stray strands of hair that had broken free of it. The way the warm, musky scent of him lingered on his cloak and kept the winter's chill at bay better than the cloak's fur lining. The way he'd given up his cloak to keep Gerrick warm without Gerrick so much as asking him for it. The way he'd been looking after Gerrick ever since they'd started traveling together.

After spending most of the last six years taking care of Daisy, it was nice to have someone take care of him. Gerrick wondered if that was what it would feel like to have a wife back home. Or what it would feel like to have Moranthus back home.

Gerrick sighed in frustration. Dismissed those thoughts as the impossibilities they were. If Moranthus were a woman, it would make sense for Gerrick to think of him that way. But Moranthus *wasn't* a woman. Gerrick couldn't let himself forget that just because he felt lonely raising Daisy on his own.

Moranthus raised an eyebrow at him. "Are you all right?"

"I'm fine. And you're right; we are doing everything we can to save the rest of the company. You just… Your hair's coming loose. I thought you'd want to take care of that."

"Is it?" Moranthus ran a hand over his braid, then nodded to himself. "It is. Thanks for telling me," he added, crossing his arms behind his head as he lay down on his bedroll. "It's been a long day. I'm going to sleep. You're welcome to join me if you want, or keep to yourself if you don't. It makes no difference to me either way."

Gerrick kept to his own bedroll for a moment. If sleeping next to Moranthus last night had left him this confused, he might be better off spending this one cold and alone. But the icy fingers of winter creeping under his borrowed cloak and the memory of Moranthus's comfortable warmth pushed his worries aside, and the easy sense of calm he felt after settling in beside Moranthus kept his mind peacefully clear until he drifted into sleep.

Twenty-One

Moranthus hadn't wanted to add to Gerrick's worries over losing most of their food stores by agreeing with him, but Gerrick was right. The squirrels Moranthus had caught before leaving the forest got them through that first night, and they'd carried enough waybread on them to last another week if they were careful about rationing. But no matter how they rationed it, they'd be going hungry before they reached Knurlath's stronghold if they couldn't find another source of food.

They stayed clear of any settlements they passed along the way; the risk of running into someone who knew enough of Knurlath's plans to be suspicious of Moranthus's and Gerrick's interest in him was too high, and the loss of their remaining funds with the rest of their food stores meant that they couldn't have bought more supplies if they'd wanted to. Whenever they stopped to make camp, Moranthus went out hunting for either the white, short-legged rabbits that bounded across the winter snows or the few scraggly, edible plants that grew so

"

far north. Most nights, he came back with something, even if it was barely enough to take the edge off their hunger. On the nights he didn't, they got by on the last of their dwindling supply of waybread.

Moranthus had expected Gerrick to start lagging behind. He didn't look like he'd ever gone hungry in his life. No one grew that tall—for a human anyway—and broad—by anyone's standards—unless someone was feeding them right, and Moranthus wasn't certain how Gerrick would react now that no one was feeding him much of anything. But a bit of hunger seemed to give him an edge he hadn't had before. It was as though he looked forward to reaching the final stretch of their journey, even knowing what lay at the end of it for him. If he hadn't pulled out that locket of his every time they stopped to rest when he thought Moranthus wasn't looking, Moranthus would've thought he had a death wish.

Moranthus wished he could share in Gerrick's enthusiasm. He'd spent more years hungry and cold than Gerrick had spent alive, but as they drew nearer to the heart of the swath of land Knurlath had carved out for his clan, Moranthus was the one whose feet started dragging. The weeks they'd spent on the road should've given him more than enough time to harden his heart against Gerrick and resign him to doing what he knew was best for both of them. Moranthus would get to go home, and Gerrick would die knowing he'd saved the rest of his company and secured a future for his daughter. It was as close to a perfect outcome as the world ever allowed.

But Moranthus's heart hadn't hardened. If anything, it had melted for Gerrick instead, in a way he hadn't felt since Ryllorin. And a way he'd never expected to feel again.

He tried to convince himself it was just a natural result of spending every night since they'd left the forest pressed up against Gerrick, trying to keep him warm in the absence of the campfires they couldn't risk building when they were within sight of a settlement. Of seeing Gerrick's attachment to his daughter. Of the cold and hunger gnawing away at his mind until he simply didn't have the mental capacity to think rationally about things.

They were good excuses, all of them. Unfortunately, Moranthus knew better than to let himself fall for any of them.

He'd spent his entire duskblade training sharing a bunk with another apprentice, huddling against him for warmth, and he hardly remembered the man's name. Knowing about his marks' families had never gotten in the way of him doing his job before. And he'd never have survived as long as he had in his line of work if a bit of cold and hunger were enough to dull his wits. Gerrick was something special. Someone Moranthus would've given anything for a chance to get closer to. And Moranthus was sending him to his death. A death that was entirely Moranthus's idea.

Moranthus didn't want any part of this. But it was what needed to be done if Moranthus didn't want to live out the next few centuries as a traitor to his homeland. There was no victory for him in this any longer. Just a less catastrophic form of defeat. He didn't know if losing Gerrick was worth that. Then again, he supposed that wasn't his choice to make. It was Gerrick's, and Gerrick had chosen to die. Unless Moranthus could think of a better plan to rescue Orthenn, he needed to accept that.

That thought haunted Moranthus as he returned to their camp, a scrawny, old rabbit slung over his shoulder, on what he knew would be one of the last nights they spent on the road. The settlements they passed had grown larger and more permanent as they traveled farther north, so it seemed inevitable that the next one would be Knurlath's stronghold. No goblin would risk building something on such a grand scale if they didn't know their warlord was nearby to defend it.

They were far enough away from the last settlement they'd passed to build a campfire, but Moranthus couldn't see even the beginnings of a plume of smoke as he approached the copse of trees where he'd left Gerrick and Storm. When Moranthus reached them, he found Gerrick sitting beside a pile of firewood, his hands shaking as he failed to strike a spark from their flint. From the look of it, he'd been at it for quite some time. If Moranthus had known Gerrick would have so much trouble, he would've started a fire himself before he left. He didn't like leaving Gerrick alone in the cold for so long. Not when the man didn't have so much as a pair of mittens to protect his hands.

Moranthus crouched down beside Gerrick and put a hand on his wrist, tensing at how cold his skin felt. "Let me try. If you spend much longer in this cold, you'll end up as purple as I am. And you don't need me to tell you that it wouldn't look nearly as good on you."

Gerrick sighed in frustration but let go of the flint. "I almost had it."

Moranthus shrugged. "If you say so." His hand lingered on Gerrick's wrist—perhaps longer than it should have, but if Gerrick noticed, he didn't care enough to pull away. In that moment, Moranthus wanted nothing more than to take Gerrick's shaking hands in his and rub some warmth back into them. To pull him closer and try to shield him from the screaming wind around them. But Moranthus knew better. Gerrick liked women. Only women. Gerrick sharing a bedroll with Moranthus for a while hadn't changed that. Still, Moranthus couldn't stop himself from wondering what that rough, callused skin would feel like, pressed between his palms.

Moranthus gritted his teeth in frustration and struck the flint, hard enough to send out a shower of sparks that set the campfire ablaze in an instant. Skies above, what was wrong with him?

"Don't suppose you could hit that bird, could you?" Gerrick asked, shattering what precious little presence of mind Moranthus had left. "Damn thing's been circling around since you left. Starting to make me dizzy."

"Well, we can't have that now, can we?" Moranthus cast a half-interested glance at the cold, gray sky above them. If they'd startled a crow out of its roost, it wouldn't make a bad meal if he could bring it down. It was worth a try, at least.

But the bird circling above them wasn't a crow. It was a Moonridge snowhawk, far from anywhere a Moonridge snowhawk would naturally fly. Unless it was carrying a message.

Moranthus called to the snowhawk with the complex pattern of short, shrill whistles that would let it know he was authorized to inspect whatever it was carrying. He hoped Ilendra hadn't trained her birds to respond to new signals after she'd taken Moonridge's throne. If he had to kill it, she'd know someone had tampered with her correspondence.

The snowhawk circled over their heads once more, then swooped down and alighted on his shoulder. Even through his leather jerkin, he could feel its sharp talons digging into him. If that snowhawk had been in the area for long, it went a long way toward explaining why rabbits had become so scarce.

"What's this about?" Gerrick's eyebrows were raised halfway to his hairline.

"My question, exactly." Moranthus untied a small roll of parchment fastened to the snowhawk's leg, unfurled it, and held it up to catch the last of the light seeping over the horizon.

Ilendra had sent it, all right. It was bound for Knurlath's stronghold, discussing payment for services rendered and announcing the arrival of a group of frostguards operating under radically different orders than she'd given Moranthus. But its final lines couldn't have spoken more clearly to Moranthus if Ilendra had addressed them directly to him. Hastily scrawled onto the parchment below Ilendra's signature, as though they were nothing more than a casual afterthought, they read: "If you have trouble with a duskblade operating under the mistaken impression that he has orders to rescue Prince Orthenn from your stronghold, you may dispose of him as you see fit. Should you choose to show him mercy, kindly inform him that he has failed his mission and he is expected to act accordingly."

Moranthus carefully tore off the lines regarding him, leaving the parchment's lower edge as smooth and even as possible, and tossed the section he'd torn off into the campfire. As Ilendra's condemnation of him burned, he rolled up the remaining parchment and tied it onto the snowhawk's leg again. With another whistle, he sent the snowhawk back into the air.

"It seems Knurlath isn't to blame for having your prince kidnapped," he said, turning his attention back to Gerrick.

"Who is?"

"My Matriarch."

"I thought she wanted to stop him from getting kidnapped."

"So did I. It seems she didn't find it necessary to share the finer details of her plans with me." Or he'd never factored into her plans at all; she'd just wanted an excuse to be rid of her father's former lover that didn't make her look petty. "She still wants Orthenn rescued from the goblin territories in her name, but Knurlath only sent a raiding party after him in the first place because she paid him to do it. Once her agents have Orthenn in hand, they have orders to bring him to Aurora as a hostage. She didn't say why, but I can only assume she wants to squeeze a piece of land out of your king by taking credit for his son's rescue."

"Why not just use her own people to kidnap him, then? If they're anything like you, they would've had an easy enough time of it."

"Because if she got caught sending an organized band of soldiers over the Dawn's Gate border, she would've risked starting a war that Moonridge isn't ready to fight. By using a goblin lord as an intermediary, she could deny her involvement in Orthenn's kidnapping if things didn't go according to plan."

Gerrick's eyes narrowed. He probably thought Moranthus was about to betray him. Under any other circumstances, he wouldn't have been wrong about that. "What does this mean for us?"

"We get there before her soldiers do and proceed as planned from there: convince Knurlath you're the real Orthenn, trade you for Orthenn and the rest of your company, and get them out of Knurlath's stronghold before Ilendra's people arrive and start asking too many questions." Moranthus sat down next to Gerrick and gave him a pat on the shoulder. "How does that sound?"

"Like you're betraying your Matriarch. Why?"

Moranthus's shoulders slumped. He was. And, by extension, he was betraying his Patriarch too. But he was done living as an isolated half-exile and carrying out fool's errands at the behest of a woman who hadn't wanted him under her command to begin with. Done going against his conscience on behalf of a man who hadn't even counted him as something worth living for. It was time for him to start living again.

"She was never going to let me come back. Even if I go along with her plans, I won't have done anything to redeem myself in her eyes. No matter what I do, I'm spending the rest of my life in exile." Moranthus gave Gerrick a rueful smile. "So I might as well save you while I'm at it."

Gerrick shook his head. "You aren't saving me. I still need to take Orthenn's place."

"You do. But that doesn't mean we need to leave you in his place once he's safely out of Knurlath's reach. You'll be Knurlath's prisoner at the end of all this, but I won't. Once we've traded you for Orthenn, I'll ask if I can join up with his clan. I'll have just saved him from embarrassing himself when Ilendra's agents come to collect Orthenn. He won't need any more convincing to accept me into his service. After that, we'll give Orthenn and the rest of your company as much of a head start as we can; then I'll break you out of wherever Knurlath decides to keep you, and we'll run like we've got his entire clan after us. Because we will once he finds out what's happened."

Moranthus expected Gerrick to relax. Maybe even smile. But he only looked more confused as he asked, "Why don't we just let your Matriarch's soldiers take me to Moonridge? Orthenn goes free either way."

"Once she finds out she's been tricked, Ilendra's even more likely to kill you than Knurlath was. I can't let that happen."

"That's better than both of us dying. You should save yourself."

Moranthus shrugged. "If it comes to that, maybe I will. But I'm not leaving you to die without at least trying to save you first."

"If you do this, you can never go home. You're sure you can live with that?"

"I've been treated like an exile for ten years, Gerrick. I don't know what home is anymore." And being here with Gerrick… Well, it wasn't home, but it was the closest Moranthus had come to being happy in the last ten years. That was good enough for him.

"Thank you." Gerrick covered Moranthus's hand with his own and gave it a light squeeze. "Whatever comes of this, you'll always have a home with me."

Moranthus started and turned to look at him. Gerrick had leaned in close, his ice-blue eyes shining with a gentle warmth that stole the air from his lungs. "What do you mean?"

He leaned in closer to Gerrick—even though his hearing was good enough that he could have understood Gerrick's reply if Gerrick whispered it from twenty paces away—and shut his eyes. They were close enough that he could feel the mist of Gerrick's breath on his face and hear the rhythm of Gerrick's heartbeat. Just a hair closer and their lips would meet, and they wouldn't have any further need for words. One of them just needed to make the first move.

Moranthus steeled himself against his fears of what might happen if he closed that last bit of distance between them and put a hand on the back of Gerrick's neck.

"Sorry to interrupt, but it sounds like we have some unfinished business left between us," a rough voice called out from the far side of their camp.

Moranthus pushed himself off Gerrick and scrambled to his feet, blinking in the firelight as he reached for his dagger. A heartbeat later, Gerrick stood beside him, sword at the ready.

"Don't get ahead of yourselves," the voice said. "I just want to talk."

Moranthus had to squint to see into the twilight beyond the campfire, but he could just make out the shape of a goblin missing half an ear. Gralnag. He had a bow in his hand, but he hadn't nocked an arrow onto it. Their paths couldn't have crossed again by coincidence; he must have followed them. But why?

Moranthus forced a smile onto his face, but kept a hand on the hilt of his dagger. "I didn't expect to see you again so soon. If I'd known you were well enough to travel, I would have asked you to come with us."

Gralnag let out a cold, humorless laugh. "You sure about that? You were awful quick to run out on me. Don't suppose you'd want to tell me why?"

Moranthus winced. "I didn't realize you felt—"

"Don't bother with more of those pretty lies. I know you're not really trying to join up with my clan. You're too attached to that braid of yours for that. This has got something to do with you two trying to pull one over on my warlord, right?"

So he'd overheard their plan. Or he'd just made a lucky guess. "I don't know what you're talking about."

"Playing dumb, eh? That's fine by me." Gralnag pulled an arrow from his quiver and nocked it onto his bowstring. "If you won't talk to me, maybe you'll be more eager to explain yourself to my warlord. I'm sure he'll be happy to hear how you're planning to double-cross him. Can't promise he'll be happy with you though."

"Is there really no way I can talk you out of this? This is all just a misunderstanding. I know I've kept my braid for longer than I should have, but I can assure you that my life in Moonridge is well and truly behind me. Joining Clan Stoneheart will be a welcome change from living on the road. Why would I do anything to jeopardize that?" Moranthus wondered if he could move fast enough to throw his dagger at Gralnag before Gralnag loosed his arrow. He couldn't afford to arrive at Knurlath's stronghold as a prisoner. If he did, Knurlath wouldn't believe a word that came out of his mouth. Especially the truth. He and Gerrick would spend the rest of their days rotting in a goblin dungeon.

"Let me guess: your royal guard friend's just a misunderstanding too? And I'm sure that him turning up in that border settlement so soon after I brought his prince there was just a happy coincidence."

"As a matter of fact, it was." Moranthus let out a small, nervous laugh. Gralnag had spoken with Willem. Of course, he had. Anything else would have made life entirely too easy for Moranthus. "Funny how these things work out sometimes, isn't it?"

"So funny I think Knurlath needs to hear it himself." Gralnag's voice had a low, dangerous edge to it. "Weapons on the ground. Now."

"All right. If that's what it takes to clear this up, I'm happy to go along with it." Moranthus breathed a sigh of relief when he heard Gerrick drop his sword. That would help put Gralnag at ease. Maybe even get him to lower his guard.

"You too, lovely." Gralnag drew his arrow back farther.

Moranthus held his breath to keep his hands from shaking as he unbuckled his sword belt and knelt to set it on the ground. He allowed himself one last glance through the haze of the campfire to pinpoint Gralnag's location before easing his dagger out of its sheath. If he couldn't see much of Gralnag, then Gralnag couldn't see much of him either. He had his opening. As long as he didn't hesitate, he'd be fine. Moranthus got to his feet and hurled his dagger at Gralnag's chest in a swift, clean motion.

The moment the dagger left his hand, he heard the twang of a bowstring. He hadn't been fast enough. He was going to die for that. Before the thought could fully form in Moranthus's mind, Gerrick threw himself into the arrow's path, crashing into Moranthus's side hard enough to knock him off his feet. Gralnag's arrow sank into Gerrick's shoulder with a solid, sickening thud, and Gerrick fell to his knees beside Moranthus, his mouth hanging open in a silent cry of pain.

Moranthus's chest tightened. "Gerrick—"

"I'm fine," Gerrick said through gritted teeth. "My mail caught the worst of it. Go finish him off."

Moranthus nodded and sprinted across the camp to where Gralnag lay on the ground, his mouth twisted into a snarl as he tried to ease Moranthus's dagger out of his own shoulder. The blade had sunk into Gralnag's flesh almost up to its hilt, but it hadn't hit anything vital. Moranthus would need to fix that.

Moranthus knelt beside Gralnag, yanked the dagger out of his shoulder, and pressed its blade against Gralnag's throat. "You should have let us go."

Gralnag grimaced and pressed a hand against his shoulder to stanch the flow of blood from his wound. "You're sure you want to kill me?"

"I can't see any reason not to."

"All right. You don't want to save your human friend; that's fine by me." Gralnag attempted a nonchalant shrug that ended with him clutching tighter at his shoulder and hissing in pain. "Just thought I'd warn you first."

"He doesn't need saving. His armor stopped the arrow. The worst he's going to suffer from that is a small scar and some nasty bruising. I don't think he'll have any trouble surviving." Moranthus pressed his dagger harder against Gralnag's throat.

"Is he also immune to poisons?"

Moranthus's blood turned to ice in his veins. "What?"

Gralnag smirked. "You think I'd wander these parts on my own without giving myself a bit of an edge? It won't kill your friend fast; as long as he gets himself an antidote in the next day or two, he'll be fine. But if not…"

"And how, exactly, is keeping you alive necessary for me to accomplish that?"

"It isn't. Unless you want me to tell you where to find a healer who knows what they're doing. Or what your friend's poisoned with."

"I'm listening."

"Put that knife away, and maybe I'll talk." Gralnag raised a conspiratorial eyebrow at him. "Maybe I'll even help you and the human with your little plan. Clan Stoneheart shouldn't be crawling back to your Matriarch like a kicked dog after she pulled that treaty out from under us. Seems to me like we're setting ourselves up to get burned again."

Moranthus tensed. If Gralnag passed Moranthus's and Gerrick's plan along to his warlord, they were both dead. That made him a liability. But if Moranthus killed him before he found out how to heal Gerrick, that plan would be ruined all the same. He had no choice but to hear Gralnag out. He eased his dagger off of Gralnag's throat. "I'd say that last part's for your warlord to decide, not you."

"I am Clan Stoneheart's warlord. Knurlath's on his death-bed, if he isn't dead already. When I get home, the clan belongs to me."

"How can you be certain of that? You only knew he'd fallen ill the last time we talked."

"Who do you think made him sick?" Gralnag's eyes took on a cold shine. "And paid his servants off to make sure he stayed that way while I was gone? The old bastard's held our clan back too long. I lost a damn good scout and two of my best fighters playing along with your ice queen's scheming. I'm not giving up anything else for her."

"You might have done better to turn on your warlord before he agreed to kidnap Orthenn for her, then."

"Maybe I would have. But it would've cost me a chance to off him without his death getting pinned on me and half the able-bodied men in Clan Stoneheart trying to challenge me for his throne. It was worth it. And it'll be more worth it when I take the coin she's sending my clan and send her people home to her empty-handed—with a little help from you and your human if you're serious about turning on your Matriarch."

"I am." Moranthus would have preferred not to phrase it that way, but Gralnag wasn't wrong. "But why involve us at all? You seem to have things well in hand already."

Gralnag got to his feet and dusted himself off with his free hand. "We can talk details when you meet me at my strong-hold. For now, you'll be wanting to get your friend fixed up, right?"

As if in response, a thin, pained cry sounded be-hind Moranthus. Gralnag's face paled in a way that made Moranthus's stomach turn. He felt the blood drain from his own face as he asked, "What's wrong?"

"He usually the whining type?"

"No."

"Then the poison's not acting like it should. You have less time than we thought. Get him on that horse of yours, get back on the road, and ride north for a few miles. When you see a dirt path turn off the road, follow it. There's a cottage at the end of it. Tell the woman inside that I sent you, and I'm the one who did this to your friend. She'll know what to do."

"Where will you be in the meantime?" Moranthus couldn't keep an accusatory tone out of his voice. Whatever had gone wrong with Gralnag's poison, Gralnag had played an active role in causing it. It only seemed logical that he should also play an active role in fixing his mistake.

"Home. There'll be some things I need to sort out before your Matriarch's people come calling. And I've got a wound of my own that needs patching, thanks to you. Do what I told you and your friend should be fine."

"I hope you're right about this." If Moranthus lost Gerrick now, after all they'd been through… He shook his head. Thinking about it would just get in the way of him stopping it from happening.

"I am. Trust me." With that, Gralnag left the camp. Moranthus only waited long enough to wipe the blood off his dagger before hurrying back to Gerrick's side.

He found Gerrick sitting, ashen-faced, on the ground, staring at the arrow he'd pulled out of his shoulder. Its tip, stained red with blood, glistened in the firelight. Gerrick's hazy eyes locked onto Moranthus, his brow furrowed in confusion.

"What happened?" Gerrick asked, his voice slow and slurred. "Why didn't you—"

"I'll explain later." Moranthus kept his voice level to hide the panic rising inside him. "You're poisoned. There's no time to talk now."

"Oh." Gerrick dropped the arrow. "That's why I can't…feel my legs. What do we do?"

"We're getting you to a healer. I need you to help me get you on my horse." Storm wouldn't have it easy, carrying both of them, but she could manage until they reached the cottage. On horseback, it wasn't far.

Moranthus hauled Gerrick onto his feet and supported most of his weight while he half dragged Gerrick to where they'd left Storm. With one final burst of strength, Gerrick hoisted himself onto her saddle. He held himself upright until Moranthus finished tying him to it, then lost consciousness, slumping forward in a way that made Storm snort and flick her tail in agitation. She knew something was wrong, and she wanted no part of it. But she kept herself steady until Moranthus packed up the few things in the camp they couldn't go without and climbed onto her saddle behind Gerrick. The moment his heels touched her sides, she raced off across the frozen plains, faster than Moranthus could have hoped for.

The weather-beaten cottage Gralnag had directed them to didn't look like much, but the smell of herbs that emanated from its walls was reassuring. The small, wrinkled goblin woman who answered the door didn't seem the least bit surprised at his frenzied knocking, or Gerrick's condition when Moranthus cut him free of Storm's saddle and dragged him into her home. She nodded in recognition when he told her Gralnag had sent them to her.

After they'd gotten Gerrick settled on a small straw pallet on the floor, Moranthus asked, "Can you help him?"

The goblin woman held out her hand, her voice gentle, but firm as she replied, "What's it worth to you?"

Moranthus tensed. "Gralnag didn't say anything about payment."

"He didn't say anything about sending the two of you to my door tonight either." The goblin woman gave him a hard look and repeated, "What's it worth to you?"

Moranthus untied the amethyst cameo of Ryllorin from the cord around his neck. He held it tight in his hand for a moment, clinging to the last remaining fragment of his old life, then dropped it into her outstretched palm. "This is all I have."

The goblin woman turned the cameo over in her hand. A warm smile played across her lips as she replied, "It will do. You've got a long wait ahead of you. I suggest you find a way to keep yourself busy."

Twenty-Two

Gerrick woke to a throbbing ache in his left shoulder, in a room he didn't recognize. He lay on a hard straw pallet. His mail and bloodstained shirt sat in a neatly folded pile beside him. The walls around him rose up into a low ceiling and were lined with shelves filled with sealed jars and dried herbs. Bright light filtered in through cracks in the wooden shutters over a small window set in the wall across from him. The only other piece of furniture in the room—a small, wooden chair pushed up against the wall near the window—was occupied by a sleeping, disheveled Moranthus. His eyes had dark circles beneath them, and several strands of hair had come loose from his braid, falling across his face like streaks of blood.

When Gerrick raised a hand to his shoulder, he found his shoulder wrapped in a bandage far too large for the small wound he'd suffered. Curious, he pressed down on it and cried out at the sudden flash of pain it caused him. Whatever that arrow had been coated with was still affecting him. He didn't like the thought of that.

The sound of his voice jolted Moranthus awake. He kept a hand on the hilt of his dagger as he cast a worried glance around the room.

His gaze went soft when it landed on Gerrick. "You're awake." The smile his face broke into lit up the room better than opening the shutters would have.

"What happened?"

Moranthus's face fell. "You got yourself poisoned taking an arrow for me, that's what happened. You almost—" His voice cracked. "—you almost died. If I hadn't brought you here in time…"

"You did. That's what matters." The crack in Moranthus's voice made Gerrick want to reach out and comfort him. They didn't have time for that. They didn't have time for Moranthus to start crying either. "Where are we?"

"Just north of our last campsite. Gralnag told me the woman who lives here was our best chance of getting you healed. And it seems he was right about that, thank the skies."

"But he tried to kill us."

Moranthus didn't look like he was lying, but he wasn't making any sense. The scar-faced bastard from the inn hadn't seemed like the sort who'd send a man to a healer after sticking him with an arrow. And Moranthus should have killed Gralnag, not asked him for directions.

"What changed?" Gerrick asked.

"He told me where to find a healer for you in exchange for his life. And he wants to keep Orthenn out of my Matriarch's hands just as much as we do. We're going to help him with that once we get to his stronghold."

"You trust him?"

"I don't know. Maybe." Moranthus wouldn't meet Gerrick's eyes. "But we don't have a choice if we want to save your prince.

He'll have taken over as his clan's warlord by now. Whether we trust him or not, we're stuck with him."

Gerrick blinked at Moranthus in confusion. Goblin strongholds didn't change hands easily. He must have been out longer than he'd thought. "How long have we been here?"

"Three days."

"That long?" Gerrick reached for his shirt.

"You're lucky it wasn't longer," a sharp voice chimed in. Gerrick turned and found a wizened, old goblin woman standing in the room's doorway. She nodded at him in greeting as she continued, "You had a bad reaction to that poison. Anyone else would've lost you."

"Thank you." Gerrick pulled his shirt over his head, wincing at the pain that flared up every time he moved his shoulder.

"Someone's in a hurry." The goblin woman tutted at him. "I suppose there's no talking you boys into another day or two of rest. No matter how badly you could use it."

Gerrick gave her an apologetic look. "We can't—"

Moranthus cut him off. "That depends on how badly he needs it. How much risk is he putting himself at if we leave today?"

"You can stop fretting over the boy now. It's not so dire as all that. Keep his bandages fresh, and he'll finish healing just fine." The goblin woman gave Moranthus a dismissive wave. "Whatever my grandson wants you for, I'm sure it's important. He always was an impatient little thing; don't keep him waiting on my account."

Moranthus's posture relaxed, and his expression brightened. "Thank you. I don't suppose you have any supplies you could spare? We don't have any payment left to offer you, but—"

The goblin woman raised her hand in a silencing gesture. "You've paid me enough already. And I didn't work so hard to save your friend just so I could let him starve. I can spare enough food to get you where you're going. You just worry about getting your friend back on his feet." With that, she left the room.

"What did you pay her with?" Gerrick asked. The only thing of value he and Moranthus had left were their weapons and armor, and Moranthus looked like he still had all his gear.

"Nothing you need to worry about," Moranthus replied. "And nothing I regret losing when it paid off so well in the end. Now, can you stand on your own, or do you need me to help you?"

Gerrick got to his feet well enough. But his legs were wobbly, and his mail hauberk made his shoulder feel like it was on fire. He was leaning on Moranthus for support before they even made it out of the cottage. Once Moranthus and the goblin woman loaded a few days' worth of food and an armload of bandages and ointments into Storm's saddlebags, Moranthus insisted on getting Gerrick onto Storm's back too. Gerrick didn't have the strength to argue with him.

Gerrick didn't have the strength to argue when Moranthus insisted on changing his bandages for him when they stopped to make camp that night either. He was stiff and sore enough that he was grateful for the help. But the feel of Moranthus's long, archer-callused fingers brushing against his bare skin as Moranthus peeled the bandages off his shoulder kept dragging Gerrick back to the way Moranthus's hand had felt under his the last time they'd stopped to make camp. The way Moranthus's hand had felt on the back of his neck, warm in spite of the biting cold around them. He'd liked it then. And he couldn't deny he liked it now.

Moranthus drew in a sharp breath, and his eyes went wide as the last of the bandages fell away from Gerrick's wound. Gerrick took in a startled gasp of his own when he got his first look at the damage.

The arrow itself had left behind only a small, puckered wound, already well on its way to scabbing over. But a vast swath of skin around it had flared into an angry, red color that darkened to an almost purplish shade around the wound's edges. He was glad he'd been unconscious when it was at its worst if it was this bad after three days of recovery.

"Why did you do this to yourself?" Moranthus asked, a pained look in his eyes. "That arrow was meant for me."

"Because..." Because watching Moranthus bleed out on the ground would've been worse than bleeding out himself. Because, before Gralnag had shown up, Gerrick had been a heartbeat away from crossing a line with Moranthus he could never turn back from. And that scared him less than it should.

"Because?" Moranthus gave him that same sweet, soft-eyed look he'd had at their last camp, and Gerrick felt the last of his resolve crumbling.

Gerrick turned away from Moranthus. He couldn't afford to let that happen. Rescuing Orthenn took priority over everything. Gerrick's life included. If he let himself do anything that could make Moranthus forget that, he'd failed in his duties as Orthenn's body double. Gralnag hadn't interrupted them; he'd saved them. "We came here to save Orthenn. That's all that matters. I can't do that without you, but you can do it without me. So I had to keep you alive. It's as simple as that."

"Of course." Gerrick could hear the disappointment in Moranthus's voice. "You're right. Orthenn comes first. We can't forget that." Moranthus pulled out the long leather cord he wore around his neck and looked almost as surprised as Gerrick when he saw that his pendant wasn't hanging from it. With a sigh, he let the cord fall against his chest, a chagrined look on his face.

"What *did* you pay that healer with?" Gerrick asked, as though he didn't already know the answer.

Moranthus's hand drifted to the leather cord again. "I already told you. Nothing important. And I truly don't regret losing it."

"But your Patriarch—"

"Has been dead for more than a decade now. You're still alive. I'd say that makes you more of a priority, wouldn't you?"

"I suppose it does. Thank you." Gerrick felt a twinge of guilt as he watched Moranthus pull the leather cord over his head and shove it into a pocket in his jerkin.

That night, Gerrick dreamed of his final sparring session with Willem. But when he blinked the dirt from his eyes and looked up at the man pinning him to the ground, Moranthus had taken Willem's place on top of him. And instead of pushing Gerrick away when he got hard, Moranthus just smiled and pulled him closer.

Four days later, the walls of Clan Stoneheart's stronghold came into view. They were built from rough-hewn logs that stood nearly as tall as the pines they'd come from, and their tips were sharpened into spikes. A squat stone castle peeked out over the top, thick plumes of smoke billowing out of its chimneys and the braziers built along its outer walls. As they drew closer, Gerrick heard the squealing grunts of a full stable of boar and the harsh voices and metallic clangs of goblin soldiers training inside the stronghold's walls. If Moranthus's plan didn't work, they'd never fight their way out of there. Or into there, if Moranthus couldn't convince the guards posted at its gate to bring them to their warlord.

As they approached the gates, they came across a sight that stopped them in their tracks. Four horses of around the same size and build as Moranthus's stood tethered outside its walls. Each one's back was covered by a gray blanket emblazoned with Moonridge's emblem: a white bear encircled by interwoven lines of gold and violet.

Moranthus caught hold of Storm's reins and motioned for Gerrick to dismount. "This is going to complicate matters."

"It's going to do more than that," Gerrick grumbled as he slid off Storm's back. His legs were sore and stiff after spending days in the saddle, but they were steady enough beneath him. And his shoulder had healed enough that it didn't bother him anymore. He was ready to stand on his own two feet again. "If your Matriarch's men are already here, your goblin friend might've decided he couldn't afford to wait for us and handed Orthenn over. We're too late."

"Not necessarily." Moranthus's voice was calm and even. But he'd bitten his lower lip and was worrying Storm's reins between his fingers. The horses had thrown him off-balance too. "If they're still here, they don't have Orthenn yet. And I don't think Gralnag would give up on his plans that easily."

"What were those plans anyway? You still haven't told me what he wants from us."

"I don't know what he wants from us, or what he's planning. We were supposed to discuss that with him when we got here." Moranthus shrugged. "But he made it clear he has no intention of honoring his predecessor's arrangement with my Matriarch. He might not have expected her agents to arrive so soon, but he knew they were coming and he knows he can't keep Orthenn away from them without a fight. It'll be more difficult this way, but if we can distract them long enough for me to have a private word with Gralnag, I'm almost certain there's still a way for us to work around them. We'll figure something out."

Gerrick could almost see the wheels turning in Moranthus's head. He just hoped they were turning in the right direction this time. "How do we distract them?"

Moranthus smirked. "We walk in there and tell them that they're paying a ransom for the wrong Orthenn."

Gerrick thought back to the night Moranthus had taken him from Orthenn's camp. The cold look in his eyes as he'd held a knife to Gerrick's throat. The way he'd almost drawn his sword on Gerrick when he found out he'd kidnapped the wrong man. Gerrick would need to face that again, multiplied by four, for Moranthus's plan to work. "Are you sure they'll fall for that?"

"Of course, they will." Moranthus clapped him on his good shoulder. "You made a good enough Orthenn to fool me, didn't you?"

Gerrick didn't know if he could manage that a second time. But he didn't have a choice in the matter. Neither of them did. "I'll try. But I can't promise it'll work."

Moranthus gave him a rueful smile. "Neither can I."

Orthenn's name alone was enough to get them through the stronghold's gates and into Gralnag's throne room. It was small, but the rich tapestries hanging on its walls and the fur rugs that covered its floor gave it an air of grandeur all the same. Gralnag's throne—built from the same rough-hewn logs that made up his walls—stood on a raised dais against its back wall. A dozen guards, dressed in patchwork armor that stood in jarring contrast to the opulence of the room around them, lined its walls.

Gralnag himself had never looked better. He'd traded his battered traveling clothes for a fine set of leather armor edged with white rabbit fur, and he lounged on his throne like he'd been sitting on it all his life.

The space in front of Gralnag's throne was occupied by four elves. Each wore a full suit of slate-gray plate armor, and visored helmets covered their entire faces. Moonridge frost-guards. Gerrick had never seen one before, but he'd heard stories. Each one was hand-picked by Moonridge's ruler for showing exceptional strength, brutality, and loyalty, in equal measure. They were tall, even by elven standards, and broad enough to make Moranthus look like a scrawny youth. Their Matriarch had sent her finest for this job. Gerrick didn't like his chances against any of them if they caught him in a lie.

"You'd better have a damn good reason for barging in here like this," Gralnag said as they entered the chamber. "I have important guests here; guards should've told you that."

"They did." Moranthus's reply wouldn't have sounded any smoother if he'd rehearsed it a hundred times. "Your important guests are the reason we've come here, in fact. Am I correct in assuming they've come to collect Prince Orthenn?"

Gralnag shrugged. "Could be. What's it to you?"

"Nothing, really. I just thought you'd all like to know that you have the wrong Orthenn. The real Orthenn's been traveling with me for the past several weeks." Moranthus threw an arm across Gerrick's shoulders. "The man you kidnapped was only his body double."

"You sure about that? He doesn't look like anything special." Gralnag raised a skeptical eyebrow at Gerrick.

Moranthus's face broke into a wide, easy smile. Gerrick wondered how he managed it with four blank, metal faces staring at him. "I'll admit, he's long overdue for a bath, but I assure you, he's the genuine article. Elven glowstones don't lie, and mine led me right to him. If I hadn't lost it to a group of bandits a few weeks back, I'd be happy to show you."

"You're asking me to take your word for it, then." Gralnag gave Moranthus a hard look. "Still, you've gone far out of your way to tell me the worst lie I've ever heard if you're playing me false. I'm not saying I believe you, but I'd say that makes your Orthenn worth a closer look. But it's not just me you need to convince of that, is it?" He nodded toward the frostguards at the base of his throne.

One of the frostguards pulled off his helmet. His snow-white hair was pulled back into a braid so elaborate it made

Gerrick's eyes hurt. His steel-gray eyes were narrowed in suspicion, and his lips curled into a cold smile as he said in a low, nasal voice that set Gerrick's teeth on edge: "You'll forgive me if I'm somewhat more skeptical of your claim. If your Orthenn is truly the genuine article, then why have you brought him here instead of delivering him to our Matriarch?"

Moranthus didn't even flinch. "I tried taking him straight to Moonridge, but he was adamant about seeing to the welfare of his men before allowing himself to be escorted to safety. He stopped eating after I took him out of his camp, and I had no way of getting him to the border before he starved himself. I had no choice but to bring him here."

"Of course, you didn't." The frostguard curled his lip in disdain. "I'd ask how you've lasted so long in your line of work if keeping a single human under control was so difficult for you, but I suppose I shouldn't expect anything more from a man who built his career on his former Patriarch's affections rather than his skill in the field."

Moranthus's eyes narrowed. "As I recall, I'd made a name for myself as a duskblade before I caught Patriarch Ryllorin's attention, but you're welcome to form your own opinion on the matter."

"Indeed, I am." The frostguard cast an appraising glance at Gerrick. "You're certain this is the real prince?"

"Look him over for yourself if you don't believe me," Moranthus replied. "We've got nothing to hide."

Gerrick flinched as the frostguard gripped his chin between his armored thumb and forefinger. The cold edges of the frostguard's gauntlet dug into Gerrick's skin, hard enough that he was afraid it might draw blood. The frostguard kept his face neutral as he turned Gerrick's head one way, and the other, and then made a small noise of approval in the back of his throat and let go of Gerrick's chin. "It's a good likeness, I'll give you that. You certainly look the part, but then, so does the Orthenn locked away in our host's dungeon."

Gerrick squared his shoulders and looked straight into the frostguard's eyes. He did his best impression of Orthenn's usual curt, commanding tone as he replied, "Of course, he looks like me. He's my body double. What did you expect?"

"Why do I get the distinct impression that your double would offer me a similar reply if I was to ask him the same question?"

"He might. But he'd be lying. And he'd stop lying pretty damn fast if he knew I was here. He knows his place. He wouldn't knowingly go against me."

"I believe I'd like to see that for myself. My companions and I will escort you to our host's dungeon and present you to the other man who has laid claim to Orthenn's identity. Whoever you are, you certainly possess an adequately princely demeanor, and you've shown me considerably more courtesy than your companion in the dungeons. I hope, for your sake, that he behaves as you expect him to." The frostguard patted his shoulder. "I'd hate to have to cut out the first polite tongue I've encountered in this part of the world."

Gerrick fought to keep his voice steady as he said, "He won't give you a reason to." Or at least, he hoped Orthenn wouldn't.

"Good. As for you…" The frostguard turned to Moranthus, wrapped Moranthus's braid around his gauntlet, and gave it a single, sharp tug. "I suggest you run along now and decide what to do with that razor of yours. You've made yourself useful today, but that won't be enough to redeem you in the eyes of our Matriarch. She is quite finished with offering second chances to her father's old bedwarmer. Your role in this ends now. Stay out of our presence for the remainder of our stay here, or there will be…consequences."

Gerrick expected Moranthus to have a comeback for that, like he did with everything else. Something that would make the frostguard look like the ass he was, in front of the entire throne room. Instead, Moranthus just snatched his braid out of the frostguard's hand and took a step back, murder in his eyes. His mouth hung open, but no words came out.

Gerrick stared at him. Moranthus getting sent away from Gralnag's stronghold wasn't part of their plan. "No," he said, flinching under the frostguard's cold glare as it snapped back to him. "He stays with me. He was a fine companion on our journey here. If you don't want him in Moonridge, then I'm taking him with me when I return to Dawn's Gate."

The frostguard sniffed. "Very well then. It seems he's found himself a new master. Let's hope he serves you better than he did the last one." He turned his attention back to Gralnag. "If this Orthenn proves to be the genuine article, I'll see to it that you're notified. I trust that you'll see to it that he and his… companion are given more comfortable accommodations than his double, in light of his more agreeable disposition? I hardly think shackles are necessary for this one."

"Don't you worry your pretty little head about that." Gralnag gave the frostguard a dismissive wave. "I know how to treat my guests, and I know how to deal with liars. Just find the right prince. I'll do the rest."

Gerrick's heart pounded against his chest like a war drum as the frostguards led him out of the throne room, leaving Moranthus alone with Gralnag. If he couldn't convince Orthenn to play along with his act, he was a dead man.

Twenty-Three

Moranthus shook with barely suppressed anger as he watched the frostguards lead Gerrick out of Gralnag's throne room, their leader's "old bedwarmer" remark still echoing in his ears. His relationship with Ryllorin had earned him more unflattering names than he could count, but he'd only ever heard one man refer to him with that particular turn of phrase. And there was no mistaking that low, nasal voice. Ilendra had sent one of the frostguards who'd betrayed her father to recover her prize.

Moranthus raised a hand to his throat, recalling the cold sting of the frostguard's blade cutting into his skin. Shuddered at the memory of helplessly watching Ryllorin bleed to death under the frostguard's impassive gaze. Moranthus would never forget what that traitor had done to him, or what he'd done to Ryllorin. And judging by the frostguard's taunts and his rough handling of Moranthus, the frostguard hadn't forgotten him either.

"You going to be all right there?" Gralnag eyed him as though he were a rabid dog broken free of its tether.

Of course, he wasn't all right. If that frostguard had grabbed his braid like that in Moonridge, and Moranthus wasn't a half-exile, Moranthus would've been within his rights to kill him for it. But they weren't in Moonridge. And Moranthus was a half-exile, soon to be a full one.

"I'm fine," Moranthus snapped.

"Whatever you want to tell yourself." Gralnag shrugged. "Guess this means I don't need to worry about you changing sides on me, at least."

"I'd sooner die." Moranthus dug his nails into his palm, focusing on the pain until his breathing evened out and he could get his thoughts straight again. He had work to do. He couldn't let the frostguard make him forget that.

"I believe it. Can't say I blame you either. He's an arrogant motherfucker. All four of 'em are. Don't know what things are like where you elves come from, but in these parts, it's bad manners to insult a man in his own throne room." Gralnag smirked down at Moranthus, a dark look in his eyes. "I'd say it's time we brought them down a peg or two."

"Why have you waited this long? They're already in your stronghold, and your soldiers have them heavily outnumbered."

"Because I don't want to lose any more of those soldiers than I have to. The frostguards have been cagey ever since they found out they won't be dealing with Knurlath. If I try anything now, they're going to see it from a mile off, and I'm going to have a bloodbath on my hands. Not a good way to start my reign."

"I hope you weren't expecting me to convince them to trust you. You've seen what they think of me. My word's worth less than nothing to them."

"Exactly. Compared to you and your fake prince, I look trustworthy. And if your friend convinces them that he's the real Orthenn, I look like a fool for bringing them the wrong man. That makes me look like I don't have the smarts to pull one over on them, so I'm less of a threat. They let their guard down, I let them think Orthenn's theirs until I get the payment I'm due, and then I take them prisoner if I can and see what your Matriarch's willing to pay to get them back."

Moranthus nodded. It was a sound plan, if somewhat lacking in detail. He had no objections so far. "How are you going to subdue them?"

"Tomorrow morning, I'll send for you and your human friend. You'll bind his hands and bring him to me. The frostguards will be here waiting for you, thinking I'm about to hand Orthenn over to them. I can't have any more guards on duty than I do now without looking suspicious, but there'll be more of them waiting outside the door to pitch in when we need them.

"After the frostguards give me my payment, you'll act like you're trying to help your human friend escape. Get him out of his bindings and get a weapon into his hands if you can. That'll keep the frostguards distracted while my guards get them surrounded. Once that's taken care of, they'll surrender if they know what's good for them."

"And if they don't?" Moranthus didn't like the thought of facing four frostguards on his own. They'd keep Gerrick alive as long as they thought he was Orthenn, but they wouldn't hesitate before killing Moranthus. They'd probably enjoy doing it too. If Gralnag's soldiers weren't quick about getting into position, Moranthus wouldn't live to see it happen.

"Then they'll die. And probably take you down with them." Gralnag gave him an almost apologetic look. "I'd say I'm sorry for asking you to take the fall on this, but better you than one of my guards. You're free to say no of course. But then I might have to decide I'm not quite ready to forgive you and the human for that knife in my shoulder."

"There's no need for threats. I'll do what you're asking. Happily." Going along with Gralnag's plan meant facing the same impossible four-to-one odds he'd faced on the day he'd lost Ryllorin. Moranthus wouldn't have survived them then, and there was a good chance he wouldn't survive them now. But he'd be armed this time, and no one had him pinned to a headboard with a sword at his neck. Even if he couldn't save himself, he had a chance to save Gerrick. That was more than worth whatever it cost him in the end.

"You're damn loyal to that human of yours, aren't you? Stupid of you, but it's your life. Throw it away however you want." Gralnag shook his head. "Can't say I'm not a little jealous. He'd better appreciate what you're doing for him."

"I'm sure he will," Moranthus replied. "What happens after the fighting's done?"

"You and your friend are free to go, and you can take Orthenn with you. A hostage like that is a headache I don't need once word gets out that I have him, and I'm too far from Dawn's Gate to ransom him back home without that ransom getting stolen on its way here. Clan Stoneheart has always kept its interests in the north. I'm not going against that."

"What about Orthenn's men?" Moranthus had brought Gerrick into this under the assumption that he could save the rest of his company along with Orthenn. If Gralnag taking Knurlath's place as his clan's warlord had changed that, Gerrick deserved to know sooner rather than later.

"He's welcome to them. So long as he understands that me letting them go means that he and his father remember it was an elven plan that got him kidnapped, not a goblin one. I don't want any southern clans getting attacked over Knurlath's mistakes and coming after me for it once the dust has settled."

"That's generous of you."

"Nothing generous about looking out for my own best interests." Gralnag scoffed. "My quarrel's with Moonridge, not

Dawn's Gate. I want to keep it that way. That's all. You got any more questions, or are we done here?"

"You've told me everything I need to know. Thank you." Moranthus breathed an internal sigh of relief. He hadn't made a mistake in trusting Gralnag. As long as Gerrick could pass himself off as the real Orthenn, they'd both be fine.

"Good. Let's go see how your fake prince is handling himself."

Moranthus's stomach turned at the thought of facing the frostguards again. "Are you sure it's a good idea to bring me along? Their leader made it quite clear that he'd prefer not to have any further dealings with me."

"This is my stronghold, not his. You can go where you want." Gralnag rose from his throne with a heavy sigh. "But you have a point. He'll be easier to handle if we keep him docile; let's not piss him off—yet. I'll send a servant in to find a room for you. Get yourself cleaned up and get some rest. You look like you need it." With that, Gralnag strode out of the throne room, four of his guards trailing after him.

Twenty-Four

The frostguards were silent behind their helmets as they led Gerrick down the steep, dimly lit stairs to Gralnag's dungeon. At the bottom of the stairs, they entered a wide, low-ceilinged hall that stretched past the range of Gerrick's vision in either direction. Its walls were lined with iron-barred cells on one side and torches held in regularly placed sconces along the other.

The cold, damp air that filled the dungeon gave Gerrick an excuse for the shiver that ran down his spine at the sight of it. Just looking at those cells made a heavy, hopeless feeling settle into his bones. It wouldn't take long for a man to break, locked inside. And if Moranthus hadn't stolen him from Orthenn's camp, he'd be sitting in one now. Gerrick hoped Orthenn and the rest of his company hadn't been stuck here for long. None of them deserved to be trapped in a place like this.

The frostguards led him down the hall's left side. Most of the cells they passed were empty, and the few prisoners they saw didn't spare them so much as an upward glance as they huddled on the piles of straw that served as their beds. When they crossed paths with one of Gralnag's guards, she only gave them a lethargic nod in greeting as she shouldered past them. Shivering in the damp chill that filled the place, she didn't look any happier to be there than the prisoners under her watch.

They found Orthenn and the rest of his company at the hall's end, two of them chained to each other at the ankle in each of the last five cells on that side of the dungeon. Orthenn was in the cell closest to the dungeon's left wall, paired off with Aldous. They were streaked with dirt and stripped of their arms and armor, but neither looked like anything more than his pride had been injured.

Aldous's face broke into a warm, wide smile when he noticed Gerrick. Questions filled his eyes. Gerrick couldn't answer any of them. Couldn't smile back, without giving himself away. He gave Aldous a shallow, disinterested nod, then looked away.

Orthenn was easier. He'd gotten to his feet, an incredulous look on his face. "What are you doing here?" he asked.

"Ending this," Gerrick replied. "You've served me well, but it's time to drop the act. You're relieved from duty."

"You need to drop your act. You don't have the authority to relieve me from anything." Orthenn fixed Gerrick with an icy stare. His time as a prisoner hadn't made him any less stubborn. It might even have made him worse.

Gerrick fought to keep from flinching under Orthenn's gaze. He was disobeying a direct order from his prince. "I do. We both know that. I'm sure they gave you the same threats they gave me over what they'll do if they find out you're lying to them. But I can promise that if you stand down now, they won't touch you."

Orthenn shook his head. "This is madness. I don't know what you're trying to do, but it won't work. I'll have no part of it."

"I'm only trying to save you before this goes too far. That will work." Gerrick gave Orthenn a pleading look, willing him to understand. "Trust me. This is your last chance."

"I trust you. But my status is the only thing that's kept my men safe. I can't let you—"

Aldous silenced Orthenn by clamping a heavy hand down on his shoulder. At some point while Gerrick was focused on Orthenn, he'd gotten to his feet. "Give it up, Gerrick," Aldous said in the same voice he used when one of his sons got too rowdy. "You've gotten us this far, lad. Let Orthenn handle the rest. He won't let us come to any harm if he can help it."

Orthenn turned his icy glare on the frostguards' leader. "Is he telling the truth? If I admit that he's the real Orthenn, there won't be any repercussions for me or the rest of my men?"

The frostguards' leader responded to Orthenn's glare with a withering look. "If Prince Orthenn insists."

"I do," Gerrick said.

Orthenn took a deep breath, shifting his weight from one foot to the other. He looked from the frostguard to Gerrick and back to the frostguard, then relaxed his posture, a resigned look in his eyes. "Then I admit it," he said. "He's the real Orthenn. I'm just his double."

The frostguards' leader nodded. "Good. I'm glad we were able to resolve this matter without resorting to…messier tactics." He turned to Gerrick. "Are you certain you don't want this man punished for his insubordination? I would be more than happy to offer my personal assistance in the matter."

"Leave him. I'll deal with him myself. Later."

The disappointed look on the frostguard's face made Gerrick's skin crawl. "Very well. My offer still stands, should you reconsider your decision."

"The man's made his choice. Respect that; he outranks you." Gralnag's voice echoed off the dungeon's walls as he approached them. A pair of his guards flanked him on either side. Moranthus wasn't with them. Gerrick wished he knew if that was a good sign.

The frostguard's eyes narrowed. "I assure you, I have shown him nothing but respect."

"Sure, you have." Gralnag didn't look convinced. "I take it this Orthenn's the real one, then?"

"So it would seem. Consider yourself fortunate that he arrived when he did."

Gralnag shrugged. "What's it matter to me? I would've gotten paid either way. And speaking of payment, it's time we talked specifics on that. Old Knurlath didn't leave many notes behind, and I want to know just what I'm getting out of this." He gestured at one of his guards. "You. Get our new guest settled in. He doesn't need to be here for this."

With a decisive nod and a slight bow to his warlord, the guard whisked Gerrick out of the dungeon and handed him off to a pair of servants. Gerrick's thoughts lingered on Orthenn as he sat through Gralnag's servants forcing him into a bath and dressing him in a set of fine clothes that the real Orthenn would've hated—as though there was any point to making him look like a prince when he'd be back on the road in a day or two. As long as Gralnag was still planning to side with Gerrick and Moranthus over the frostguards, Orthenn would be fine. Just kept in a cell a bit longer. And Gralnag had to be on their side in this. If he was working with the frostguards, Gerrick would never have made it this far. He found a small sense of comfort in that as Gralnag's servants led him to the room he'd be staying in.

The room was small, but richly furnished. Thick rugs covered the floor around its oversized bed, and a mirror hung over the elaborately carved stand of its washbasin. Its walls were illuminated by a pair of bright oil lanterns. A small, unadorned cot had been shoved into a corner of the room.

Gerrick found Moranthus sitting, shirtless, on the cot, his hair still damp from a wash and hanging, unbraided, over his shoulder. He slowly turned a razor over in his hands. The same one Gerrick had seen him fiddling with on the night he'd told Moranthus he was only Orthenn's body double.

"Are you all right?" Gerrick asked, careful to keep his eyes off Moranthus's hair.

Moranthus shrugged and kept his eyes locked on the razor. He didn't so much as touch his hair.

Gerrick furrowed his brow. Something was wrong. He shut the door behind him, then sat beside Moranthus. "Did something go wrong with Gralnag?"

Moranthus shook his head and flipped the razor's blade back into its handle. But he still wouldn't meet Gerrick's eyes. "No. Everything's fine there. He wants our help getting the frostguards out of the way, but once that's done, he'll let Orthenn and the rest of your company go free. He doesn't want to put himself in conflict with Dawn's Gate."

"How's he planning to deal with the frostguards?"

"He's going to bring you into his throne room again tomorrow morning under the pretense of exchanging you for the payment they've brought him. The frostguards will be there waiting for us. When the trade's been made, our job is to cause a commotion by making it look like I'm trying to help you escape.

"While we have the frostguards distracted, Gralnag's guards will form up and get them surrounded. He'll have the same number of them on duty as he did today, and more of them will come in to help when they hear us trying to escape. There'll be too many of them for the frostguards to fight. Once they realize that, they should surrender."

"What happens if we can't keep them distracted?" They wouldn't be able to hold the frostguards' attention for long. Moranthus had to know that.

"Things get considerably messier." Moranthus curled his fingers tighter around the razor. "But it shouldn't come to that. They can't kill you without getting exiled for it. That'll put them at a disadvantage."

"What about you?"

"I know how to handle myself in a fight. I can last long enough for Gralnag's soldiers to get into position; it won't take them long."

Gerrick wasn't convinced. "Why do you need to be part of this? They'll still be distracted if I try to escape without your help."

"You'll be bound and unarmed when Gralnag hands you over to them. Someone needs to cut your bonds and get a sword into your hands, and Gralnag doesn't want to risk losing one of his soldiers on that."

"If it's too dangerous for his men, he shouldn't be asking you to do it either."

Moranthus shook his head. "We don't have any other choice, Gerrick. It's a small price for all the help he's giving us. I'm happy to pay it."

"Fine." Gerrick still didn't like the sound of the part Moranthus was playing in Gralnag's plan. But if Moranthus had already agreed to it, it was too late for Gerrick to do anything about it. There was no point arguing any further. "If you're happy with the plan, then what's bothering you?"

"Nothing. I'm just…tired. It's been a long day."

"So tired you don't care about me seeing you with your hair down?"

Moranthus tensed. Gerrick was on to something.

"It's something to do with that frostguard grabbing your braid, isn't it?"

"Yes." Moranthus's voice was little more than a whisper. "It shouldn't be affecting me like this, I know. But if you knew what that meant…"

Gerrick didn't know. But it had to be serious if it still had Moranthus this off-balance. "Whatever it means, he was wrong to do it."

"You think too highly of me." Moranthus gave him a small, sad smile that made his heart ache. "I'm just an exile. There was nothing wrong with him treating me accordingly."

"Maybe that's all you are to him. But you're more than that to me. I don't think any better of you than you deserve after everything you've done for me." And after everything Moranthus was *still* doing for him. Without thinking, Gerrick reached out and cupped Moranthus's face in his hand. Brushed a stray strand of hair behind his ear.

Moranthus sighed and leaned into his touch. Then, with a start, he pulled away. "I'm sorry," he murmured.

"Don't be." Gerrick was done pretending he didn't know what Moranthus wanted. Done pretending he didn't want the same thing. He pulled Moranthus closer, tangled his fingers in Moranthus's luxuriously soft hair, and kissed him. Moranthus tensed, and for a moment, Gerrick was afraid he'd pull away. Then, Moranthus smiled against his mouth and kissed him back, wrapping his arms tightly around Gerrick like he was afraid someone would try to pry them apart.

Gerrick felt no shame. Just soft lips, a warm, inviting mouth, and a clever tongue.

He didn't know how much time had passed when they finally pulled away from each other. Just that it wasn't enough. That they hadn't been close enough. He wanted to be closer, whatever that meant.

He ran his hand down Moranthus's exposed chest and belly. Started to work at getting Moranthus's belt undone.

Moranthus caught his wrist. "Are you sure about this?" he asked, his eyes dark and his breathing heavy.

"I am. I want to know what this feels like."

Moranthus let go of his wrist. "So do I. But there's no need to rush; we have the whole night ahead of us." His lips quirked into a smirk that make Gerrick feel weak in the knees.

Gerrick let out a shaky breath he didn't know he'd been holding in. "A-all right. What do you want me to do? I've never…" he trailed off. He didn't trust himself to say anything more without making a fool of himself.

Moranthus slung a leg around Gerrick's waist and made himself comfortable straddling Gerrick's lap. "Relax," he breathed, his lips hovering a hair's breadth away from Gerrick's. "I'll show you."

And he did. It wasn't so different from being with a woman once Moranthus helped him through his first, awkward fumblings. But where a woman would've been soft and pliant, Moranthus was firm and insistent, claiming every inch of Gerrick's body as his own with hands, lips, and tongue. There was nothing feminine in his harsh gasps and low, pleasured groans as Gerrick did the same to him. Nothing feminine about the shape of his body, in spite of his slight frame and smooth, hairless skin. Even when Gerrick had Moranthus on his back underneath him, Gerrick's cock deep inside him, Moranthus still had that masculine surety of himself that had never come naturally to Gerrick. And it lit a fire in his belly that he'd never felt with a woman.

It was almost enough to bring tears to his eyes, after. Now he knew what he'd been denying himself for so many years. What had been missing when he'd spent the night with a woman and been left wanting in the morning. Why, on the day that Edith had broken things off with him, tears running down her cheeks as she asked him why he didn't want her the same way she wanted him, he hadn't been able to find the words to answer her. After spending his entire adult life wondering and cursing himself for his own confusion, he understood. His heart felt lighter than it had in years as he drifted into sleep.

Gerrick woke with Moranthus still in his arms. Moranthus's back was toward him, his hair tickling at Gerrick's nose every time Gerrick breathed in. Gerrick reluctantly let go of Moranthus to brush the hair out of his face, then let his arm fall back around Moranthus's waist.

Moranthus stirred and turned in Gerrick's arms, a sleepy grin smeared across his face. "Morning," he said, wrapping his arms around Gerrick's neck as he leaned in to kiss him.

Gerrick wanted to let him. Last night was like a dream he still hadn't woken from. He never wanted to wake from it, when he'd never felt as good—as right—as he did lying here with Moranthus in his arms. But he couldn't let it go on any longer. He'd let it go on too long already. It wouldn't be fair of him to let Moranthus get his hopes up any higher before he let Moranthus down. He tensed and pulled away.

Moranthus froze, his smile falling into a worried frown. "Is something wrong?"

Nothing was wrong. Gerrick had never felt better. That was the problem. He liked men; there was no denying that after last night. His night with Moranthus had been one of the best of his life, but he couldn't let it happen again. Something dangerously close to a sob caught in his throat at the thought. He wished things were different. Things would be different if he'd met Moranthus when he was younger. Before he was Orthenn's body double, or Daisy's father… Back when his life still belonged to him, and he was free to make his own choices, they could have stayed like this forever. That sweet face and warm, sleepy smile, made all the sweeter by the fact that it was just for him, could have been the first thing Gerrick saw every morning for the rest of his life. And his nights… It would be harder to spend them alone now that he knew what he'd be going without.

But Gerrick was Orthenn's body double. And Daisy's father. He'd ruin Orthenn's reputation if someone mistook him for Orthenn while he and Moranthus were together. Daisy would face years of cruel teasing from the other children if Gerrick gave her a second father in place of the mother she'd lost. And Moranthus deserved better than a man who, at a moment's notice, could be called on to give his life in his prince's place. He'd lost one lover to an early death already; it wouldn't be fair of Gerrick to do that to him again.

Gerrick sighed. Fought back the urge to hold Moranthus close to him and never let him go and said, "Yes."

Moranthus pushed himself as far away from Gerrick as the narrow cot would allow. "You're having second thoughts about last night, aren't you?" His voice wavered.

"I'm sorry. It was good. You were…more than good. But…"

"But it was a mistake, and you don't want to do it again." Moranthus's voice was steady again. "Right?"

Gerrick forced himself to nod. Pretended he didn't see the tears welling up in Moranthus's eyes. Blinked away the tears that threatened to form in his own at the sight of them.

"All right. We'll just write this off as a pity fuck and forget it ever happened." With a smile that didn't reach his eyes, Moranthus mimed a signature. "There. It's done. Now that's behind us, let's get back to rescuing your prince. After all, those frostguards aren't going to distract themselves."

Gerrick's heart was heavy as he rose from the cot and set about dressing. He'd done the right thing. He knew that. He and Moranthus would both be better off for it in the end, so why did it feel so wrong?

Twenty-Five

Moranthus's hands shook as he hurriedly braided his hair. He knew the end result was sloppy and loose, but he couldn't bring himself to care. He wouldn't be wearing it much longer anyway.

He was almost grateful when a knock sounded on the door moments after he'd finished dressing himself. Gralnag's guards had arrived earlier than he expected, but that wasn't necessarily a bad thing. He wouldn't have a chance to dwell on the growing ache in his chest now, and the tears prickling at his eyes wouldn't get a chance to fall.

He had no right to feel this way. Gerrick hadn't promised him anything serious last night, and Moranthus had been a fool to assume that what they'd done was anything more than Gerrick satisfying a bit of curiosity. Gerrick had said it himself: he just wanted to know what it felt like. Now he knew, and it wasn't to his liking.

But in the moment, Gerrick hadn't *acted* like a man who was only trying to satisfy his curiosity. There'd been a naked sincerity to his unpracticed caresses that made Moranthus dare to hope for more than just one night with him. An adoring look in his eyes as he entered Moranthus that seemed to promise he wanted more than just sexual gratification from their coupling.

Gerrick had stayed when it was over too. Instead of retreating to the bed, he'd spent the night on Moranthus's cot, cradling Moranthus in his arms like he was the most precious thing in the world. When Moranthus had woken to find Gerrick still holding him, he'd felt whole again, like he'd found a piece of himself he hadn't known was missing. And before he could fully appreciate that feeling, that piece was torn out of him again, leaving him as empty and cold and alone as the day he'd lost Ryllorin.

Except that he *wasn't* alone this time. Or at least, he didn't need to be. He'd still have a place with Gerrick in Dawn's Gate in the end—Gerrick had given Moranthus his word on that, and Moranthus trusted him not to go back on it. It wasn't the place in Gerrick's life he wanted to occupy, but once the initial sting of Gerrick's rejection had worn off, it would be enough for him. He'd rather have Gerrick as a friend than not have him at all.

Another knock sounded against the door, and Moranthus strode across the room to open it. When he found himself face-to-face with the frostguards instead of Gralnag's soldiers, his blood froze in his veins.

"What are you doing here?" he asked, hoping against hope that this was somehow part of Gralnag's plan.

"Isn't it obvious? We've come to collect what's ours," their leader replied. Moranthus didn't need to see his face to know he was sneering behind his helmet.

"I thought Gralnag was planning to hand Orthenn over to you later in his throne room. He told us to stay here until he sent his guards for us. What changed?"

"I don't trust this new warlord to deal fairly with us. Our Matriarch reached an agreement with Knurlath, not Gralnag. As Knurlath is now dead, we are no longer obligated to honor the terms of that agreement. We will collect Orthenn and his double, and we will leave this place before our host is any the wiser. You may assist us, or you may die. It makes no difference to me."

"I'll help you." Moranthus slumped his shoulders and hung his head to make himself look defeated. It wasn't difficult; after the way the morning had started, he was halfway there already. "But why collect the double too? He isn't worth anything to our Matriarch, and getting him out of the dungeon will slow us down."

"It occurs to me that it would be…irresponsible to leave such a convincing fake in the hands of a goblin warlord. By removing him from Gralnag's possession, I am protecting our Matriarch from the complications he has the potential to cause." The frostguard shoved a length of rope into Moranthus's hands. "Now bind the prince and follow me. Any further questions on this matter will be treated as a display of rebellion, and you will be punished accordingly. Do I make myself clear?"

Moranthus nodded.

"Good. If you continue to be this cooperative, you might just convince me to put in a good word for you with our Matriarch upon our return home." The frostguard gave him an overly familiar pat on the shoulder.

"Thank you." Moranthus hoped the frostguard wasn't stupid enough to think that Moranthus believed he was in any position to sway Ilendra's judgment. From what Moranthus had heard, Ilendra preferred her men with soft bodies and biddable temperaments. The frostguard possessed neither of those qualities.

Gerrick gave Moranthus a questioning look as he approached him with the rope, eyes begging Moranthus to tell him that this was part of their plan. Moranthus shook his head and set about binding Gerrick's wrists. He kept the ropes as loose as he could without arousing the frostguards' suspicion. Gerrick wouldn't have much room to work with, but if he struggled enough, he'd be able to get at least one of his hands free. As he tied the last of the knots holding them in place, Moranthus slipped a finger under Gerrick's bindings and tugged at the slack he'd left there, hoping it would be enough to make Gerrick realize that Moranthus had given him a way to free himself.

In a final, discreet act of rebellion, Moranthus left Gerrick's sword belt on the floor of their room and made sure the door stayed open behind them after the frostguards led them out of it. That would have to be enough to alert Gralnag's soldiers that something had gone wrong when they came to collect Moranthus and Gerrick. Moranthus couldn't risk anything more.

Moranthus studied the frostguards as he followed them to the dungeons, looking for any weaknesses he could exploit. He didn't necessarily need to kill them to stop them, and he didn't want to if he could avoid it. As long as he could incapacitate them long enough for Gralnag to realize something was amiss, he and Gerrick would be fine. That made things easier.

The dungeon was cold and dank, lit only by flickering torches placed at wide intervals. Most of the iron-barred cells they passed were empty and open. Some had shackles, in varying states of rusted disrepair, bolted onto their walls. Moranthus fruitlessly scanned the hall for any sign of Gralnag's guards. Either none were on patrol at this hour, or the frostguards had already dealt with them. He and Gerrick needed to do this on their own.

One frostguard took his helmet off as they neared the cells where Orthenn and the rest of his company were being kept.

He probably thought it would help him see better in the dungeon's dim light. He'd just made himself into Moranthus's first target.

Moranthus drew his dagger from its sheath and struck the helmetless frostguard on the temple with its pommel. Without so much as a gasp, he crumpled to the ground, his armor making a loud, clanking noise as it crashed into the stone floor. If Moranthus had put the right amount of force behind the blow, he'd be unconscious for a few minutes and too disoriented to do much of anything when he woke up. If Moranthus had miscalculated and hit him too hard, there was a chance he'd never wake up at all.

Out of the corner of his eye, Moranthus saw Gerrick struggling against his bindings. Moranthus needed to keep the remaining frostguards distracted, or they'd restrain Gerrick before he got his hands free, and Moranthus would need to face all of them on his own.

Without a moment's hesitation, he slammed his dagger's pommel as hard as he could into another frostguard's helmet, wincing at the loud, ringing sound it made. He couldn't imagine what it must sound like inside that helmet, but the frostguard's screams as he clutched at his head with both hands made it clear it wasn't pleasant.

While he was distracted and off-balance, Moranthus shoved him into a cell and clamped one of the shackles dangling from its rear wall shut around his wrist. As he turned to look for his next opponent, he caught sight of Gerrick grappling with a frostguard on the ground. He'd gotten his bindings off, but it wasn't clear whether he or the frostguard had the upper hand. Moranthus dashed out of the cell, trying to think of the best way to get a grip on the frostguard and pull him off Gerrick.

A heavy hand grabbed hold of his braid and gave it a sharp yank. Moranthus stopped cold, a pained cry on his lips.

"Forgetting something?" a low, nasal voice asked. The last frostguard left standing was their leader. And he'd caught Moranthus with his back turned.

Moranthus turned to face the frostguard and caught a backhand across the face for his trouble. The frostguard let go of his braid and let him stagger backward, his vision blurry from the impact and the taste of blood in his mouth from where the blow had forced him to bite the inside of his cheek. The frostguard wouldn't kill him quickly after Moranthus had humiliated him by incapacitating two of his comrades so easily. He'd want to draw things out and make them hurt.

Moranthus could use that to his advantage.

He sheathed his dagger and drew his sword. It wasn't his weapon of choice, but it was the only thing that could save him when the frostguard decided to stop playing games and come at him with the blade that hung from his own sword belt. "I didn't forget you," he said and spat a mouthful of blood onto the floor. "I just assumed that if you were that slow to react, you weren't much of a threat. But you're welcome to prove me wrong."

The frostguard took off his helmet and dropped it on the floor. He sneered as he asked, "You're sure you want to face me? This is your last chance to run, Exile. I suggest you take it."

"I just faced two of your friends and came out of it looking better than they did. Maybe Ilendra will let me have your job once you're out of the way." Moranthus tried to circle around the frostguard. He'd need some space to fall back when the frostguard started advancing on him.

The frostguard drew his sword and rushed Moranthus before he could take a single step. Moranthus barely got his own blade up in time to block his strike, and the impact shook his entire body. If things came down to a contest of strength between them, he didn't have a snowflake's chance in summer of winning.

Moranthus twisted out of the block and landed a solid blow on the frostguard's jaw with his elbow. The frostguard grunted and staggered backward, but kept his footing. He turned on his heel faster than the bulk of his armor should have allowed and lashed out at Moranthus with his blade. Moranthus's answering block was clumsy and weak. He lost his grip on his sword and watched with dismay as it slid across the stone floor, far beyond his reach.

A quick glance at Gerrick revealed that he was equally beyond Moranthus's reach. The other frostguard's helmet had fallen off, and his bloodied nose looked broken, but he still had Gerrick effectively pinned to the floor.

The frostguards' leader smirked and returned his sword to its scabbard. Before Moranthus could back away or make a dive for his own sword, he grabbed Moranthus by the collar of his shirt and lifted him into the air.

"You should have run." With a smile, the frostguard slammed his fist into Moranthus's face, then threw him to the floor.

After that, everything was a blur of pain. Moranthus curled in on himself, catching as many of the frostguard's kicks on his arms and legs as he could. But eventually, one caught him in the ribs with a sickening *crack*, and he rolled onto his back, the thought of defending himself long forgotten. He clutched at his chest, each gasping breath plunging him deeper into a sea of burning agony. Getting slapped by a bear felt like a friendly pat on the back compared to this.

The frostguard knelt beside him. "This has been quite the diversion, but I'm afraid it's reached its end." He put a hand around Moranthus's throat and started to squeeze. "It will be a pleasure, watching the light leave your eyes. I haven't had such a satisfying kill in quite some time. Thank you."

Moranthus tried, with both his hands, to pry the frostguard's hand off his neck, but there was no loosening his grip. With trembling fingers, he clawed at the frostguard's face, driving his thumbs into the frostguard's eyes.

The frostguard wrenched his head free with a pained snarl and gave Moranthus a tooth-rattling backhand across the face. Stunned, Moranthus went limp in his grip, too weak to resist when the frostguard grabbed both his wrists with his free hand and pinned them over his head. He kicked feebly at the frostguard's legs. The frostguard chuckled and tightened his grip on Moranthus's throat.

This was the end. Moranthus stopped struggling and turned his head, his eyes scanning the room for Gerrick as his vision grew spotty around the edges. But all he could see was a slate-gray mound of armor.

He heard a solid *thud* somewhere above him, and the frostguard's grip on his throat loosened, then let go entirely. Moranthus turned his gaze upward to find Gerrick standing over him, an unlit torch in his hand.

Twenty-Six

Gerrick had never felt more helpless as he watched Moranthus struggle to get himself upright, coughing and clutching at his throat as he gasped for breath. Gerrick should've gotten there sooner. He'd taken too long breaking free of the frostguard holding him. He was lucky he'd gotten free at all. Moranthus hadn't given him much room to work with in those bindings, and he never would've won a fight with that frostguard if the frostguard hadn't been holding back out of fear of hurting him. But all the excuses in the world wouldn't have stopped him from blaming himself if he hadn't gotten to Moranthus in time.

He knelt beside Moranthus and reached for his arm, ready to pull Moranthus to his feet if he needed it.

Moranthus shrank back from him. "I'm sorry," he wheezed. "But I really…need you not to touch me right now."

Gerrick winced. He knew things wouldn't be the same between him and Moranthus after what he'd done, but he hadn't expected it to hurt this much. "That's fair. Can you stand on your own?"

Moranthus nodded and tried to push himself off the ground. He barely managed to get onto his knees before he pitched forward, a harsh coughing fit wracking his body. When the coughing subsided, he gasped, "All right. Help me up."

Gerrick gently took Moranthus's hands in his own and pulled him to his feet. Moranthus pushed himself off Gerrick, swaying on his feet as he struggled to hold himself upright. He tensed when Gerrick wrapped an arm around his shoulders to keep him steady, but didn't pull away.

"I'm sorry for..." Gerrick's words failed him. He tried again. "It was nothing to do with you. I just…"

"Gerrick, please. Don't. You're only making this harder." Moranthus had that wounded look in his eyes again as he slumped against Gerrick.

The sound of heavy footsteps echoing off the dungeon's walls startled them both. Gerrick cast a panicked look around them, worried that one of the downed frostguards had gotten up, but they were all where Moranthus and Gerrick had left them.

A moment later, Gralnag and a handful of goblin soldiers came into view. Gralnag ordered his soldiers to a halt a few paces away from them. He let out a long, low whistle at the sight of the downed frostguards around them and the state Moranthus was in. "Looks like you've already got things under control here. Nice work."

"We didn't have much choice in the matter," Moranthus croaked. He rubbed at his throat before continuing, "It certainly took you long enough to get here."

Gralnag shrugged. "Didn't know anything was wrong until my guards found your room empty. You're lucky this was the first place I looked for you." He gestured at the downed frostguards and turned to his soldiers. "You lot. Get these bastards locked up before they come to. I don't want a repeat of this."

While his soldiers scrambled to carry out his orders, Gralnag shifted his attention back to Gerrick and Moranthus. "I want you two with me. I need you to keep that prince of yours in line when I let him out of his cell. He's not going to be happy to see me, and I don't want any more fights down here today."

Orthenn didn't spare Gralnag so much as a word as he stepped out of his cell, Aldous trailing behind him. He looked at Gerrick, the remains of his bindings still hanging off one wrist, then at Moranthus, bleeding from a split in his lip and a long cut over his right eyebrow as he leaned against Gerrick for support. His eyes were hard, and he'd set his mouth into a grim line. "One of you had better explain to me what happened here."

"You mean, other than us rescuing you and you being exceedingly ungrateful?" Moranthus asked.

Gerrick started and almost dropped him. That was no way to speak to a prince. Moranthus should know that. "He's taken a few blows to the head. He doesn't know what he's saying."

"I know exactly what I'm saying, and I'll say it again if I need to. I just threw away my only chance of ever seeing Moonridge again for the two of you. The least he could do is say 'thank you.'"

Orthenn scoffed. "You expect me to be impressed with that after you broke into my camp, tied me to a tree, and kidnapped my body double?"

"That was entirely your fault. You're the coward who decided to hide behind a body double instead of facing your enemies directly. Don't try to blame that on me."

Gerrick considered putting a hand over Moranthus's mouth to shut him up. "He's not a—"

"Don't speak for me," Orthenn snapped.

Gerrick bowed his head. "My apologies."

"Why are you apologizing to him? You let yourself get kidnapped on his behalf and would have died for him, too, if I hadn't intervened."

"I know. I'm his body double. That's what his father is paying me to do." Gerrick rubbed Moranthus's shoulder in an effort to calm him. They wouldn't get anywhere with Orthenn while Moranthus was in this state. "That's part of why I shouldn't be with..." Gerrick stopped himself. He'd said too much already. This wasn't something he should let Orthenn hear.

"That's a shitty excuse, and you know it." Moranthus started to pull away from him.

Gerrick tightened his arm around Moranthus to hold him in place. He still wasn't steady enough on his feet to hold himself upright. They both knew that. Gerrick wasn't going to let Moranthus hurt himself just because Gerrick had let his tongue slip.

Moranthus cried out and doubled over in pain, clutching at his chest.

Gerrick's stomach churned. "Are you all right?" he asked, easing his grip on Moranthus.

Moranthus took several shallow, rasping breaths before replying, "I'm fine. Frostguard probably just cracked a rib or two. Please don't squeeze me again."

Gralnag raised an eyebrow at him. "Seems like your friend there's hurt worse than he looks. He should get that looked at."

"He should," Gerrick replied, ignoring the daggers Moranthus was glaring at him. "Is there a healer in your stronghold?"

"Of course, there is. He's not my gran, but he knows what he's doing. One of my guards'll take you to him."

"Thank you. I'll make sure he gets there." Gerrick gave Orthenn a respectful nod. "If you'll allow it."

Orthenn gave him a hard look. "I will. It looks like you and the elf have some things to sort out. So get them sorted. Then you report back to me. You still owe me an explanation. Make it a good one."

Gerrick nodded again. "Of course. Thank you for your patience, my prince. You won't regret—"

"Just go." Orthenn pinched the bridge of his nose. "Earth Father spare me from this madness."

As Gerrick turned to leave, Aldous gave him a sympathetic look and mouthed, "Good luck, lad."

Gerrick gave him a strained smile in return before half dragging Moranthus down the dungeon's hallway.

G ralnag's healer was tall, by goblin standards. He wore a set of simple, gray robes that hung loose on his rail-thin frame. "What happened here?" he asked as Gerrick brought Moranthus into the infirmary.

"Frostguards," Moranthus replied, his body limp in Gerrick's arms as Gerrick helped him onto one of the narrow cots that lined the infirmary's walls.

"This is why you don't do business with elves," the healer tutted. "Present company excluded, of course, assuming you aren't a frostguard yourself."

"If I were, they wouldn't have done this to me." Moranthus ran a hand over the livid finger marks covering his neck.

"Is the strangling what you're here for, or is there something else?"

"I got kicked in the chest. I think it might have broken something."

"I'll have a look at it, then. I'll need you to remove your shirt." For the first time, the healer turned his attention to Gerrick. "Help him with that if he needs it. If the two of you will excuse me for a moment, I've left a rather important poultice unfinished in my quarters, and if I leave it alone much longer, the whole thing is going to dry out, and I'll have to start over again. I'll return shortly." With that, the healer crossed the room and disappeared through a rough-hewn wooden door set in its far wall.

As Moranthus shrugged out of his jerkin and pulled his shirt over his head, Gerrick winced at the sight of the swollen, reddish-purple marks that covered Moranthus's torso. He'd be covered in bruises soon. Bruises that should have been inflicted on Gerrick instead. He was the one the frostguards had wanted. The one they would have killed if they'd gotten him out of Gralnag's stronghold and figured out who he was. But he'd walked away from that fight almost unscathed, while Moranthus had almost died.

"You should've let them have me," Gerrick murmured. "They didn't bind you. You could have run. Why didn't you?" Moranthus would've had every right to leave Gerrick to his fate after what Gerrick had done to him. But he'd stayed anyway. Gerrick didn't know if he deserved that.

"You say that like you don't already know the answer."

"I don't."

Moranthus sighed. "Because I think I'm falling in love with you, and leaving you with those frostguards when I know what they would've done to you would've hurt worse than anything they could've done to me. I know you don't feel the same, and I'm sorry if this makes things awkward, but that doesn't change how I feel."

"Moranthus…" Gerrick wondered if he'd made a mistake that morning. He'd broken things off between them before they could begin because he thought it would be easier that way. Safer for both of them. Instead, he was just needlessly hurting both of them. But it was too late to turn back now.

"I'm sorry." Moranthus turned away from him. "That wasn't fair of me. Forget I said anything."

"You've got nothing to be sorry about. You almost got yourself killed protecting me. I should be apologizing to you."

"You don't have anything to be sorry about either. You didn't ask me to do any of this. I did it because I wanted to." A bit of Moranthus's old smirk crept onto his face. "And those bastards had it coming anyway."

"They did." Gerrick took Moranthus's hand in both of his. Felt a smile warm his cheeks when Moranthus didn't pull away. "I just want you to know…what happened this morning doesn't change anything. I still want you to come back to Dawn's Gate with me. And you still have a place in my home if you want it. I haven't forgotten everything you've done for me."

"By the skies, Gerrick…" Moranthus shook his head. "I know you haven't. And I appreciate the offer. But I don't know if I can do that anymore. This is hard enough for me as it is."

"Please. I don't want to lose you."

Moranthus snatched his hand back. His voice was sharp as he replied, "Then maybe you should've thought about that this morning. Or last night, when I asked you if you were sure of what you wanted."

"I'm sorry. If I'd known—"

"I know, Gerrick. You've apologized enough. Just… I'm tired, and I'm hurting, and if you keep this up, I'm going to say things I'll regret later. I can't do this right now. Please… just go."

Gerrick left the infirmary feeling tired and defeated. Finding Orthenn waiting for him outside its door didn't lift his spirits. "How long have you been waiting?" Gerrick asked.

"Not long," Orthenn replied. "You two work things out?"

"I don't know."

For a moment, Orthenn's expression softened. "That's too bad." His face returned to its usual stern, cold look as he added, "But I still need to know why you're working with a man who tried to kidnap me."

"It's a long story." And one that Gerrick was in no mood to tell.

"We have time." Orthenn cast a distrustful glance at the infirmary's doorway. "But not here. Walk with me."

"All right." Gerrick followed Orthenn down the hall. When they'd left the infirmary a ways behind them, he took a deep breath, then began, "Moranthus found out I'm your body double a couple days after kidnapping me. That made him stop pretending he was working for your father and admit that his Matriarch sent him after you. I didn't believe him at first, but he had a set of orders from her that looked real, and I didn't want to take any chances.

"His orders made it sound like his Matriarch just wanted you rescued, so I agreed to go back to your camp with him. But by the time we got there, you were gone. If he hadn't helped me track Gralnag's raiding party, I never would have caught up with you. You have him to thank for your rescue. I'm just lucky he let me tag along."

Orthenn scoffed. "Those frostguards made it clear that their Matriarch only wanted me rescued so she could ransom me back to my father herself. Your elf friend was a part of her scheme just as much as they were."

"He wasn't. As far as he knew, he was supposed to meet up with a group of soldiers at Moonridge's border and help them escort you home. He didn't know Knurlath was working for his Matriarch."

"How can you be sure of that?"

"He wouldn't have spent weeks chasing after you if he knew his Matriarch was the one who wanted you kidnapped. He spent the entire time planning to convince your captors that I was the real Orthenn so he could hand me over to them in exchange for them letting you go free. And he was just as surprised as I was when he intercepted a message bound for those frostguards that explained what his Matriarch was really up to."

Orthenn raised an eyebrow at him. "That doesn't explain why he turned on her. *If* he turned on her."

Gerrick kept quiet for a moment, trying to think of a way to explain Moranthus's change of heart without bringing up what had happened between them. What would still be happening between them if Gerrick hadn't pushed Moranthus away. "The message also said that she was planning to exile him. He took a liking to me while we were traveling together, and I was able to convince him to go ahead with helping me save you, even if it meant betraying his Matriarch. I guess he just didn't want to lose a friend so soon after losing his home."

Orthenn kept his eyebrow raised, but the rest of his expression softened as he gave Gerrick a reassuring nod. "All right. I believe he isn't a threat to us. You were right to trust him. What do you suggest I do about him now that this is over?"

"Offer him a place in Dawn's Gate. He can't go back to Moonridge after what he's done, and we shouldn't abandon him here after everything he's done for me. For you. For your company." Gerrick knew Moranthus wasn't sure about Dawn's Gate anymore, but he hoped Moranthus would respond better to the offer if it came from Orthenn.

Orthenn was quiet for a moment before replying, "I'll consider it. But it's his choice to make, not yours."

"Of course."

"Now that's taken care of, we're wanted in our host's great hall. He's given our company a place at his table, and they'll want to thank you for that. Try to enjoy yourself."

Twenty-Seven

Moranthus kept himself upright, posture erect as he watched Gerrick leave the infirmary. He forced himself to stay that way until he could no longer hear Gerrick's and Orthenn's footsteps. Only when he was certain there was no chance of Gerrick turning back for him did he let himself collapse onto the cot and, burying his face in the pillow, let loose the tears he'd been fighting back all morning.

Every sob rekindled the fire burning in his rib cage, but the pain was nothing compared to the deep, gnawing ache in his heart. His hopes of a future with Gerrick were dashed; he'd been beaten and strangled within an inch of his life in Gerrick's defense in spite of that, and still, Gerrick insisted on acting as though nothing had changed between them. As though things could ever be the same between them after last night. How could Moranthus ever move past Gerrick's rejection of him when Gerrick insisted on bringing it up every time they spoke? Gerrick's lingering kindness toward him only poured salt in the wound.

And still, Moranthus couldn't bring himself to be properly angry with Gerrick. Or fully reject the notion of following Gerrick back to Dawn's Gate. He knew himself well enough to know that once the healer tended his wounds and the day's pains had faded, he'd be back at Gerrick's side in a heartbeat. He cared too deeply for Gerrick to do anything less.

The sound of approaching footsteps echoed in the hall. Moranthus got himself upright again and shot an irritated glance at the infirmary's doorway. He'd spent the better part of the last ten years alone; why was it suddenly impossible to have a moment to himself?

He wiped his tears on the back of his hand, sniffling in what was probably a futile effort to keep his nose from running. He'd already been thoroughly humiliated today. The last thing he needed was a random stranger seeing him in this state. Hopefully, whoever the footsteps belonged to was too caught up in their own reasons for needing a healer to pay any mind to a stray weepy elf.

Gralnag strode into the infirmary a moment later, absently rubbing at his shoulder. The same shoulder Moranthus had struck with his dagger.

Gralnag's brow furrowed when his gaze landed on Moranthus. "I thought you'd be patched up and sent on your way by now. What happened?"

Moranthus shrugged. "Your healer had an important poultice to attend to."

"Ah. That'll be for me." Gralnag seated himself on the cot across from Moranthus's. "Serves you right for putting a knife in my shoulder, I suppose."

Moranthus gave him a tired look. "Isn't it time you stopped bringing that up? If you're really so keen on retribution, why didn't you just lock me in your dungeon instead of sending me to your healer?"

"Because I like you." Gralnag chuckled when the only response Moranthus could muster was a surprised blink. "Besides, it looks like your human's already hurt you worse than I ever could. I'm not competing with that."

"You don't know what you're talking about."

"Don't bullshit me. I've seen enough to know what's going on between you two."

Moranthus wiped his eyes again. "Is there a point to this, or do you just enjoy taunting me?"

Gralnag smirked. "Little of both. But I did want to thank you for what you did today. It took balls, taking on those frostguards. I wasn't sure you had it in you."

"I said I'd take care of them, didn't I? What did you have to be unsure about?"

"You've said a lot of things. Most of them haven't been true. I don't think I got a single honest word out of you back at that inn, for example."

"Fair enough." Moranthus cringed. "For what it's worth, I do regret my initial dishonesty. And I apologize for taking you to bed under false pretenses. If I'd known we'd share a common goal by the end of all this, I would have acted differently."

Gralnag gave him a dismissive wave. "Don't apologize for that. I got what I wanted out of you. And now I know I can trust you. So good on you for keeping your word."

"I don't know that I had much choice in the matter, but thank you."

"You could've run, couldn't you? Or you could've gone along with their scheme and stolen your human and his prince out from under my nose. Would've saved yourself a world of hurt that way too."

"So I've been told," Moranthus replied. "But I couldn't have done anything else without getting Gerrick killed. He's worth a few bruises."

Gralnag shook his head. "Everything comes back to that human with you, doesn't it?"

Moranthus sighed. "That…isn't an unfair assessment." It wasn't as though he had anything to lose by admitting that to Gralnag; he was just confirming what they both already knew. Still, saying it out loud made it feel more real, somehow. And more disheartening.

"But things aren't so rosy between you two anymore, are they?"

"Obviously." Moranthus shot Gralnag a glare.

"Don't give me that look. I'm not poking fun at you. I'm just hoping you might be ready for a change."

"And what change would that be?"

"Joining my clan. I have a place for you if you're interested. I don't have your Matriarch's resources at my disposal, but I pay well, and I know a valuable asset when I see one. You'd do well here."

Moranthus raised an eyebrow at him. "What value do you think I'd add to your clan? You weren't even sure you could trust me until today."

"When word of this gets back to Moonridge, things might get ugly between me and your Matriarch. I'm going to need every sword I can get under my command. And who better to help me fight her than one of her own people?"

Moranthus recoiled at the suggestion. He had no regrets over thwarting Ilendra's plans, but his quarrel was with her, not all of Moonridge. Betraying his homeland like that was un-thinkable. "No. I won't take up arms against my own people."

Gralnag gave him a sidelong glance. "That didn't stop you from going after those frostguards."

"That was different." The frostguards had given him little choice in the matter. And he'd had a score to settle with their leader.

"Sure it was." Gralnag's expression was unreadable. "So, what? You're bound for Dawn's Gate now? Thought they burned people like you there."

"I was told they abolished that practice a century ago. I'll be fine."

Gralnag raised an eyebrow at him. "You're sure you trust the man who told you that?"

"Of course, I do." The words left Moranthus's mouth almost before Gralnag finished his question. Gerrick had his flaws, but he wasn't a liar. And he'd proven himself as a reliable friend before and after their ill-fated stint as lovers. Moranthus had no reason to doubt his word.

"Sounds like there's no talking you out of it, then. Hope it works out for you."

"Thank you. I…hope things end favorably for you here."

Gralnag snorted. "No, you don't. But it's a pretty lie. I'll pretend I believe it."

Moranthus gave him a wry smile. "I do excel at lying prettily. Or so I've been told."

"Don't let it go to your head." Gralnag got to his feet, rolling his injured shoulder. "Now that's settled, I'm asking after that poultice. This is taking too damn long."

After a moment's hesitation, Gralnag added, "That offer doesn't expire, you know. For as long as I'm warlord, you're welcome in Clan Stoneheart. If things don't work out for you in Dawn's Gate… Maybe you'll be ready to reconsider fighting under a goblin banner."

Gralnag had made himself vulnerable by extending the offer to him again. Moranthus wouldn't insult him by throwing it back in his face. Regardless of what the future held, it was good to know he still had a friend in this part of the world.

"Thank you," he replied. "I'll keep that in mind."

Twenty-Eight

Gerrick couldn't put his heart into joining his brothers-in-arms' celebration of their freedom. He forced a smile onto his face any time one of them thanked him and put as much enthusiasm as he could muster into answering their questions about where he'd been and why he wasn't dead. But without Moranthus at his side, his victory felt empty. They should be enjoying this together. They would be enjoying it together if Gerrick hadn't driven a wedge between them.

Once Gerrick's welcome had run its course and his brothers-in-arms had started into what was probably the first proper meal they'd had in weeks, Gerrick drifted into silence. As soon as he could, he slunk away from the table and the merriment around him.

Before he could find a servant to ask where his company would be sleeping that night, a heavy hand grabbed his shoulder. He felt a twinge of guilt when he turned to find Aldous standing before him, a worried look on his face. Aldous should be enjoying himself with the rest of the company, not chasing after Gerrick.

"Where are you off to?" Aldous asked. "The night's only just begun."

"Bed. I've had a long day."

"You're sure that's all? You look like something's troubling you." Aldous gave him a knowing look. "Or *someone*."

"I'm just tired. Really." Gerrick shrugged Aldous's hand off his shoulder and turned to leave. He didn't need to drag Aldous into what had happened between him and Moranthus. It was Gerrick's burden to bear.

"It's something to do with the elf, isn't it?"

Gerrick stopped. Turned to face Aldous again. "How did you know?"

"I've been married for over fifteen years, lad. I know a lovers' quarrel when I see one. What happened?"

"It doesn't matter. I broke things off with him this morning."

"Did you want to?"

"No."

"Then why did you do it?"

Gerrick furrowed his brow in confusion. It should be obvious. "Because we're both men."

"And?"

"What would the rest of the company think?"

"Most of them think you like men already, lad." Aldous gave him a sympathetic pat on the shoulder. "Them knowing you like men isn't going to make much difference."

Gerrick ran a frustrated hand over his beard. Aldous should be telling him he'd made the right choice, not trying to talk him out of it. He tried again. "It could start rumors that Orthenn likes men too. I'm his body double. If the wrong person saw me with a man…"

"If Orthenn's worried about that, he can find himself a wife. It'd probably do wonders for that sour mood of his."

"Daisy would get made fun of for having two fathers. I can't put her through that."

"If she doesn't get made fun of for that, the other children'll find something else to pick on her for. It's what they do. Your girl's a sturdy little thing; she'll be fine."

Gerrick let out a shaky breath. Felt the last of his resolve crumbling away. "What if, after all that, it just doesn't work? What if he doesn't like Dawn's Gate? What if he decides he doesn't like me?"

Aldous's eyes were soft as he slung an arm around Gerrick's shoulders. "Then at least you'll know you tried. This is the first time I've seen you take an interest in someone. Don't throw that away."

Gerrick slumped his shoulders. It was good advice. But it had come too late. "I already did. I can't turn back from that."

"You can't know that unless you try. Go have a word with the elf. Tell him how you feel. If he's as torn up over this as you are, I'm sure he'll take you back." Aldous winked at him as he continued, "And keep that hangdog look you're wearing; that always brings my wife back around when I've gotten on her bad side."

Gerrick couldn't stop a small laugh from escaping. "You're sure? If he takes me back, I won't be marrying your wife's sister."

Aldous shrugged. "She'll find someone else. To tell you the truth, she wasn't sure about the thought of meeting you either."

"I should be going, then." Gerrick stepped out from under Aldous's arm and clapped him on the shoulder. "Thank you. I needed to hear that."

"Don't get all sappy on me now. I just want to see someone put a smile on that stony face of yours. That's all. Now go on. I'll cover for you if anyone asks where you've wandered off to."

Gerrick found Moranthus sitting on his cot in the infirmary, trying to buff the scuffs from the frostguard's beating out of his jerkin. Under Moranthus's shirt, Gerrick could see the outline of a thick wrapping of bandages around his chest. Aside from an oil lamp on the floor beside Moranthus's cot and a thin sliver of light shining out from under the door to the healer's quarters, the room was dark.

Gerrick stopped and knocked lightly on the infirmary's doorframe on his way in. He didn't want to startle Moranthus with the sound of his voice.

Moranthus looked up from his jerkin. Gerrick couldn't read his expression as he said, "You came back."

"I did."

"Why?"

"I've been thinking. About what you said earlier."

"And?"

"I…" Gerrick struggled to find the right words. Moranthus wasn't going to make things easy on him this time. But he had to try. His tongue felt thick and dry as he said, "It isn't just you. I think… I think I might be falling in love too."

"Then why…" Moranthus paused. It seemed like he was also having a hard time finding the right words. "Why did you want to end things with me this morning?"

"I didn't want to hurt you if things didn't work out. I want them to work. I want… I want you. But I can't make you any promises. I'm Orthenn's body double. That's dangerous work. And I have my daughter to think of. I'm sure you'll get on with her just fine—she's a friendly little thing. But if you don't, she has to come first. I'm her father before I'm anything else. There are easier men for you to be with. You might be happier with one of them than you would with me."

"And if I'd still rather have you, even if you can't make me any promises?" Moranthus's hands shook as he clutched his jerkin.

Gerrick crossed the distance between them. Sat beside Moranthus on his cot. "Then I want to see if we can make things work between us if you'll let me. Even if I can't promise this will last… I promise I'll try to make it last."

"That's good enough for me." Moranthus dropped his jerkin onto his lap. With a sweet, lopsided grin, he wrapped his arms around Gerrick's neck and kissed him. "I'll take you for as long as I can have you."

Twenty-Nine

Moranthus woke to the warm security of Gerrick's arms encircling him. Gerrick was still asleep, a serene expression on his face and the faintest hint of a smile on his lips. Moranthus's breath left him in a happy sigh at the thrill of seeing Gerrick like this. He rested a gentle hand on Gerrick's cheek, lazily running his thumb over the thick, bristly strands of Gerrick's beard.

Gerrick stirred, and Moranthus tensed, steeling himself against the possibility of Gerrick pushing him away now that the dawn had broken and the world had caught up to them. It had happened once; it could happen again. But Gerrick pulled Moranthus closer as his eyes fluttered open, and he covered Moranthus's hand with his own, giving it a reassuring squeeze. "How are you feeling?" he asked.

"I've never felt better." Moranthus had a dull, throbbing ache in his chest from the broken rib the frostguard had given him yesterday, and he felt like he'd been kicked in the head by a horse, but it was nothing that wouldn't heal. And nothing he wouldn't happily put himself through a hundred times over for a morning like this.

Gerrick didn't look convinced, but he nodded, letting go of Moranthus's hand in favor of settling his arm around Moranthus's waist again. "That's good." His voice took on a heavy, regretful tone as he continued, "I wish I could stay with you like this all day, but I need to get back to Orthenn. I've been gone too long already. You should report to him, too, when you're feeling up to it. I spoke with him yesterday, and he's agreed to let you travel back to Dawn's Gate with the rest of the company."

"If you don't have any objection to it, I'm feeling up to going with you now. I just have a broken rib; that's nothing to stay bedridden over. I'd just get bored staying here by myself."

"You're sure you shouldn't give yourself at least one day of rest?"

A warm, tingling sensation spread over Moranthus at the concern he saw in Gerrick's eyes. "I'm sure. I know my limits. I won't push myself too hard. And I'll have you there to help me if I need it."

"All right." Gerrick's expression lightened and his eyes smiled, even if his mouth didn't, as he brushed his lips against Moranthus's cheek, his beard scratching pleasantly at Moranthus's skin. "We should get moving. Orthenn's not a man you want to keep waiting."

Moranthus reluctantly disentangled himself from Gerrick's arms, dragged himself out of bed, and shouldered into his jerkin. "We'll meet up with your company soon enough. But first, there's one last thing I need to attend to. My career as a duskblade is over. It's only right that I hand in my resignation before starting a new one."

He pulled the razor out of his pocket, flipped it open, and set about sawing his braid off. It took longer than he expected—the razor was made for shaving hair, not cutting through it—and his head felt strangely light when he'd finished. But it didn't tear at his soul the way it had the first time he'd shaved himself. This time, it was his choice. His severed braid wasn't a mark of shame, symbolizing everything he'd lost; it marked the start of his new life and everything he hoped to gain from it. He had nothing to be ashamed of.

When he'd finished with his braid, Gerrick asked, "Are you going to shave the rest of it?"

"I could." Moranthus grimaced as he ran a hand over what was left of his hair. "But I think this is enough. It'll get the point across to anyone who sees it. That's what matters."

Gerrick nodded. "It will." A faint blush colored his cheeks as he added, "I… I think you look nice like this."

"Do I?" Moranthus felt his own face go a bit warm as the compliment sank in. Awkward as it was, the sincerity in Gerrick's voice made it sound almost poetic. "I suppose I'll have to keep that in mind when I deliver this"—he wound his severed braid around his hand—"to the leader of our frost-guard friends, and he starts sneering at me again."

"Why do you need to do that? Isn't cutting your braid off enough?"

"It is, but only if word of that gets back to Ilendra. She won't be happy about this, but as long as she knows I've accepted exile as the consequence of my actions here, she can't touch me. Without my braid, I'm dead to her and everyone else in Moonridge. She can't so much as acknowledge my existence without breaking her own laws."

"Do you want me to go with you?"

"He's nothing I can't handle." Moranthus took a step toward the door and came dangerously close to losing his footing. He was still a bit unsteady after the beating he'd taken yesterday. "But I might need some help getting to him."

The frostguards' leader sneered at Moranthus as he approached his cell. He didn't look nearly as imposing out of his armor, and the chains around his ankles gave him an utterly defeated look. "Have you come to kill me, Exile?" he asked.

"Of course not. *Someone* needs to tell our Matriarch what happened here." Moranthus tossed his braid into the cell. "You seem like the most logical man for the job. Give this to your Matriarch when she ransoms you back to her, will you?"

The frostguard's face paled. He was probably dreading having to explain this to Ilendra. She'd already be furious with him over his failure to deliver Orthenn to her; finding out Moranthus had played a role in that failure wouldn't do anything to improve her mood. If the frostguard hadn't almost killed Moranthus yesterday, Moranthus might've pitied him.

The frostguard's voice was missing its usual mocking tone as he said, "You can't ask me to do this."

"Why not? It is, after all, past time I decided what to do with my razor. I'm sure she'll be happy to know I've made my choice."

"And what do you intend to do if I decide not to pass your message along?"

Die, most likely. But Moranthus doubted it would come to that. "Are you planning to lie to your Matriarch? Betray her the same way you betrayed her father?"

The frostguard leapt to his feet and lunged at Moranthus through the bars of his cell. The chains around his ankles kept his grasping fingers a safe distance away from Moranthus, but he took a step backward regardless. Best not to take any chances with this one.

"Do not speak to me of betrayal, Exile," the frostguard snarled. "I have ever been a loyal servant of Matriarch Ilendra."

"So, you *will* pass along my message. Thank you." Moranthus allowed himself a satisfied smirk.

The frostguard scowled but pulled away from the bars and bent to pick up Moranthus's severed braid. "I will. I know where my loyalties lie, Exile. Can you say the same?"

The question silenced Moranthus for a moment. He had no regrets, but he *had* just put an end to a century and a half of service to Moonridge's ruling family. That was no light matter.

But more than that, his thoughts were drawn to Gerrick. To the life they planned to start together in Dawn's Gate. To the clear conscience he was enjoying for the first time in ten years. And he had his answer.

"As a matter of fact, I can." Moranthus turned on his heel and strode off toward the dungeon's stairs. He'd let the frostguard waste too much of his time already. They were done here.

Moranthus ignored the string of threats and obscenities the frostguard hurled after him as he climbed the stairs out of the dungeon. And into Gerrick's warm embrace. He was going home. And for the first time in ten years, he had something worth going home to.

He'd never felt so alive.

Acknowledgements

This book began as my MFA thesis, so I think it's only fair that I start my acknowledgements there. Thank you, David, Andrea, and Marty, for accepting my application and letting me run amok with my elves and goblins and swords. Thanks also to Lori, Jenny, and Mario for your invaluable advice and guidance through my early drafts.

Thanks to everyone at NineStar Press for making my publishing dreams a reality.

Thank you Deanna (D.M.) Rasch for being the best accountability buddy I could ask for.

Special thanks to Jesse Kuiken for your encouragement of my early writing attempts.

And thank you, Kal, for your love and patience and for listening to all my crazy ideas. Also for reminding me to eat. And sleep.

About Shannon Blair

Shannon Blair is a fantasy author with a fondness for elves, goblins, and general otherworldly goodness. Their love of fiction and storytelling drove them to pursue an MFA in Creative Writing from Regis University, where a short writing exercise spiraled out of control and eventually became Dawn's Light. When they aren't on a quest to make the fantasy genre a more LGBTQA-friendly place, Shannon can be found inventing whimsical backstories for the colorful crafts and vendors at the craft market where they work. They live on the outskirts of the Denver metroplex with their partner and two spoiled rotten cats.

Email

TheWriterShannonBlair@gmail.com

Facebook

www.facebook.com/profile.php?id=100012031608767

Twitter

@SBlairAuthor

Website

www.shannonblair.com

Also from NineStar Press

He Dreams Magic by Emme C. Taylor

Ren has always wanted to leave, to escape his quiet village life. He wakes up from gold-tinged dreams with his heart pounding and a yearning for something he can't name, can't hold. He longs to experience something magical just once in his life.

Nico's monsters don't lurk under the bed. They walk in daylight. They haunt him every day of his life. He's possibly the strongest magician of his time, yet he's trapped. All he wants is an out.

At a magical carnival in the middle of a forest, Ren and Nico collide. They've been on this collision course their entire lives, always hurtling toward each other. For both men, escape is now. They have no choice but to flee together. Monsters and betrayal hunt them across strange lands. They find themselves on a journey to save each other—and possibly the world. All they have is one another, Nico's magic, and a lifetime of half-remembered dreams. But finding each other, finally having someone to rely on, might be the strongest magic of all.

Sorcery of the Blood by Alice G. Holmes

Kingston St. Louis and Martin Von Brandt are vampire hunters of the highest caliber. That is until Kingston is made a vampire and they discover too late that the city is being taken over by vampires in a bloody coup.

Branded as outlaws, they're forced into hiding with an unexpected ally. For their plan to stop the coup to work, Kingston will have to overcome his prejudices and train the very vampires he used to hunt, and Martin must learn magic.

All the while, they struggle with their feelings for each other. Love can be a weakness, and they can't afford weakness when hiding from a powerful enemy.

Flicker by Elizabeth Tybush

Stripped of his magick and exiled to Earth, Solin Felwing vows to redeem himself. He committed a lot of bad for "the greater good" and the only way to make up for it is to give back to those he stole from. Incognito, of course, to avoid being brought to justice by humankind.

Solin volunteers at a soup kitchen, but his redemption is thrown into disarray when his best friend Jemier arrives to profess his love. Sam, Solin's one-man support group and only human friend, thinks Solin deserves better.

When old enemies resurface, Solin fears his attempt to change is over for good. He could easily wipe his foes from existence—if he had his magick. Saving his friends—and himself—means compromising in new ways, but the temptation to sin remains. Everything could change in a flicker.

Connect with NineStar Press

Website: NineStarPress.com

Facebook: NineStarPress

Facebook Reader Group: NineStarNiche

Twitter: @ninestarpress

Instagram: NineStarPress